WITHERING HEIGHTS

WITHERING
HEIGHTS

Dorothy Cannell

ST. MARTIN'S MINOTAUR
New York

This is a work of fiction. All of the characters, organizations, and events portrayed in this novel are either products of the author's imagination or are used fictitiously.

www.minotaurbooks.com

Design by Kathryn Parise

LIBRARY OF CONGRESS CATALOGING-IN-PUBLICATION DATA

Cannell, Dorothy.
    Withering heights / Dorothy Cannell.—1st ed.
        p. cm.
    ISBN-13: 978-0-312-34337-8
    ISBN-10: 0-312-34337-X
    1. Haskell, Ellie (Fictitious character)—Fiction.   I. Title.

PS3553.A499W58 2007b
813'.54—dc22

                                                2006048906

First Edition: April 2007

10   9   8   7   6   5   4   3   2   1

This book is for Master Jack, who invented the game Tree Fort versus Castle, and for the two princesses, Grace and Kate, who always cleverly escaped from the dungeon behind the sofa. With kind regards, from Mr. Small and Mrs. Tiny. And grumbling apologies from the Wicked Warlock.

WITHERING
HEIGHTS

1

꧁꧂

The storm hurled itself against the blurred contours of the house like an angry sea. Thunder roared, lightning flared, and the wind moaned, subsiding for a moment, then whooshing back with renewed ferocity. Clouds drifted across the bruised and bloated sky. It was early afternoon, but it might well have been the dead of night, fit only for human beasts of prey and the shadowy vigils of unholy spirits denied respite beneath a sanctified churchyard earth.

A tree branch brushed my arm with skeletal fingers as I scuttled across the courtyard after parking my car in the old stable. I screeched but did not panic, until a wildly flapping moon-colored thing made a dive for me as I neared the back door. Stumbling sideways, I still became entangled in its clammy folds. No bird this, but a shroud in search of a body. (Well . . . it could be I overreacted a little. My husband, Ben,

1

claims I do that sometimes.) Having fought my way free, I reassessed the situation. Perhaps I was merely dealing with a sheet blown off the line. But a very nasty evil-minded sheet, for sure.

I was glad to step into my bright kitchen at Merlin's Court. Setting down my handbag and packages, I peeled off my raincoat and hung it on a hook in the alcove, then shook out my damp hair before weaving it back into a plait. Living on our part of the English coast, with its cliffs and rocky shoreline, we are prone to ferocious storms. But I had stayed up late the previous evening devouring the final gripping chapters of *The Night Visitor*, so it wasn't surprising that my imagination had started to run amuck on the drive home through the blinding rain.

Tobias the cat was seated on the broad window ledge, where he is never supposed to be. Typically, he looked at me as though I were the one about to get into trouble. Apart from his twitching whiskers there was no sign of life. All was neat and tidy, a kitchen on its best behavior. The copper pans hung in gleaming precision from their rack. Not a cup or saucer was out of place on the Welsh dresser. No stray crumbs on the quarry-tiled floor. No plastic horse tethered to the rocking chair. No sign or sound of husband or children. They had left for London in the Land Rover the previous morning with scarcely a backward wave. The twins, Tam and Abbey, age seven, and five-year-old Rose were to spend the next fortnight with Ben's parents. I didn't expect him home till early evening. The unaccustomed quiet was unnerving. Even my household helper, Mrs. Malloy, was conspicuous by her absence. Either she was occupied somewhere else in the house or she had thrown in the duster and gone home. Tobias gave me a smug look from the windowsill, as if to say how pleasant it was just being the two of us. I made myself a cup of tea and poured him a saucer of milk. He was right. What could be cozier? A woman alone with her cat, a cup of tea, and a plate of digestive biscuits.

The rain was still hammering down in a most unsuitable way for July as I seated myself at the scrubbed wood table. When a few minutes had gone by without a disembodied voice asking me to pass the sugar, I forgave the weather and was glad I had paid the second-hand bookshop in the village a visit. Under the Covers is a great place to forage for out-of-print titles. I had even grown quite keen on the smell of mildew that assaults one on entering its quiet gloom.

That day I had been buying not only for myself but also for the thirteen-year-old daughter of Ben's cousin Tom Hopkins. I'd only met young Ariel once, a couple of years previously, at my in-laws' flat above their greengrocer's shop in Tottenham. Ariel was in the company of her paternal grandmother. Oblivious to the tea tray with its assortment of jam tarts and iced cakes, she'd sat with feet and hands together, looking bored to rigor mortis. Seated next to her, I did my best to bridge the child–adult gap. Mercifully, just as I was ready to abandon all hope of drawing her out of the sulks and putting something like a smile on her face, she informed me somewhat fiercely— clearly daring me to approve—that she liked black-and-white movies: especially ones set in spooky old houses. I responded casually that I enjoyed them too and didn't object to novels of the same sort. What followed was a pleasant half-hour chat. Ariel stopped curling her lip and asked me for names of authors and titles. By the time her grandmother intimated it was time to leave, I was quite sorry to say good-bye to the whey-faced girl and asked if she would like me to sort through my collection and send her a couple of the books we had discussed. Unless her parents would object, I added responsibly.

"It'll be all right with Dad," said Ariel.

"And your mother?"

"Betty's my step." A toss of the sandy pigtails. "She won't care what you send me."

Not particularly heartened by this information, I got the Hopkinses' address from my mother-in-law and a few weeks later sent off a package of books, addressing it to Tom and Betty, with a letter enclosed. I never heard back from either of them. But Ariel wrote to thank me with an enthusiasm that suggested the genie had been let out of the ink bottle. On paper she was a different child, impish and insightful. She had loved *The Curse of St. Crispin's* so much that she was dying—underlined three times—to read everything else by its author. That was the beginning of our correspondence, and it became an enjoyable one for me. Over the course of the next eighteen months, I sent Ariel several more books and always looked forward to discussing them with her in letters.

Then something earthshaking happened to the Hopkins family: Tom and Betty won the lottery. They sold their semi-detached home in a London suburb and bought a huge house somewhere in the north. Ben and I learned this information from his mother, but even she was not privy to their new address. And Ariel's grandmother, who would have been a likely source of this information, had died the previous year.

Now, on this day of storm, it was six months since I had heard from Ariel. I had been thinking about her quite a lot recently, wondering how she was adjusting to her new life. Given my favorite choice of reading matter, I knew all too well that the sudden acquisition of great wealth could be a murky matter, fraught with perils for the child heiress. Ben felt that if Tom and Betty did not want people to know their whereabouts, that was their prerogative. Even so, he had agreed to ask his mother, on his current visit, if she had any updated information on where the family of three had gone to earth.

There was always the chance, I had explained while looking

fervently into his marvelous blue-green eyes, that Ariel was desperately hoping I would get back in touch with her. But I had not pressed the point. Ben isn't much of a fiction reader. He prefers cookery books, which is understandable, seeing that he has written half a dozen of his own, in addition to owning and managing a restaurant named Abigail's in our village of Chitterton Fells.

Pouring myself another cup of tea, I realized I'd finished all the biscuits. Time slips by so fast when one is Ellie Haskell; blissfully married to the handsomest man outside of a gothic novel, with three lively children and Tobias to round out the family. Having decided to take early retirement, Tobias is underfoot much of the day, meowing about how much better things were when he was young. As if on cue, he demanded a second saucer of milk.

"Don't interrupt," I told him sternly. "I am busy relaxing."

And now came another distraction. Mrs. Malloy entered through the hall door, wafting a feather duster. She was looking her majestic best in a purple taffeta dress and an enormous pair of rhinestone earrings that would have done her proud at a cocktail party hosted by a royal duchess, had Chitterton Fells gone in for such swanky affairs. Her jet-black hairdo with its two inches of white roots is always her chief fashion statement. She also goes in for iridescent eye shadow, lashings of mascara, brick-red rouge, and purple-passion lipstick. That's Mrs. Malloy. And, as I have said on occasion to Tobias, who admires her fondness for fur coats, all credit to her.

Nothing would induce Her Royal Personage to slop around as I was presently doing in an old green skirt and sweater and no makeup. She routinely takes me to task for not putting my best face forward, explaining that looking like a loaf of bread is no way to keep a husband when there are plenty of fancy cakes on little paper doilies out there. Regrettably, I always let this

5

go in one ear and out the other, telling myself smugly that we can't all be slaves to fashion. Not being clairvoyant, I did not foresee the danger of ignoring such pearls of wisdom. Oh, woe to the woman who sticks her nose in a book and forgets that real life is not always destined for Happily Ever After.

"I thought you'd left for the day," I said, getting to my feet.

"What? Be drowned in that storm when no right-minded person would put a cat out in it?"

Tobias looked grateful. Had there been a saucer of milk handy, I am sure he would have offered her a slurp.

Her Mightiness began clattering around the kitchen in her six-inch heels, opening up cupboard doors as if hoping to surprise miniature burglars lurking behind the plates. The noise she made was not Beethoven to the ears, but then she has never been a woman to fade willingly into the next county.

Irritating as this can be, I've grown fond of her over the years. We've shared some good times and a number of adventures in which we have, more by luck than skill, managed to unmask evildoers bent on reducing England's population one or two murder victims at a time. A recent escapade had found us on unauthorized assignment to a surly gumshoe named Milk Jugg. Our participation was the result of a silly mistake that could have happened to any pair of well-meaning busybodies. Milk had not been overwhelmingly grateful. We had, however, solved the murder and received a nice little mention in the local newspaper. Mrs. Malloy had sent a copy to George, her son by one of her husbands. (I couldn't remember whether it was the third or the fourth—but then, neither could she.)

Now, mindful of my responsibilities as employer, I poured her a cup of tea and got out more biscuits.

"It's good of you to stay so late this afternoon getting the house really shipshape." I beamed my warmest smile.

"And nice of you, Mrs. H, to take the trouble to ignore me

when I've been telling you the same thing twice over. Warms the cockles of me heart, it does, but then it never takes much to make me feel appreciated." Mrs. Malloy teetered into full view on those stilt heels to strike a dramatic pose, one hand on her hip, the other still holding the feather duster aloft.

"I'm sorry. What have you been saying?"

"Nothing that important, Mrs. H."

Now I felt guilty, something I do rather well. Had I been into nonfiction, I could have written a bestseller on female neuroses, to the accompaniment of a great many footnotes. Mrs. Malloy is devoted to the children, and it helps enormously to be able to leave them with her when Ben and I occasionally go out in the evening. My cousin Freddy, who lives in the cottage at the end of the drive and is second in command at Abigail's, also helps out in this regard. Except when, as was currently the case, he is desperately in love with some hapless female who fails to grasp that he is already married to his motorcycle.

"I didn't mean to ignore you," I told Mrs. Malloy through a mouthful of digestive biscuit. "I was thinking about *The Night Visitor* and that ghost child, Oriole, tapping on the window when Miss Flinch was aching to be alone with thoughts of Sir Giles's refusal to explain his avoidance of a certain corner of the shrubbery on the anniversary of his wife's disappearance."

It was the right ploy for making amends. Mrs. Malloy had recommended the book to me. She is every bit as keen on this sort of literary gem as are Ariel and I. Among our favorites are those set in Yorkshire, featuring—nine times out of ten—the orphaned heroine. A young woman who leaps at the chance to become a governess in a decaying mansion where Something Unspeakable is shut away in the north tower and melancholy music drifts up from the crypt. Her charge is frequently a plain child who has not been right in the head since taking a peep through the lepers' squint and seeing Nanny stuff a body into the priest hole. Given these unhappy circumstances, along with the fact that he only inherited Darkwood Hall because his twin brother drowned in the hip bath, the master of the house tends to be somewhat morose. Sadly, this prevents him from telling the heroine (when first encountering her at dead of night on the secret staircase) that he adores her pale, prim face. Behind the masterful control of his emotions is a searing need. He yearns to explain that if she can overlook his limp, his missing ear, and the scar slashed across his right cheek, he will be willing to forget that his first wife died in childbirth and ravish her on the spot.

Setting the teacups on the kitchen table, I wondered if Lord Darkwood would have doted on the governess quite so passionately were she the one needing an immediate appointment with a plastic surgeon. Probably not. But never mind: there is something utterly beguiling about the image of a man tortured by the realization that he is unworthy of even a stray smile from the woman he adores. It is one of those vagaries of life that enable Ben to look fabulous in old blue jeans and a sweatshirt while I, a part-time interior designer dressed much the same way, look like an assortment of fabric swatches I would avoid using in my work.

Suddenly the air was rent by a piercing scream. It was only the kettle whistling. Mrs. Malloy, however, wilted into a chair as if she had received a mortal shock of her life, and only flickered back to life when I passed her a cuppa.

"I'm a bit unsettled today." She smiled wanly up at me as she stirred in the third spoonful of sugar. "Yesterday evening I went on a journey . . . a long long journey."

"Shopping in Pebble Beach?" I asked, receiving a scowl in return.

"It wasn't that sort of journey. Something quite different.

It's what I was wanting to tell you from the moment you walked in, but it soon became clear you wasn't listening."

"Well, I am now." Seating myself opposite her, I shifted the refilled plate of digestive biscuits her way. "Don't keep me in suspense. You're sounding delightfully mysterious."

Mrs. Malloy mellowed visibly. "I went to see a psychic named Madam LaGrange. My friend Maisie from the Chitterton Fells Charwomen's Association had been to her and said she was quite wonderful. Of course, she charges quite a bit. . . ."

"Why *of course?*"

"She's a specialist."

"Not your ordinary general practitioner?" I was wondering if another digestive biscuit would cross my path in the near future. Mrs. Malloy had put a couple on her plate and then proceeded rudely to ignore them. Not that I was one to talk about good manners. If I'd paid attention when she was trying to talk to me earlier, I would already have the scoop on Madam LaGrange. Probably named Mrs. Smith when serving up hubby's dinner instead of staring into her crystal ball.

"Oh, she does some standard fortune-telling, because that's what most people want." Mrs. M smirked disparagingly. "She told me, at no extra charge, to be careful of standing at bus stops when it's thundering and lightning because she saw a woman with an umbrella take a tumble and go under a double-decker."

"Cheerful!"

"She didn't think it was me, more likely someone I knew or would meet in the future."

That's right, Madam LaGrange, I thought, keep it vague.

"She also said"—Mrs. Malloy pursed her butterfly lips and stared into space—"that a woman of my acquaintance whose first name begins with *E* should stop living in a dream world, seeing as her hubby's old girlfriend is going to show up and this time around she'll stop at nothing to get him."

Suddenly, I wished that Madam had been a bit more vague. Did it make any difference that my name was really Giselle, although almost everyone called me Ellie?

"Or she may have said beginning with a *B*." Mrs. Malloy waved a negligent hand. "I can't say as I was listening that close, being eager to get on with the journey back to one or more of me past lives."

"Oh!" I stared at her, my momentary unease banished.

"That's Madam LaGrange's specialty. *Transgression* is what she calls it."

"I thought the term was regression. Never mind. What do I know?" Truth be told, I was a little hurt. Mrs. Malloy and I are not joined at the hip, but we share more than a working relationship. She must have known I would be interested in discovering whether I'd ever hobnobbed with Cornish smugglers or queued up in a past life to get the Brontë sisters' autographs. Unfortunately, being grown-up means having to rise above wounded feelings. "Tell me what happened. I'm dying of curiosity. Did Madam LaGrange hypnotize you?"

" 'Course not! She told me I'd have to take a couple of trains and then a taxi the rest of the way!" Mrs. Malloy curled her purple lip, before settling back in her chair and sipping her tea.

"Thanks for the sarcasm. I meant, did it work? Did she succeed in putting you into a trance?"

"Madam LaGrange said I was a very good subject. I went all lovely and floaty, like I was made out of gossamer."

"Weren't you nervous?" I asked, inching the plate of biscuits toward me.

"Well, I was a bit at first, Mrs. H, sitting in that room with the curtains drawn and dance-of-the-seven-veils music piping up from the old-fashioned gramophone. But then I decided it was silly to get the willies over a little thing like being sent back in time. What's the worst that could happen? That's what I said to meself."

"You could have found yourself stuck back in the eleventh century without your toothbrush or a change of underwear. What if Madam hadn't been able to bring you back? I'm not sure it does to play around with this stuff."

"Thought you might see it that way. It's why I didn't say anything when I got here this morning! Or could it be you're jealous?" Mrs. Malloy stuck her nose in the air.

I felt myself blush. It was true. I'd always had a sneaking desire to discover if my interest in gothic romances sprang from having once been a Victorian damsel in distress. Had I glided down the turret stairs at dead of night with only the pale moon's glance to light my way toward the priest hole in trembling hope of finding skeletal evidence of mayhem at the manor? Had I mustered the moral fortitude to spurn the master's ardent advances and remind him that his invalid wife still clung to life on the edge of her chaise longue and he could never divorce her because he was a Roman Catholic and the scandal would kill his mother? Had I displayed the heroism of a Jane Eyre in refusing to become his mistress? That would depend, I supposed, on whether the darkly handsome master looked anything like Ben when he slowly removed his dressing gown. Would there be tears in his eyes and that wonderfully husky note of desperation in his voice when he begged me to let him set me up in a fabulously expensive apartment in Paris?

I was picturing the endless nights of forbidden passion, the crystal chandelier that cast its radiant glow over the Louis Quatorze bed, the tumbled silk sheets, and the dear little poodle on its monogrammed cushion when Mrs. Malloy intruded with blatant insensitivity into this most private of moments.

"You're the one off in a trance, Mrs. H!"

"Just thinking your visit to Madam LaGrange must have been an interesting experience." I poured us both another cup of tea. "Did you find out if you have lived before?"

"After she brought me out of the trance, Madam LaGrange told me I'd never stopped talking the whole time."

"How much did you remember?"

"No need to sound suspicious, Mrs. H! The veil falls back into place. That's the way it works. Anyway, it turns out I was in the circus in two previous lives. The first time I was married to one of the clowns and the mother of seven. So it didn't leave much time for making it up the ladder—"

"To the trapeze?"

Mrs. Malloy eyed me coldly. "Put it that way if you like. The ladder of success is what I was getting at."

Did the tattered remnants of disappointed ambition explain why she'd emphasized early in our relationship that she didn't do any jobs that required going up stepladders with a bucket? "Seven children." I sympathized. "No wonder George is your one and only this time around."

"My second life in the circus was lots better. I had a thing going with the ringmaster and the man that trained the elephants, but mostly I fixed on me career as a tightrope walker." Mrs. Malloy attempted, but failed, to look modest.

I visualized her walking the length of our clothesline in her ultra-high heels and a taffeta dress, not a hair out of place. The mind boggled.

"Any other lives in your résumé?"

"Well, yes, so Madam LaGrange said, but I'm not so sure about the last one." Mrs. M eyed me now with a mixture of awkwardness and defiance. "Leastways, not like I was about the first two."

"The circus ones do sound completely credible." I tried not

12

to look at Tobias, who was clearly smirking behind the paw with which he was pretending to wash his face.

"I got the faintest suspicion that Madam LaGrange might be making up stories at the end."

"No!" If a cat could guffaw, Tobias would have done so. I was truly shocked. Were Madam a fake, she might at least have had the integrity to appear genuine and not crush her client's fantasies as they flourished. We all need a little escapism, even when completely content with our lives. I with my idyllic marriage and wonderful children was proof of that. And it hadn't taken long after getting to know Mrs. Malloy to realize she hid the heart of a romantic within her taffeta bosom.

She now studied the hanging rack of copper pans. "It crossed me mind, Mrs. H, that Madam LaGrange could be working from bits and bobs of information I'd given her about meself when I rang up to make the appointment. Seeing that was last week, I couldn't remember for certain what I'd said about this or that, but I'm almost sure I told her me maiden name."

"Is that important?"

"I'm getting to that. There we was yesterday evening, sitting at the table with the shadows drifting about and that Taj Mahal music piping away like it wouldn't stop even if you smashed the gramophone. All properly spine-tingling, I was thinking, Mrs. H, when it came to me that Madam LaGrange seemed a mite bored. Once or twice I caught her looking at her watch, and all at once she says that me last incarnation, before this one, was as a cat in the late eighteen hundreds."

"A cat?" I reached yet again for the plate of biscuits. This required at least two digestives. "I suppose that would explain why you're so fond of fur coats. What sort of cat? A pedigree or a regular old—" I was silenced by a baleful glare from Tobias.

"Old tabby? That's what you was going to ask, wasn't it?" Mrs. Malloy's false eyelashes twitched.

"No, I wasn't!" I said, through a splutter of crumbs. "Not that there is anything wrong with being a tabby. Tobias is one"—I shifted my chair away from him—"and he's always thought he was the whiskers. I've known lots of other tabbies, wonderful people—I mean cats—all of them. Every one, without exception! But I am sure you were a pedigree, Mrs. Malloy. Probably a Persian. Or a Siamese?"

"Tabby was me maiden name."

"Oh!"

Mrs. Malloy sighed deeply. "I think it's one of the reasons I got married so many times, trying to put the sound of it as far behind me as possible. You've no idea, Mrs. H, what it's like to have a name that makes you the butt of spiteful jokes."

She was wrong about that. Being named Giselle is not conducive to happiness when you are a plump child completely lacking in grace and athletic ability. There had been no malice aforethought on my parents' parts. It was understandable that my mother had hoped I would follow in her satin shoes and become a ballerina and that my father had naively assumed I would inherit her ethereal beauty rather than his portly build. Having soon realized their mistake, they had done their fond best to put matters right by adjusting to an Ellie who was not born to pirouette. Even so, there had been no getting away from my full name completely. It is impossible to keep dark secrets from your schoolmates, especially the ones whose mission in life is to make you wish your parents kept you prisoner on a diet of bread and water.

"I can't count the times the other kiddies teased me, calling out, 'Here, puss, puss! Come and have some Kittycat, puss!' " Mrs. Malloy sat staring into space. "But I've got to remember as how it's been worse for me sister, not getting married even once and so being stuck with the name Tabby for life."

Now I was the one to stare. Mrs. Malloy had never previously said peep to me about having a sister. "I thought you were an only child."

"We don't speak. Haven't done for years."

"A quarrel?" I was always good at suggesting the obvious.

"Me and Melody never did get on."

"Melody?" I found this harder to grasp than the concept of Mrs. Malloy being a tightrope walker . . . or even a cat. There is that little matter of age appropriateness when it comes to names. Mrs. Malloy, although she would have denied it to the death, was in her early sixties. Presumably, her sister was of a similar age and should by rights have been a Barbara or a Joan or maybe a Margaret. A Melody is never supposed to be older than fifteen, either in books or in real life. It isn't possible to believe there will ever be nursing homes peopled with residents named Tiffany, Megan, or Stacie.

"She's older than me by a couple of years. But never no maturity. Our relationship went from bad to worse when we was teenagers. She accused me of stealing her boyfriend."

"Did you?"

"'Course not!" Much affronted, Mrs. Malloy sat up straighter in her chair. "I borrowed him, is all. And only for an afternoon, at that. But you'd have thought when I gave him back it was with tea stains all over him. Such a carry-on I got. Miss Melody Dramatic, I called her."

"If she was in love with him—"

"Nothing of the sort. I don't think he'd ever washed his neck. He was just someone to get Melody's mind off the other one."

"Unsuitable?"

"A doomed relationship from the word go."

"Oh, dear! A married man?"

"Mr. Rochester."

"As in . . . ?" I'd stuck my elbow in my saucer and toppled the cup, much to the chagrin of Tobias, who was sitting on my lap.

"That's him. Edward Fairfax Rochester."

The man against whom all other gothic heroes must be judged and the majority of them found wanting! The storm had picked up again. Thunder rolled and rumbled in the distance. Lightning flashed. Rain rattled against the kitchen windowpanes. When it ended, would we be left with a blighted oak on the grounds?

"Melody couldn't think how to get Mr. R to leave Jane Eyre for her. She said no one else would ever come close."

Some might think this a little odd, but having felt much the same way before meeting Ben, my heart went out to the unhappy Melody. I found myself wondering if it might not be possible for her to begin life again, even at this late date, as a primly garbed governess—after establishing, of course, that there was no mad wife in the attic.

"You shared a love of great romantic fiction. Doesn't that count for something?" I asked Mrs. Malloy.

"After sobbing herself to sleep for five years, it seems Melody turned in her library card and vowed never again to darken the threshold of a bookshop. All her cooped-up passion went into learning to type. She's worked for the last forty years as secretary to an accountant in Yorkshire, some small town not all that far from Haworth."

"Home of Charlotte Brontë and the rest of her famous family! But why would your sister torture herself that way? Why not get as far away as possible from painful associations with the man of her dreams?"

"Never happy unless she's miserable herself and depressing everyone around her. The boyfriend moved home and never again let go of his mother's apron strings. I've not met her boss, but my guess is she's done a number on him too."

"That sounds unkind, Mrs. Malloy." Tobias wandered off my lap onto hers.

"I suppose it does." She had the grace to look shamefaced. "Truth be told, it bothers me the way I never could stand her. My chums in the Chitterton Fells Charwomen's Association get on me all the time. 'Your own sister,' they say, 'and the only contact you have with her is exchanging Christmas cards. Go and see her. Make up your differences!'"

"They're right."

"You *would* say that, Mrs. H! But there's no explaining it even to meself. Just looking at Melody's photo gets me hopping mad. That daft expression on her face! Like she's afraid if she don't smile just right the camera will zoom in and suck off her nose. I'm not saying as I'm proud of it, but I remember looking at her when she was two years old and thinking, You're a miserable little cow, Melody Tabby, and always will be."

I was doing some laborious arithmetic. "Wouldn't you have been a newborn at the time? You said she was a couple of years older than you."

"Did I?" The rouged cheeks turned a deeper brick-red. "Maybe it's the other way round. Melody always seemed elderly. By the age of nine you'd have thought she'd started collecting her pension and going on coach rides to Margate with a bunch of gray-haired old biddies. Still, I knew girls at school like that and they didn't drive me up the wall quite the same way. But then again, none of them was me own sister. I can see what you're thinking, Mrs. H, but it wasn't a case of having me nose put out of whack when she came along. This was something different, almost like . . ."

"Go on!" I urged.

"Well, almost like . . . I'd known her before."

"Before what?"

Mrs. Malloy heaved a pained sigh that inflated her bosom and conveyed clearly that I was being even dimmer than usual. "Before we was born. Into this current lifetime is what I'm getting at. But maybe I was wrong."

"No sign of Melody floating around the periphery of your trance?"

"Not a hint. Madam LaGrange didn't mention her."

Even Tobias looked sorry. And I wondered if I should invite her to spend the night. I pictured myself sitting up with her through the small hours, holding her hand to make sure she didn't have the vapors or go into a decline. Doing so was something I wouldn't begrudge, even though with the children gone I'd made other plans for an evening alone with Ben. These had included my sea-foam green nightgown, music from *Phantom of the Opera* playing in the background, and an atmospheric arrangement of chamomile-scented candles on my dressing table.

I reminded Mrs. Malloy that it was something to discover that she had been a person as exciting as a tightrope walker in a previous life. And a cat too, if one discounted the possibility of Madam LaGrange's having made that part up. Come to notice it, in close proximity Mrs. Malloy and Tobias did bear a certain rememblance to each other, around the eyes and the twitch of their mouths.

"Go on, say it, Mrs. H; you think she's a fraud."

"But sincere about it," I consoled. "It could be she'd do better in another specialty."

"She did say she's just finished a postdoctoral course on séances and is thinking about going into them full-time."

"Well, there you are! Her heart wasn't really in her session with you."

"Still, I don't think it'd be wise for me to dismiss that bit about her seeing a woman falling in front of a bus in the rain." Mrs. Malloy's pious gaze shifted to the windows, where the storm was still going at it, hammer and tongs. "Or that business about the old girlfriend showing up. That sort of thing can ruin the best marriage."

"Possibly."

"Take Mr. H, for starters."

"Yes, do let's." Had Tobias presently been within reach, I would have thrown him at her.

"Not that I think he'd seriously misbehave himself." Mrs. Malloy solemnly shook her head. "But there's no getting around it, he's a very attractive man, besides being able to cook like a dream at home as well as at work. An old girlfriend might go all out—plunging necklines, skirts up to her knickers—to win back the chance she'd missed. Of course, like I said, it wouldn't come to anything in the end, but—"

"Interesting you should mention Ben's culinary talent." I got up to put the tea things in the sink. "His latest cookery book will be out next month. There's a review of it, an excellent one, in the magazine *Cuisine Anglaise* that arrived in this morning's post. But getting back to Melody, I think that having given Madam LaGrange a try you should attempt the more conventional approach. Go see your sister."

"It wouldn't do any good. There's never been no talking to Melody when she's in one of her snits." Mrs. Malloy came up beside me with the teapot. "Like I told you, this one's lasted close on forty years."

"That's nothing." I added more washing-up liquid. "For Moses that was a walking tour in the desert, hardly enough time to get sunburn. And speaking of fresh air and relaxation, it occurs to me that you're due for a holiday. Now don't argue." I held up a soapy hand. "With the children away at their grandparents' and my not having any decorating jobs going at the moment, this would be the ideal time to reunite you with Melody."

"There is that." Mrs. M picked up a dish towel and stood with it draped over her arm as if auditioning for the part of a waiter. "And Madam LaGrange did say I was about to take a trip to foreign parts, which I suppose could be Yorkshire, seeing as the people there talk different from the way we do. Then again, I'm not so sure I want to spoil a nice long tiff with Melody by trying to make it up. Especially if it means having to go and see her on me own."

I knew exactly where this was leading and I wasn't having it. There would be no twanging on my heartstrings. My loving duty was to my husband, who I knew was desperate to be alone with me without fear of our three imps capering into the bedroom. As for a former girlfriend daring to show up, I wasn't worried as I scrubbed the shine off a couple of plates. Hadn't Ben assured me when he asked—begged—me to marry him that I was the only woman he had ever loved? And aren't men always especially truthful at such glowing moments?

The answer, that all dark-browed romantic heroes have their secrets, should have stared me in the face. But, alas, I was as blindly foolish as any gothic miss descending the darkened staircase of a gloomy manor house at dead of night with only a candle's frail flickering light to ward off the terrors awaiting her.

2

O ur drawing room at Merlin's Court lends itself to tran-
quillity. It was early evening, and the storm had ceased
several hours before. Sunlight skimmed the polished surfaces.
The scent of roses drifted in through the open latticed windows, and the portrait of Abigail Grantham, first mistress of
Merlin's Court, smiled serenely down from above the mantel-
piece. Unfortunately, there was nothing remotely tranquil
about Ben's mood that evening.

He was seated in the fireside chair across from mine. A
softly lit table lamp dramatically highlighted his profile. He
was looking dangerously attractive in faded blue jeans and a
worn sweatshirt: a lethal combination, as I had often told him.
He was wearing his reading glasses, which only added to his
appeal. But far from sending loving glances my way, he appeared oblivious to my presence. Eight years of marriage had

accustomed me to these occasional down moments. Even so, this was to have been a special evening. If he resented Mrs. Malloy's spending the night, that wasn't my fault. I had just persuaded her she'd be better off mulling over a reconciliation with Melody in her own house when he'd walked in and announced that it had been hell driving home in the storm and anyone with any sense would stay put for the evening. She had graciously agreed with him and gone upstairs immediately to lay out guest towels for herself.

The silence thickened. Ben's dark head was bent. He was gripping a glossy magazine with agonized intensity. It was the latest issue of *Cuisine Anglaise*, the one that contained the review of his soon to be released book, *A Light Under the Stove*. As I had told Mrs. Malloy, I had thought it extremely complimentary. I even thought it improved the seventh or eighth time Ben read it aloud to me. Alas, being prey to the tortured sensibilities of a man of letters, he had fixated on one line— the one that described his prose as somewhat *floury*.

My attempts to convince him the comment was not as damning as he thought had fallen on determinedly deaf ears. Reminders that his other books had done extremely well had failed to cheer him. Sensing that he needed time to savor the savage belief that his writing career, if not his life, was over, I focused on my regrets. It seemed my hopes for a romantic evening were doomed to disappointment.

Such a pity! Ben had, without raising a dark sardonic eyebrow in my direction, reminded me why I had known on first meeting him that there would be no joy in my remaining an unattached overweight female with a bunch of finely tuned neuroses. So much had happened since. I know longer needed two mirrors to get a good look at myself. But I still thrilled to the image of him striding across the moors with the wind whipping his black hair to a wild tangle. The intent set of his shadowed jaw, the opal fire of his blue-green eyes, and the way his mouth curved in wry amusement all mocked the impudent folly of the elements in enlisting him as an opponent.

A wife, however, knows when it is time to reenter the fray. I didn't put on a pair of boxing gloves, not having any readily to hand, but I did speak sternly. "Darling, put that magazine down; you've been wallowing long enough. It's bad for the complexion."

His response was a weary grimace.

"Do I have to take it away from you?"

"No." He tossed *Cuisine Anglaise* across the room. I sucked in a breath as it narrowly missed the yellow porcelain vase on the secretary desk before landing in a flutter of pages on the bookcase. Watching him slump back in his chair caused my patience to dwindle.

"It isn't a bad review, and even if it were it's not the end of life on earth."

"You're right." He spoke in a toneless voice.

"Think about it! How many people read that silly magazine anyway?" It was of course the absolutely wrong thing to say, totally insensitive and unsympathetic. But I wasn't used to dealing with Ben in this attitude of pale sorrow. I would much have preferred him to leap three feet in the air and clutch at his head before pounding up and down the room, as was customary when he was severely upset. Turbulence I could deal with, knowing I only had to count to ten and it would be over. I would straighten any pictures that had been sent askew, and whatever was wrong would get sorted out over a cup of tea or, when the rare situation warranted it, something stronger.

"*Cuisine Anglaise* has a wide circulation, Ellie."

"Among people who call beef *boeuf*." I couldn't keep my hoof out of my mouth. "And they aren't the sort to buy your cookery books by the dozens."

"Thanks a lot!" Removing his reading glasses, he set them down with painstaking precision.

"It was meant as a compliment, Ben. Your strength is real food, eaten by real people, not trendy fashion food for the beautiful and bored. You appeal to the average person. Getting meals on the table isn't a form of artistic expression for them. More likely it's a matter of Mum and Dad getting the children to eat what's put in front of them rather than dropping it on the floor for the dog or gagging on it until they're ordered out of the room."

"Why didn't you tell me this before I wrote the damn book? I could have stuck to advice on putting frozen dinners in the microwave," said Ben. "That wouldn't have required any 'floury' prose." His smile did not take the edge off the words. But I didn't have the sense to stop while I was behind. I was too upset that our evening had been ruined and he'd hardly told me anything about his overnight with his parents or how well the children had settled in before he started for home.

"You're not the only one to get less than bubbling praise at times." I stirred restlessly in my chair. "But I don't go to pieces when a client finds fault with a room design I've spent days working on."

"It's not the same, Ellie. Being criticized in print is far worse—"

"Than being told to my face I've done an inadequate job?" I got to my feet and had the sherry decanter in hand when Mrs. Malloy came teetering into the room, again with the feather duster. I had been picturing her snugly tucked up in the guest room with my copy of *Lord Rakehell's Redemption*. But here she was, a possible bright spot or at the very least an interruption, in an otherwise bleak moment. Tobias followed in her wake. Sensing disharmony, which he had made clear in the past was not good for a cat of advancing years, he settled on the bookcase and turned convincingly to stone.

Ben, who had risen for our overnight guest if not for Mr. Tobias, pointed an outraged quivering finger. "He's sitting on *Cuisine Anglaise!*"

"Good!" I flared. "He'll stay sitting on it if I have anything to say about it!" Having poured myself a liberal glass of sherry, I returned to my seat and did my own impersonation of cat staring into space.

"One look through *Cuisine* Whatsit the first time it arrived for you was enough for me, Mr. H!" Mrs. Malloy swayed with the breeze, or possibly the effects of a nip of gin in the kitchen, on her ridiculously high heels. But it was clear she had summed up the situation, as behooved a woman who had once commandeered Milk Jugg's private detective agency. "As if I want to eat at those restaurants they write about. The ones where they put marigolds on your salad and hold up the bottle of wine so you can bow to it! And me a Christian woman! Idolatrous, the vicar would call it!"

With Ben standing there like a bottle of sauce, I felt compelled to stem the flow of Mrs. M's tirade. "*Cuisine Anglaise* is the periodical of choice for the person with the professionally trained palate."

"Biffy for them!" Mrs. Malloy's bust having inflated to a dangerous size, I waited uneasily for the sound of an explosion. "If the review wasn't all that complimentary about your new cookery book, Mr. H, I'd be pleased as Punch. Your recipes are for the sort of meals that taste lovely and give you a warm, dreamy feeling when you remember them years later. It's the same with books. Shakespeare may be good for you, but like I was saying to Mrs. H earlier, it don't warm the cockles of your heart like a nice story about a wicked house-

25

keeper and the family ghost appearing of a nighttime at the windows."

Had she said that? My eyes went to the portrait of Abigail. Her serene smile promised as clearly as if she had spoken that her ghost would never show up at any of our windows. Enormously comforting! Thrilling as such things are to read about, one does not necessarily wish to experience them in real life.

"You have a point, Mrs. Malloy." Ben looked less like a bottle left in the middle of the floor for someone to trip over.

"That's the ticket." Mrs. Malloy teetered over the chair he had vacated. "You stop worrying about being remembered five hundred years from now for your *Poulet à la* Whatsit. Go on writing recipes for the sort of food that keeps people coming back for more at Abigail's. No one can touch you, Mr. H, when it comes to your Welsh rarebit. The one that's a lovely shade of pink because of the diced beetroot you put in it. And then there's the Dover sole with the Gruyère sauce and the steak-and-mushroom pie with the vermouth. Who needs anything fancier than that?"

Tobias charged the feather duster she had discarded. At his approach it came to life and put up quite a fight.

"You're the voice of reason, Mrs. Malloy." Ben smiled at her. It was good to see the light back in his eyes, but I wished I could have been the one to put it there. "How about a glass of sherry? Would you like another one, Ellie?" It was impossible to tell whether or not he was still irritated with me.

"I think I'd rather have a cup of tea."

"Same here," Mrs. M surprised me by saying. "Just the thing with that sky darkening up like it's getting set to storm again. A good thing I gave in and agreed to stay the night or I could have got caught in it good and proper."

Not if she had left earlier, I thought, and immediately felt guilty.

"In these heels"—she looked down at her spindly shoes—"I need to see where I'm putting me feet or I could trip on the bus steps and break me neck." This reference to Madam La-Grange's warning about the perils of bus stops should have reminded me of her other prediction.

Having closed the window and drawn the curtains, Ben said he would make the tea and be back in a jiffy. On his way out of the room he paused to touch my hair lightly, and the world shifted back into place.

"Was it just the magazine business that got to him?" Mrs. Malloy inquired, the moment he was out the door. "Or did the children get upset when he left them with his parents?" Here was the reason she had refused the sherry and most uncharacteristically opted for tea. She had known Ben would offer to get it, thus providing us with a few minutes of private chitchat.

"All three of them always enjoy being with Grandpa and Grandma. They love staying in the flat above the greengrocery. They think it a great adventure to help out at the cash register and hang up the bananas."

"Well, I'll tell you what I think." Mrs. Malloy's pious expression would have suited the vicar when leaning over the pulpit to announce that more help was needed for the foreign missions. "Children don't need a holiday near as much as their mum and dad do. So how about you and Mr. H taking off for a few days instead of staying cooped up here?" Her gaze shifted around the room. "It can get depressing, Mrs. H, with the walls closing in and always the thought of how much dusting there is to do."

For which one of us? Although that might be a moot point now that Tobias had disemboweled the feather duster.

"Where would we go at such short notice?"

"Well, Yorkshire do spring to mind, seeing as Melody lives there. But I'm not just looking out for meself. Think on that good bracing air you get in the dales and up on the moors!" In a moment she would start humming a casual tune.

"Mrs. Malloy," I said gently but firmly, "I told you this afternoon that Ben and I have things we want to get done around the house while the children are gone."

"You'd only be away a couple of days. And like I told you, where Melody lives isn't far from Haworth. You could go and see the parsonage where the Brontës lived."

"I've been there. Seventeen times. I used to make a semiannual pilgrimage before I married Ben."

"Well, maybe he'd like to see it."

"Perhaps." I was wavering, and Mrs. Malloy was every bit as good as Tobias at moving in for the kill.

"I just hate the thought of facing Melody on me own. She can be very intimidating in her way. Tossing out facts: what was said, where it was, and, as if that's not enough, the date and the hour when it happened."

"What does she look like?" It was impossible not to be curious.

"A moth-eaten stuffed rabbit."

"No resemblance then to yourself?"

Mrs. Malloy was looking understandably outraged by this tactless suggestion when Ben came back into the room with the tea tray, which he placed on the Queen Anne table between the sofas. Nicely within reach of Mrs. M and myself, should we feel inclined to reach for a second slice of his delectable chocolate raspberry cake. Scratch that thought. How many digestive biscuits had I eaten that afternoon? Never mind. I could already feel the pounds creeping on. Exercise was needed if I didn't want to wake up in the morning to face a blimp in the mirror. Getting to my feet, I handed Mrs. Malloy the cup of tea Ben poured for her. The brush of his shoulder against mine sent a thrill coursing through me.

Was it possible we would have our romantic rendezvous in the bedroom after all? It was that time of day when dark stubble shadowed his face, adding a hint of mystery to familiarity. The smile he gave me, as he handed me my cup, made my heart beat faster. Perhaps he was only thinking that it felt good to have our squabble behind us, while I was seeing myself slipping into the sea-foam green nightdress before unpinning my hair so that it fell in a languorous silken swirl down my back. There was that bottle of expensively seductive perfume on the dressing table that I reserved for the worthy occasion, there were the candles that glowed amber when lighted . . . and now there was Mrs. Malloy's voice breaking into my highly personal dream.

"No one makes a cup of tea like you do, Mr. H!"

His smile became a roguish grin. "You're too kind, Mrs. Malloy."

"It's all in the way he drops the teabags in the pot." I eyed him impishly.

"Flattery!" He picked up his own cup and saucer. "I suppose you two still think I'm in desperate need of cheering up."

I sat back down, avoiding eye contact with the cake sitting so prettily on its paper doily. "What Mrs. Malloy thinks you and I need is a few days' holiday in Yorkshire while the children are gone."

"Why Yorkshire?"

"I've got a sister there," supplied the voice from the chair opposite mine.

"That we could take her to see," I explained to Ben, "in between all the wonderful exploring you and I could do."

The expression on his face wasn't promising. "I'd no idea you had a sister, Mrs. Malloy."

"We haven't seen or spoken to each other in close on forty years."

"Isn't that sad?" I leaned forward. "Don't you think, darling, that it's important for Mrs. Malloy to take the initiative and try to put things right by going to see Melody?"

"Melody?" he echoed, looking as nonplussed as I had felt on first hearing the name. "Does she sing or play any musical instruments?"

An understandable question. It would be the only excuse to call a woman of middle years Melody.

"Tone-deaf. Always was. Of course there's no saying as how she hasn't taken up the tambourine or one of them play-themselves pianos in the last forty years. It'd be comforting to find out she's got more in life than her typing job for that solicitor." Mrs. Malloy continued to make inroads on the generous slice of chocolate cake on her plate.

"You must go and see her." Ben strode over to the windows and back. "It doesn't do to let these old quarrels go on and on. And it will make a nice trip for you and Ellie."

"What about you?" I set my cup rattling back in its saucer.

"I'd be a third wheel."

"No, you wouldn't."

He came and perched on the arm of my chair and placed a hand on my shoulder. "As you said, it will only be for a few days and I could use that time to start getting recipes together for another book, before I lose my nerve and decide I'm a has-been." His laugh brushed my ear. Obviously he wanted me to take a lighthearted view of things. To be a good sport. Instead, I felt hurt and in no mood to don the sea-foam green nightgown anytime that night. Only for Mrs. Malloy's sake did I put on a good front.

"We could leave in a couple of days."

"Why not tomorrow?" He returned to the coffee table to pour more tea.

Couldn't he get rid of me fast enough? Not being carved

out of stone, I did the only thing a woman could do—cut myself the largest slice of cake that would fit on my plate.

"It would make for a bit of a rush." Mrs. Malloy pursed her purple lips. "And of course I do want to look me best so as to look ten years younger than . . . well, look nice for Melody, that is. But I suppose if we was to set off late-ish in the morning or early afternoon, I could manage to get meself organized."

"Don't you want to phone or write to her first?" I asked.

"She'd find reasons not to see me."

"You can't be sure of that."

"Better to catch her on the hop."

"That's settled, then." Having finished with the teapot, Ben sat down on one of the sofas and stretched his legs, crossing them at the ankles with an elegance of movement that should have charmed me back to good spirits.

"You didn't tell me much about what happened at your parents'," I said, addressing the ceiling, "other than that they were well and pleased to see you and the children."

"Mum and Pop were pretty much as usual." Ben shifted Tobias out from behind his head while balancing his cup and saucer deftly in his other hand.

"What did they have to say?"

"The usual sort of thing. This, that, and the other. Who'd said what to whom after church on Sunday. You know how they are."

"It's interesting," I told the pair of candlesticks on the mantelpiece, "that a man can explain in excruciating detail to a fellow enthusiast how he screwed the knob back onto the bathroom door, but he can't describe to his wife anything above the barest minimum of what happened during a visit at which she wasn't present."

"One of them quirks of nature." Mrs. Malloy looked ready to expound on this but, perhaps sensing my mood, closed her mouth. Ben, however, seemed blindly unaware that I was irritated. Probably his mind was otherwise occupied, concocting a recipe for a rejuvenated version of bubble and squeak that would leave the reviewer for *Cuisine Anglaise* begging for a personal taste test.

He cupped his hands behind his head and closed his eyes. "Mum put on a great lunch when we arrived. Roast beef, Yorkshire pudding, and all the trimmings. The conversation mostly revolved around Tom and Betty winning the lottery and no one hearing from then since."

"Just who are Tom and Betty, if I may be so bold as to inquire?" Mrs. Malloy had her nose, along with her pinky, elevated as she sipped her tea.

"The Hopkinses," I said. "Tom is Ben's cousin. It's his daughter, Ariel, who enjoys gothic novels."

"Oh, right! I remember you kindly let me post a parcel of them to her."

"Tom isn't a first cousin," Ben explained. "Our mothers are second cousins; I think that's how it goes. They probably wouldn't have stayed in touch but for the fact that they are both Roman Catholics and at one time attended the same church. I'd never met Tom until the year I began working at my Uncle Sol's restaurant in Tottenham Court Road."

"I've never heard about him!" Despite not letting on until today about Melody, Mrs. Malloy naturally expects to know more about our relatives than we do.

"He died before I met Ellie. The nicest, kindest bloke, who always hoped I'd follow in his footsteps. Mum asked me to put in a word with him about Tom, who was out of work, and Uncle Sol hired him on at the cash register. He was there for about a year until he got a job with more money as a mechanic. He was great with his hands and could spot why things didn't work"—Ben massaged his jaw to conceal a yawn—"but I didn't see much of him even when we were working together. I had my own life and he had a girlfriend he was pretty crazy about."

"No bothering to keep in touch?" Mrs. Malloy has a strong sense of family, when it isn't hers.

"How was I supposed to know he'd one day win the lottery? They didn't have them in those days. If someone had tipped me the wink, I'd have made him my best friend."

"Has your mother managed to get hold of their new address?" I asked him, ignoring the witticism.

"Afraid not. Of course she assumes it's Betty, not Tom, who's afraid that if his relatives know where to find them they'll all show up with their hands out, hoping for a share of the lolly."

"From the stories past winners tell, that does happen with disastrous results," I said. "The millions disappear and bankruptcy looms."

"Would Betty be the girlfriend from when you was working with Tom, Mr. H?" Mrs. Malloy pulled a passing Tobias onto her lap and proceeded to arrange him into a furry blanket. It was getting a little nippy. I found myself thinking longingly of bed for a variety of reasons, one of which sprang from the fact that Ben smiled at me tenderly while answering Mrs. M.

"No, that wasn't Betty. Perhaps it was a pity the other relationship didn't pan out. From the couple of times I met her, she seemed exactly what he needed. A real go-getter and as pretty as they come. Tom called her his wild Irish rose."

"What went wrong?" I asked.

"She wasn't a Catholic, which was a must for his parents. They put up a stink. Over their dead bodies would their son marry out of the faith. They had someone else lined up for him in no time, a girl he'd known from their first days in kindergarten. They'd gone on retreats together and even dated a few times as teenagers."

"Betty?" Mrs. Malloy and I said together, in the hopeful voices of children expecting to have stars drawn beside our names on the chalkboard.

"No, Angela. She and Tom married but only had a few years together." Ben waited for a rumble of thunder to subside before continuing. "There was a car accident and she was killed. She wasn't even thirty, and to make matters as bad as they could be, Tom was driving."

"How awful!" I pressed a hand to my throat.

"Bad weather conditions. Tom was lucky to get out of the crash with only minor injuries."

"The poor man! He must have been devastated."

"I'm sure he was. I wrote to him, of course, but I didn't go to the funeral because he wanted the immediate family only."

"Grief takes people in different ways," Mrs. Malloy proffered sagely.

"Quite shortly afterward, he met and married Betty. The family thought it indecently quick. Maybe that's another reason she's glad to be shut of them." Ben attempted to mask another yawn, a sign for me to get to my feet and begin gathering up the tea things. Time for bed.

I was thinking it was nice that Mrs. Malloy had Lord Rakehell waiting for her upstairs when an ill wind blew my cousin Freddy into the room. With his long hair, beanpole figure, and dangling skull-and-crossbones earring, he never projects the image of a young man about town, but women—including Mrs. Malloy—for some impenetrable reason dote on his every leer.

"Hello, my nearest and dearests!" He spread his arms wide, his scraggly beard parting in an ecstatic grin.

"Keep creeping up on us like this and I'll ask for your key back." I eyed him severely. "You almost made me drop the teapot, and it's irreplaceable. Woolworth's doesn't sell this pattern anymore."

"You're all wet from the rain. You need to dry off, Freddy dear." Sounding ridiculously motherly, Mrs. Malloy looked around as if hoping to find an assortment of freshly aired towels at her elbow.

"To what do we owe the pleasure?" Ben asked the source of the wet footprints.

"I thought with the children gone from the nest, an evening down at the pub might be in order. Who's game?" Freddy swept us with his beneficent gaze.

"Well, I would be," said Mrs. Malloy, "but the thing is I need to get a decent night's sleep, so's to be up with the birdies to get me packing done before setting out for Yorkshire to see me sister."

Before Freddy could say he didn't know she had a sister, I explained I was accompanying her and also needed my full ration of slumber. That left Ben to take the hint and graciously bid Freddy adieu. But that didn't happen.

"Sure, I'll come along." No sign of a yawn anywhere close to his face now. He exuded energy. "You don't mind, do you, Ellie?"

"Of course not! I'll be happy knowing you're having fun." And then I'll go to bed and look at the ceiling, I thought.

" 'Right then! We'll be off." He kissed the top of my head. "Ready, Freddy?"

Did he have no idea that I wanted to pull off his ears? In all fairness, probably not. The sunny smile I gave him would have done wonders for my acting career, had I had any aspirations to go on the stage. As Mrs. Malloy had so profoundly said, it didn't do to be a spoilsport.

"Are you sure you're all right with this, Ellie?" He had turned around and taken hold of my hand.

"Absolutely." I prodded him toward the door. "I've got a book, *Lord Rakehell's Redemption*, that I'm dying to read, if I can just lay my hands on it. I'm hoping there'll be a murder. That's always the best part, isn't it, Mrs. Malloy."

When would I learn to keep my mouth shut?

3

Shortly after Ben and Freddy left, Mrs. Malloy headed upstairs—supposedly to prepare mentally for her reunion with Melody but probably to lose herself in machinations that would ultimately result in Lord Rakehell's transformation from villain to devoted husband. Ha! I stomped into the kitchen to bewail the treachery of men in general and Ben in particular.

Feeling abandoned and heartily sorry for myself, I got busy at the sink, sloshing cups and saucers around in water both too hot and too soapy. My children were gone. My husband had left me. Even my cat had turned tail and gone outside, refusing to come back in when I called, in spite of the rain. Why hadn't I gone with Ben and Freddy to the Dark Horse?

The answer rumbled down from the thunderous night sky. Because I'd relished cutting off my nose to spite my face. Having laboriously dried the last plate, I was left with nothing to do beyond kicking myself in the shins. To go up to bed leaving Tobias outside was not an option. After another futile endeavor to lure him back inside with the promise of taking him to see *Cats* for his birthday, I trailed disconsolately back to the drawing room, where I was made further despondent by finding the dismembered feather duster buried under a chair. Reflecting that with my luck it would turn out to be on the endangered species list and I would be whapped with an enormous fine should word leak out to the Chitterton Fells Council on Conservation, I rearranged some ornaments that had been perfectly fine as they were. Then I straightened some magazines and plumped a couple of pillows. Had there been a fire in the grate, I would have poked it.

The mantelpiece clock was chiming seven P.M. when a pitiful meow sounded at the window and, feeling that life was marginally improving, I crossed the room to let Tobias in. Far from being grateful at being rescued from the elements, he shot past me in a streak of wet fur to deposit himself on a chair and assume his most ill-used expression. If it's true that misery loves company, I should have been elated. Had I been kinder, I would have told him to finish off the feather duster and forget the consequences. Instead, I turned off most of the lights, leaving only one rose-shaded lamp glowing, and sank down on the sofa facing the windows.

Immediately I found myself weighed down with fatigue. It wasn't the pleasant lassitude that is often the precursor to drifting off into untroubled sleep; I felt heavy and lumpish, beset by physical discomfort. The cushions would not conform to my back. The floor became unreachable to my feet. My shoulders wouldn't hold my arms up properly. I thought about going up to bed, but not only was it too early, there would be that slog up the wooden mountain. Added to which I wasn't entirely sure I was awake and wasn't about to take up sleepwalking. Offstage, the thunder had transformed itself into an overture for *Cats*, with a more than permissible number of wrong notes. I could hear the audience rhythmically clicking its teeth. No, that was the clock ticking away like a metronome inside my head, growing increasingly louder until it, along with the Chitterton Fells Philharmonic Orchestra, got pushed into the background by a more imperative intrusion. A bird, sent by the Endangered Species Commission, was tapping at the windows.

"Tobias, do something about that," I murmured huffily.

No meowed response. As I struggled to sit up and reach around for my feet, which I was almost sure I'd had on when I sat down, the noise got louder. The room was in shadow, adding to my foggy state of mind. Even so, it occurred to me that there might be someone—a person sort of someone, not a blackbird or thrush—trying to get my attention.

"Who is it?" I asked, through lips that didn't belong to my face.

"It's me," said a spectral voice.

"Who?" I crept forward without so much as the poker in hand to protect myself. Against the dark sweep of curtain, a wedge of open window was revealed. Realizing I must have failed to close it when letting Tobias in was not cheering. It was my own fault that I was about to die wearing an elderly bra and no earrings.

"Oriole!" At least that's what I thought the voice said.

My heart pounded and my throat squeezed shut. Here was no ordinary everyday intruder with a bad back and a wife or mother waiting at home, eager to present him with a cup of tea before hearing how he had done on the job and whether the proceeds would allow for a little extra being set aside for Christmas. Lurking behind that pane of glass was the nasty-minded child ghost from *The Night Visitor*. My mouth went dry. Ice prickled down my spine. I regretted never having learned to fall without hurting myself, this surely being an acceptable moment for a Victorian-style faint. No need for a breath-constricting corset. It took Tobias, looking at me with whisker-twitching contempt, to bring me back to reality.

"How clearly do you think when you're half asleep?" I asked him defensively. Then I again addressed the window. "Say again who you are?"

"Ariel."

"Ariel Hopkins?"

"Yes."

This was a stunner, but I didn't waste time gasping; I hurried into the hall, opened the front door, and ushered her in. She was a pitiful sight, wet and bedraggled; her feet in inadequate sandals, her sandy plaits looking as though they had swabbed decks.

"Hello, Ellie." She sized up my welcome through rain-fogged spectacles, as I peeled off the sodden raincoat and tossed it over the banister. Her face was a pale pinch-lipped blur. I envisioned Jane Eyre's friend Helen Burns and held my breath against the pathetic eruption of a consumptive cough.

"Sorry to burst in on you like this." She didn't sound regretful.

"Why tap at the window, instead of ringing the bell?"

"I didn't want to start off on the wrong foot by waking the children if they were in bed."

"That was thoughtful, but they're with their grandparents in London."

"What about Ben?"

"He's at the pub with my cousin. Let's get you into the drawing room where it's warmer." I led the way, still in something of a dream state.

"You won't believe the horrible time I had getting here. Sometimes life can be too cruel," she said, as I settled her on the sofa. "Would you believe, Ellie, there wasn't a buffet on the train? It almost made me wish I hadn't come."

"And where would that be from?" I asked, switching on extra lighting before closing the window against more visitors.

"Yorkshire."

Why was I not surprised?

"I had to wait ages for a taxi after my train got in."

"Ariel"—I sat down across from her—"do your father and Betty know you're here?"

"I told them I was going to my friend Brandy's house and that her parents were okay with my spending the night."

"Ariel!" Unable to think, I bundled a sofa blanket around her. "After I've made you a cup of cocoa and something to eat, you have to let them know what's going on. Meanwhile, take off those wet shoes and settle back comfortably. Wipe your glasses." I pointed to a paper napkin on the table beside her that I had failed to pick up earlier when tidying away the tea things. I headed for the door. "Now you're defogged you can see where you are. Try and relax."

"How can I when my life is in turmoil?"

"We'll get to that in a minute." It was good to draw breath in the hall, but before I could fully recuperate I was summoned back to the drawing room by a piercing scream.

"A cat jumped out at me." Ariel glared at me through her now-clear lenses. "A great, horrid tabby cat."

"He lives here."

"I hate cats."

"Do you?" I forced a smile. Receiving none in return, I fled back into the hall, where I beheld Mrs. Malloy descending the stairs, majestically crowned with purple hair rollers. Having been engaged in her nightly ablutions, she was only wearing one eyebrow. This did not stop her, while clutching her matching dressing gown around her chest, from informing me that I looked pale.

"I feel pale."

"I thought I heard the kettle whistle."

"That was a scream."

"Whose?" She followed me into the kitchen, the clicking of her high heels echoing through the house. "Not Mr. H, waking up to a hangover?"

"He's not back. He's only been gone half an hour."

"You, clearing your lungs?"

"Ariel Hopkins. She absconded from home."

"The girl you send the books to? The one that's parents won the lottery?"

"That's her."

"Talk about surprises. After you and Mr. H were just discussing them!" Mrs. Malloy hovered at my elbow while I made the cocoa and put a slice of chocolate cake and some digestive biscuits on a plate.

"Ariel could probably do with a sandwich or, better yet, something hot to eat," I said, picking up the tray, "but I don't want to waste unnecessary time. I need to phone Tom and Betty. She told them she was staying at a friend's house. But if they've checked and found she's not there, they'll be worried to death."

"Where did she spring from?" Mrs. Malloy graciously held the kitchen door open for me.

"Yorkshire."

"You don't say! Why's she come?"

"That's the burning question." I drew up short outside the drawing room door. "If only Ben were here!"

"No sense standing weighing down the floor, is there? Here, give me that tray." Mrs. Malloy stopped fussing with her

42

purple rollers to give an exasperated sigh. "Your hands are shaking, Mrs. H, and you've slopped the cocoa. Talk about making our little guest feel welcome!"

We entered to find Ariel sitting with Tobias on her lap.

"He climbed on and I haven't been able to get him to budge." She aimed a fierce look at me through glasses that were way too big for her face.

"I'll take him," I offered.

"He can stay if he goes on behaving himself. When he's still, he's like a hot-water bottle. And I think he's picked up on the fact that I don't put up with any nonsense. Who's this?" She pointed a finger at Mrs. Malloy.

"Got a mouth, haven't you?" Mrs. Malloy operates on the theory that children won't get the upper hand if you don't let them get taller than you, which is one of the reasons, I suppose, that her ridiculous heels keep getting higher.

Having enthroned herself in the most comfortable chair in the room, she patted the purple crown of rollers and smiled complacently down at her feet.

"I know someone who wears stupid shoes like those." The cocoa mustache Ariel now wore did nothing to diminish her hauteur. I pitied Tom and Betty, being stuck with the job of preventing her from alienating entire populations at a time. Would they offer Ben and me a substantial bribe to keep her?

"Ariel," I said firmly, "I need to phone your parents."

"Betty's not—"

"Never mind that."

"Can't it wait until I've told you everything?" She swallowed a mouthful of chocolate cake.

"Has either of them been mistreating you?"

"They won't let me have a TV in my room."

"That doesn't count. Give me the phone number."

"There's no need. I'm not the usual fussed-over child. They

43

won't check up on me at my friend's house. They're not that sort. Maybe if I had a real mother it would be different."

Impervious to this tugging at the heartstrings, Mrs. Malloy got to her feet. "I'll make the call if you like, Mrs. H; that way it can be kept short and simple. The child's here safe and sound, and you'll ring them when you've got her story. Give me your phone number, young lady."

I was grateful for this intervention; it seemed to be in the cards that Tom or Betty would blame me for this escapade, either because I had sent those parcels of books or because I happened to be living and breathing somewhere in England. Ariel mumbled her number, and before she had finished glowering at me, Mrs. Malloy returned to report she had met with incoherence from Betty, in the midst of which the phone had been handed to Tom, who'd added a couple of snorts to the dialogue.

"I expect they'll have a row deciding what to do with me." Ariel smirked. "Why have you only got one eyebrow?" she demanded of Mrs. Malloy.

"Because I was in the middle of taking off me makeup when your arrival brung me downstairs."

"I thought it might be the first sign of some horrible pestilence."

Mrs. Malloy resumed her seat with a thump sufficient to send a purple roller flying off her head. "Enough chitchat, Miss Rude Face. What brings you here?"

"To talk to Ellie." Ariel tossed back her sandy plaits. "Last night in bed it came to me she's the ideal person to help me sort out what's been going on."

"And what's that?" Displaying interest, I leaned forward in my chair.

"Finding myself living in a gothic novel. It all started when Dad won the lottery six months ago and Betty insisted on moving to Yorkshire. Their friends—Mr. and Mrs. Edmonds; I can't stand them—had gone there to live, and they raved about this grand house not far from them, with parts that date back to Elizabethan times. They thought Dad and Betty should buy it."

"Where in Yorkshire?" Mrs. Malloy was ready to handle the interrogation with all the aplomb of a chief superintendent from Scotland Yard, while I sat back like the green young sergeant, eager to learn how the great man did things.

"Milton Moor. It's about twenty miles from Haworth, if you know where that is and why it's famous." Ariel licked her cocoa mustache.

"Yes, we do know." I'd decided against playing the silent sidekick.

"Why, if that isn't something!" Mrs. Malloy evinced delighted amazement. "Milton Moor's the little town where me sister lives. I couldn't remember the name when Mrs. H and me was talking earlier."

"What's your sister's name?" Ariel gave Tobias a nudge when he attempted a nibble at the biscuit she was holding. Disliking selfishness, he got off her lap.

"Melody Tabby. She's secretary to an accountant."

"Has to be Mr. Scrimshank. He's the only one in Milton Moor, it's that small a place. He handled things when Dad and Betty bought Withering Heights." Ariel returned my stare. "That's what I call it, because an icy chill went down my spine the first time I saw it. Not that anyone listened to me. Its real name is Cragstone House. Mr. Scrimshank is a friend of Lady Fiona, as well as being her lawyer."

"Who's Lady Fiona?" I asked.

"Cragstone's previous owner. And according to Betty, now the first thrill of living in a mansion has worn off, a cold-blooded killer."

Mrs. Malloy lost another purple roller as she jerked forward in her chair. "Who's the victim?"

"Nigel Gallagher. Her ladyship's husband. He's just an ordinary mister; she was born to the title. The house and grounds had been in her family for generations. I suppose that could have made him feel a bit inferior. Anyway, Betty thinks he's buried somewhere on the grounds and one day he'll get dug up with the new potatoes."

"What put that jolly thought in her head?" Mrs. Malloy's ears were practically flapping.

"Mr. Gallagher disappeared about eighteen months ago. The police didn't make a thing of it, because it wasn't the first time he'd taken off without warning for extended periods on expeditions to foreign parts, as Mrs. Cake puts it. She says the man was always an odd duck, but better a man that likes a bit of travel than one that sits on his bum all the time finding fault with what's on the telly."

"Who's Mrs. Cake?" It seemed expedient to get a grip on the mounting cast of characters.

"The cook."

"Got the name for the job," quipped Mrs. Malloy.

"Mrs. Cake's a very nice lady who doesn't deserve having jokes made about her. She was with the Gallaghers for years. They're quite old, fifty or sixty at least." Ariel took no notice of Mrs. M's wince. "And she—Mrs. Cake—stayed on at Withering . . . Cragstone to work for us. She's the only really normal person there, which is why I think her falling down the stairs the other night and spraining her ankle is the worst thing that's happened so far."

"What else has been going on?" I noticed Tobias looking out of the window and wondered if he heard Ben's car.

"When we first moved in, it was small things that could be explained away. Pictures that fell off walls. Lights turning on

46

or off by themselves. Finding the front door wide open in the morning."

"Like you say"—Mrs. Malloy repositioned a roller—"those sorts of occurrences do happen. And nasty as it must have been for Mrs. Cake, who I'm sure is a lovely person, people do fall downstairs without some evil force being responsible."

Ariel eyed her mulishly. "It was her behavior afterward that was unnerving. At first she said she woke up in the middle of the night to hear someone moving about and got up to check out who it was. Not finding anyone and thinking they might have left by the back entrance, she was heading down to the kitchen when she tripped over something left on the stairs. But the next morning she acted really nervous and said he'd woken from a bad dream and had been imagining things. I heard her talking to Betty, and it was clear she wasn't herself."

"A sprained ankle's no fun," I pointed out.

"I know that. And Mrs. Cake hates having to sit in her chair with her foot up, unable to do more than shell peas and watch Betty let the saucepans boil over. But I'm telling you, there was more to it."

"What do you think happened?" I asked.

"I think someone was moving around that night up in the part of the west wing where the indoor servants slept in the days when there were lots of them. Now there's just Mrs. Cake, in the room closest to the stairs leading down to the kitchen." Ariel adjusted her specs. Only the wind and rain attempted to interrupt her. "I think it was a real live person up there, the one who wants us out of Withering . . . Cragstone. Betty thinks it was Mr. Gallagher's ghost and Mrs. Cake was afraid to say so in case it made her sound loopy, but the next morning decided it might make more of an uproar if it was thought there had been an intruder."

"If it were a ghost," said Mrs. Malloy, "I know just the person to—"

Unwilling to let her get started on Madam LaGrange, I cut her off. "Let's get back to what else has you worried, Ariel, beyond the incidents that you admit can be explained away."

The expression on the girl's face was hard to read. "The thing is, most of them have happened to Betty, who's far from my favorite person and likes to draw attention to herself. But she doesn't have enough imagination—seeing as she never reads anything beyond fashion magazines that don't do her any good—to make things up on a grand scale. She's a really boring person. I don't think Dad minds a bit that she moved into a bedroom of her own because of his horrible snoring. At least it stopped some of her nagging. I don't see how he could ever have been in love with her after being married to my mother. Grandma Hopkins said she was an angel that God wanted back in heaven. Honestly, I wish Dad and Betty would be sensible and get a divorce. But of course he'd never consider it because he's such a strict Catholic. He wouldn't even go for an annulment. He told me once when he heard of a couple from church getting one that such loopholes should be reserved for marriages that haven't been consummated. And horrible as it is to think about, he *has* had sex with Betty. He admitted it when he was giving me the Talk." Her voice capitalized it. "They've done it more than once, too, not just to get it over with." She shuddered. "Sometimes I wonder what I did to deserve all this grief. Perhaps I was a murderer, or something equally wicked, in a past life."

"Interesting you should bring that up—" began Mrs. Malloy.

Again I hurried to prevent the interjection of Madam La-Grange. "Ariel, what frightening things have happened to Betty?"

"She went into the study one morning—she always goes in

there first thing to have her coffee—and found a funeral wreath, a horrible moldy one that looked as if it were weeks old, hanging on the nail that used to hold Mr. Gallagher's portrait. And another time she discovered three dead ravens on her bedroom windowsill." Ariel paused, to good effect. "As I just said, she has her own bedroom, so Dad can't say whether this next thing is true or not, but last week she was woken in the middle of the night—or so she says—by a mournful disembodied voice calling her name. When she asked what it wanted, it said, "Help me, Betty, get me out of this dark place!" And then the shadow of a man with a lion's-head walking stick appeared on the wall at the foot of the bed. Mr. Gallagher has . . . had . . . a lion's-head walking stick."

Clearly thrilled to the core, Mrs. Malloy was rendered speechless, leaving me to ask Ariel if she had believed her stepmother.

"Like I said, I'm not her biggest fan, but I can't see her making it up, even to get attention. If that had been the idea, wouldn't she have screamed the house down and brought Dad running, and maybe even me? But she didn't say anything until the next day. And she was quite calm about it. She said it confirmed her suspicions that Lady Fiona had murdered her husband, and she was going to draw up a plan of the grounds and start digging in likely spots."

"Was that before or after Mrs. Cake fell, or was maybe even pushed, down the stairs?" Mrs. Malloy was on the rim of her chair.

"Before. And I know what you're getting at." Ariel shrugged. "It explains why Betty was sure Mrs. Cake had seen Mr. Gallagher's ghost."

"Okay," I said. "We have two choices here. Either Betty is producing these stage effects for her own reasons, or someone is attempting to frighten the life out of her."

"I've been telling you, Betty's not scared. She's not that sort. A bomb could go off under her and she wouldn't blink. She sees herself as a cute Miss Marple about to show the police they've had the wool pulled over their eyes. This is giving her something to do, now that she doesn't go out to work and hasn't any ideas on how to turn Cragstone into a showplace. Val's taken over that job."

"Who?" Mrs. Malloy and I inquired in unison.

"Val. She's the one who wears silly high heels like yours." Ariel eyed Mrs. M's feet disparagingly. "The weird thing is that Betty, who's not keen on getting in thick with people these days because she thinks they'll try to squeeze money out of her and Dad, seems quite okay with Val. Mrs. Cake says it's hard not to take to someone who's not only helpful but also lovely to look at. And I suppose Val doesn't look bad for someone over thirty."

"Is she a new acquaintance?" I repositioned myself as Tobias climbed onto my lap.

"She moved into the Dower House a couple of months ago to take care of her great-aunt, who was Mr. Gallagher's nanny when he was a little boy. The nanny's really doddery now and very upset that he's gone, besides being angry that Lady Fiona, whom she never liked, sold Cragstone when Mr. G wasn't around to have any say about it."

"That seems one point against her ladyship having murdered him and buried the body somewhere on the grounds. Even without Betty conducting a search, there's the risk of the grave being discovered. Far better, I'd think, for her ladyship to stay put in the ancestral home."

"She had to sell. Her finances were in a terrible mess."

"How about your dad's response to what's been going on?" Mrs. Malloy, who had patently resented the insult to her footwear, managed a smile.

"He's afraid people will get wind of Betty's suspicions about Lady Fiona and insist she's trying to destroy the woman's character. He says there'll be a lawsuit for defamation—Lady Fiona could use the money—and it will be in all the papers: COUPLE WHO WON LOTTERY ACCUSES FORMER HOUSE OWNER OF MURDER. Dad's got a horror of the press because of the articles written about the accident that killed my mother. That's one reason I want to find out what's really going on—such as Nanny Pierce trying to drive us out of the house so that Mr. Gallagher can move back in when he returns from his travels."

"A doddery old lady indulging in scare tactics?"

Ariel shifted restlessly in her chair. "Val could be helping her. Maybe that's the real reason she moved into the Dower House and has been so helpful to Betty with the decorating. It gives her the perfect excuse to be in and out of Withering . . . Cragstone all the time. Maybe Nanny has promised to leave her a nice inheritance in return for her cooperation."

I smiled. "You've read those gothic novels I sent you."

"But you're the expert on them, Ellie. You know how the plots are woven to lead readers astray . . . making us think we've figured out what's going on and then springing a throat-gripping surprise at the end. What if both Betty and I have got it wrong? What if it isn't Nanny Pierce who wants us out of Cragstone, but someone else who resents our moving in? Like Mr. Scrimshank, who's a walking creep show. Just wait till you meet him!" She gave Mrs. Malloy a pitying look. "Perhaps he's madly, obsessively in love with Lady Fiona and thinks that if we are forced out no one else will dare buy the place and she'll get it back for next to nothing."

"Or could the prankster be Mrs. Cake, the devoted cook?" I was compelled to suggest. "I know you're fond of her, Ariel, but she'd need to appear likable and trustworthy in order for her scheme to work, wouldn't she?"

"I suppose. This is why I need you, Ellie—and I suppose Mrs. Malloy as well, seeing that her sister lives in Milton Moor—to come home with me and help me solve the mystery."

"Well, now, that does seem a solution." Far from sounding vexed at Ariel's begrudging inclusion of her, Mrs. Malloy beamed like a little girl on discovering she has sprouted a head of curls as a reward for eating her vegetables.

"There's a problem," I said. "Your dad and Betty have made it clear by not letting the family know where they live that they wish, at least for the time being, to be left alone. So I can't imagine they will welcome a visit, particularly when they don't know me, let alone Mrs. Malloy."

"I know. That's why I didn't tell them I was coming here. But if you take me back they'll have to ask you to stay for lunch, at least. Dad might even want to, if Ben came too. I know it wouldn't have been easy if the children were at home, but with them being at their grandparents' it's not a problem."

"Ariel, Ben has his restaurant, and he wants to put in a lot of hours this week on the cookery book he's starting."

"Then we'll just have to come up with a way to get Betty to decide she wants you to stay for a few days. It's a pity you can't sprain your ankle, but I suppose with Mrs. Cake already having done that it would seem too much of a bad thing and you'd be shoved hobbling out the door." Ariel wrinkled her brow. "If only I could think of something really great to do for Betty to put her in a good mood."

My spirits would improve, I thought, if Ben were to walk into the room before Tom or Betty rang, wanting to know why I hadn't called back to let them know the reason for Ariel's mad escapade. These were his relatives, not mine. The first thing I would do would be to whisk him away and ask if there had ever been the least suspicion that the car accident that killed Tom's wife might not have been an accident. During the course of

Ariel's account, the nasty suspicion had crept into my mind that he of all people might be the one most likely to play games with Betty's mind in the hope that she would react in the approved gothic fashion, by casting herself off the battlements. I didn't want to think this. Tom was a cousin, and so far as I knew murder did not run in Ben's family. What I would not contemplate was that Ariel might be a child of devious intent, equal to the evil little stepdaughter in *The Hidden Forest*.

Some hopes are answered. Footsteps in the hall. I excused myself to Mrs. Malloy and Ariel, along with Tobias, whom I dislodged from my lap, and hurried from the room. Ben was in the hall, taking off his raincoat. It was one of those moments that crop up sometimes, even after all our years together, when time turns back to front and I seem to be seeing him for the first time, awed by his dramatic good looks and the energy he generates with an economy of movement. And this time there was the wonderful comfort of his arms, held open to gather me close.

"I left Freddy at the Dark Horse for someone else to bring home," he murmured against my hair. "I should never have gone out on our first evening without the children. Forgive me, sweetheart. It was that damned review!"

"I know." I returned his kiss. "Darling, you have no idea how lucky I feel. It's like winning the lottery to realize how blessed I am to have you and how our normal life is. You see, while you were gone we had a surprise visitor."

"Who?"

"You'll never believe it."

Through the open doorway I heard Mrs. Malloy telling Ariel about Madam LaGrange's expertise in the arena of the supernatural.

4

***

I'm glad you're coming," I told Ben the following morning, "but I doubt it will be more than a turn-around trip. I can't see the Hopkinses inviting us to stay for a few days. Especially after your saying Tom sounded as though he couldn't wait to get you off the phone last night."

"He was understandably embarrassed."

"It's Ariel's finger-crossed hope they'll feel under an obligation, especially as we are taking her back."

"Who knows?" Ben handed me a pair of his pajamas to put in the suitcase. We were in our bedroom, a roomy apartment with warmly aged dark oak furniture and rose-patterned chintz fabrics. Bright sunshine poured in through the windows, as if eager to atone for the storm. "Betty may enjoy demonstrating her detective skills to you and Mrs. Malloy by flaunting a spyglass when looking under rocks for the body of the missing husband."

"Who, according to Ariel"—I zipped up the case—"is in reality off on a safari or climbing Mount Everest. It seems the more probable scenario. Had his absence aroused suspicion, there would surely have been a hue and cry from the police."

Ben eyed me thoughtfully. "Has it occurred to you Ariel is hoping you'll blow the Mr. Gallagher's Ghost theory out of the water as a means of publicly humiliating Betty? That kid is a tough little customer if ever I saw one."

"That could be a front." I crossed to the dressing-table mirror and assessed my reflection critically. "She's vulnerable. That's something I can understand because so was I at her age. Where she's thin and pasty, I was podgy and pie-faced. Under those circumstances, one learns either to stand up for oneself or let the bullies reduce you to a cowering huddle."

"You were never pie-faced." Coming up behind me, Ben placed his hands on my shoulders. "Must I punish you for such statements?" His lips brushed my neck.

"That's how I saw myself. It didn't help that I sat next to the prettiest girl in our class. Her name was Bridie O'Donnell. She had beautiful black curly hair, perfect skin, and the bluest eyes. I used to go to bed at night and pretend I was her. For good measure I gave myself a wonderful singing voice, a flair for languages, and the ability to perform cartwheels."

"I bet you could give her a run for her money now."

"Nice of you to say, Mr. H." I smiled at him in the mirror and decided that I did look better than might have been hoped when I was twelve or thirteen. My hair had decided to comply that morning and stay put in its chignon, and a flick of mascara had brought out the green in my eyes, matching rather nicely the dress I was wearing. "Perfume," I said, reaching for the bottle, but Ben turned me to face him.

"I like your scent. Eau de Ellie, sunshine with a subtle bouquet of furniture polish." He kissed me deeply and there were no shadows at Merlin's Court.

"I didn't sleep well last night," I admitted. "My mind was too busy, so I got up early and had a whip round with the spray can of lavender wax. There's nothing like a little light housework for clearing away the mental cobwebs. Mrs. Malloy headed for the bus stop after breakfast. She should be back by now with her suitcase. If her sister doesn't offer to put her up, she'll be looking for a place in Milton Moor to spend the night. Which will be the same for us, if Tom and Betty send us smartly on our way."

Ben kissed me again. I inhaled the spicy scent of his aftershave and the other essence that was essentially him. There are aromatic moments that put romance back into marriage, without thought of a ticking clock or a moody thirteen-year-old girl to be returned home.

I stroked his crisply curling black hair. "What about Abigail's?"

"Freddy will handle things. We got it all sorted out over the phone while you were getting breakfast."

"I know the situation has altered since last evening, but you so much wanted to get a quick start on the new book; also, you said you'd feel like a third wheel traveling with Mrs. Malloy."

"It was the reverse. I didn't want her feeling like piggy-in-the-middle when she was already under strain with this reunion with her sister looming."

"Oh!" Talk about feeling small!

"I thought you'd guess where I was coming from."

Perhaps I would have if I hadn't said all the wrong things

about the review in *Cuisine Anglaise* and leaped to the conclusion that he was eager for some time alone. I had been petty and petulant, a prey to foolish insecurities. But I wouldn't let it happen again. From this moment on, I would trust unwaveringly in his love for me. Not a quiver of doubt would intrude.

"You're wonderful." I was bathed in sunlight, inside and out.

"Let's hope the Hopkinses do boot us out and I can prove myself tonight in a hotel bedroom," Ben murmured in my ear.

"I hope Betty doesn't know Mrs. Malloy and I have done some sleuthing in the past. If she's set on making it her mission to prove Lady Fiona murdered her husband, she's unlikely to want either help or competition."

"I don't think you need worry about that angle. There was only one article in the local paper when the two of you took over that private investigator's case and solved it—much to his chagrin."

"Poor Milk Jugg. I hope he's forgiven us."

"Time to get going." Ben picked up the suitcase and ushered me out of the bedroom.

"What's Tom like?" I asked, as we headed downstairs.

"Quiet. Low-key."

"Any hint of hidden depths beneath still waters?"

"We were never pals, even when working together at Uncle Sol's restaurant. The only times I saw any real emotion in him was when he talked about his girlfriend and then on the couple of occasions I saw them together. The one before Ariel's mother."

"Who was his parents' pick."

"Right Angela. Same religious background. Safe choice."

"For him, perhaps, but not for her. She died in a car he was driving." I paused but found myself unable to ask Ben if he thought there was the remotest possibility it hadn't been an accident. "Poor Angela! I wonder if he was ever madly in love with her. It's obvious Ariel believes, or wants to, that it was the perfect union and Betty is a poor substitute turned pain-in-the-neck."

"Then he's got double trouble: his wife *and* his daughter."

"Tom didn't insist on coming to collect Ariel?"

"A halfhearted offer. He said there was some sort of household panic going on that made it difficult for him or Betty to take off."

"Maybe they have Lady Fiona tied up in the kitchen waiting for the police to arrive." We stepped down into the hall to see the front door standing open and Tobias seated on the top outdoor step sunning his coat and lazily stirring his tail. Further investigation showed Mrs. Malloy heaving an enormous suitcase into the back of the Land Rover and Ariel standing off to the side with her skinny arms folded and a disapproving expression on her face.

"What's in there," she snipped, "the washing machine? So you don't have to wash out your knickers in the sink at Cragstone?"

Mrs. M was puffing too hard to reply.

"Let me help you with that." Ben hurried over to her, and while he was stowing our luggage along with hers, which included the addition of a couple of hatboxes and a makeup case, Freddy ambled up the drive. Though looking the worse for his evening at the Dark Horse, he smiled amiably in our general direction. Scooping up Tobias, he nuzzled him into his beard, making it difficult to say where either of them left off.

"Never fear, Ellie." He yawned a grin at me. "All will be well at Merlin's Court under my command. Don't bother to get in touch unless somebody dies."

Hardly the best send-off. But Freddy has his own brand of humor. He claims the bodies start piling up wherever Mrs. Malloy and I put in an appearance. Completely unfounded . . .

58

or, shall we say, exaggerated. Ben and I, having returned his wave, watched him head into the house and close the door. Paradise lay within: our entire refrigerator to himself.

We took our seats in the front of the vehicle while Mrs. M and Ariel got into the back. For a while we drove in silence, presumably each busy with our own thoughts. I for one was glad of the lengthy drive ahead. It would take us a couple of hours to get into Yorkshire. Mrs. Malloy had to be wondering what reception she would get from her sister, Melody. Ariel was surely somewhat nervous about being returned to the bosom of her family. Ben was probably the only one of us capable of enjoying the scenery as it slid past the windows. Or was I projecting my unease onto the two in the backseat? Maybe they only had happy thoughts in their heads. Ariel sounded chipper enough when she finally spoke.

"I hope nobody minds that I used the phone this morning."

"Not at all," I replied. "Did you ring your—"

"I'd rather not say for the moment who I spoke to."

"That's up to you," Ben told her.

"Are we stopping soon for something to eat?" she inquired, with that imperious note in her voice that I'd compassionately ascribed to a desperate need to be loved. "I'm starving."

"What, already?" Mrs. Malloy retorted before either Ben or I could flex our lips. "After that enormous breakfast you ate? I don't know where you put it. Nice and slim as you are," she added hastily, before letting out a piercing squeal.

Had Ariel pinched her? Before I could twist my head around, Mrs. M explained.

"It's the underwire of me bra poking into me. They always do it after I've had them for a while."

"Why not switch to another make?" I asked, as Ben passed a double-decker bus, only to discover it had been lumbering behind a lorry that seemed to be laboring under the delusion that it was a hay cart being pulled by a tired old nag. Making for further frustration, we were now going uphill, unable to see oncoming traffic.

"I couldn't do that, Mrs. H. Like I've told you before, I had no trouble getting rid of me husbands when they didn't work out, but I've kept me solemn vow to stay married to one make of bra for life."

"I wish Dad would get rid of Betty," muttered Ariel.

"You shouldn't talk like that," Ben replied, without shifting his gaze.

Silence pervaded the Land Rover's interior. We finally made it past the lorry and came to a roundabout, followed the arrow marked TO THE NORTH, and got off at the right exit. Had I been driving, we would have circled until we were giddy. I dozed off and wakened to hear Mrs. Malloy rustling around in her handbag; there followed the crackle of candy wrappers.

"No, thank you," said Ariel.

"Want a toffee?" A paper bag was handed up front.

"Not for me, thanks." Ben edged to a stop at a red light in a street lined by narrow-faced gray stone shops, with an open-air market glimpsed around one corner.

"Then I'll take two." I handed the bag back.

Mrs. Malloy said it was always good to have a few sweets on hand. I agreed and we sped on, leaving the town behind and entering the motorway, which we stayed on for an hour or more. We might have been anywhere in England. Everything seemed the same from one moment to the next, an unending stream of uniformity from the vehicles to the buildings. Metal and glass . . . concrete and glass . . . all stripped of color, scale, and shape. Everything moving at the same automated speed. Where were the famous dales, the mysterious, beckoning moors? Did the Yorkshire I had imagined exist anymore? Or had it been paved over and roofed in for a shopping center?

"I've changed my mind." Ariel spoke from behind my head. "I will have a toffee, Mrs. Malloy."

"Aren't you the kind little miss?" An irritable rustling of paper bag. "Didn't anyone ever tell you the word *please* hasn't been rationed since World War Two?"

"Maybe Betty attempted to clamp down on her behavior." Ben spoke in a low aside to me, but Ariel must have heard. She sucked in an infuriated breath.

"Ellie, can we *please* put him out of the car?"

"That's enough." I almost yanked my head off in turning around to face her. "I understand you're on edge—"

"I'm not. I'm perfectly calm."

"That's neither here nor there."

"You just said—"

"What my wife is attempting to explain, Ariel, is that we are fast losing sympathy for you," Ben informed her, "whatever your grievances."

I settled back in my seat, staring rigidly at the windshield. More silence. We were exiting the motorway to a view of hills as rough-hewn as the stone walls bordering the fields surrounding the outline of a farmhouse that might have been Wuthering—not Withering—Heights. Way off to our right spread a shadowy stretch of what I hoped might be moorland. But I couldn't enjoy this introduction to the county of gothic glory. Had Ben and I spoken too sharply to the girl? How precarious was her state of mind? Would Tom and Betty prove especially difficult if we returned her blank-eyed and silent?

"I don't know why I have to come off sounding bratty, at the very times when I really want to be nice so people will like me," Ariel remarked plaintively. "Like last night, Ellie, when I knew I needed to win you and Mrs. Malloy over. I could hear myself talking and it didn't sound right, but there just didn't seem anything I could do about it."

"Got one of them multiple personalities?" Mrs. M asked eagerly.

"I suppose I'm perverse."

"Probably." Ben laughed, and I felt myself relax.

"Our own worst enemies, that's what we all are sometimes." Mrs. Malloy sounded ready to enlarge on this theme. But Ariel announced that we were now within a few miles of Milton Moor.

"And we haven't stopped for lunch." I looked at my watch to see that it was nearly noon. "Should we look out for somewhere?"

"It's all right. That toffee did the trick. I'm not starving anymore. Why put off the evil hour? Of course, it'll be bread and water for me." Ariel sounded almost cheerful. It was Mrs. Malloy who betrayed uneasiness.

"I wonder if Melody will think I've aged some."

It seemed likely after a span of forty years, but I crossed my fingers and said probably not. Ben nosed the car onto a sharply steep road with buff-colored houses, grimed with smoke, butting up against the pavement. All very prim and properly Victorian, with lace curtains screening the windows and pots of stiff-looking maroon and purple flowers on the steps. It was truly like stepping back in time. Finally my heart thrilled. A woman opened her door and whacked a mat against the wall. A cat leaped out of a tree and a little boy of about three came pumping along on his tricycle. A woman with orange hair came out of a house with a BED AND BREAKFAST sign on the gatepost. I noted a couple of side streets with shops and other businesses. Then we were again looking out on more open country, bordered by the dry-stone walls and punctuated by solitary trees and outcroppings of rock. Some cultivation, but mostly a sea of coarse wavering grass. We passed a man with shaggy black hair streaked with white, striding alongside a similarly colored sheepdog, both of them completely at one with the landscape. Elemental. Timeless.

"Who said a moor is merely a lawn in need of mowing?" Ben inquired.

"I don't know." I was a little peeved that he'd broken the mood.

"You made that up yourself, Ben." Ariel actually giggled, like a real child.

"Caught out!" He grinned and I simmered down. It was good that the two of them seemed to be coming to terms. Now all we needed was a little harmony on meeting Tom and Betty.

"We're here. Time to face the music!" Mrs. Malloy tapped on her window. "Look! It says it on the brass plate on that brick wall: Cragstone House. And there's the roof and the chimneys towering up to the sky. Well, I never!" She continued her raptures as we drove in through the gateposts. "There's a cottage off to the side, but much bigger than the one Freddy lives in back at Merlin's Court. This one could house a family of six without anyone bumping walls." She had rolled down her window and stuck out her head, risking getting scratched by the shrubbery lining the drive, which gave way on either side to flower beds in a park setting.

"Oh, you're talking about the Dower House! It's rather nice inside. Lady Fiona still owns it and a couple of acres of land."

"Is that where she's living?" I asked.

"No, she's temporarily in residence at a hotel. Mr. Gallagher's old nanny is at the Dower House with her great niece, Val. Their last name is—"

She didn't get to finish. Ben had parked the Land Rover facing a flight of steps that would have seated a full orchestra. The moment called for a rousing flourish of Mozart. The handsomely carved front door opened to reveal a man and a

63

woman descending to meet us. The stiffness of their gait suggested that they were either made out of fiberboard or were rigidly controlling their emotions. I decided the latter was more likely; Ben and I got out of the vehicle as if ordered to do so by two police officers. Mrs. Malloy and Ariel followed. I didn't turn to see if they had their hands up.

The couple had reached the bottom step. Tom wasn't much of a surprise. I had pictured him as being of medium height and stocky build, with pale, slightly protuberant blue eyes and a weak mouth. And there he stood. The reality was completed by the brown tweed sports jacket and elderly cords he was wearing, perhaps in ineffectual hope of looking like a landed squire, of the kind that lived for his trout fishing and pheasant shooting and had only given up smoking a pipe when it became politically expedient to do so. Betty was another matter. I had got her all wrong. She was neither an ethereal blonde trailing organza nor a raven-haired beauty wearing spiffy riding togs. She was a diminutive redhead in a too-large pale blue suit, with a nose that had been pinched out of plastic. Her eyes were clear green glass.

"Ariel!" Her voice was a spurt of ice-cold water. "Get over here."

"Oh, Betty darling!" I was staggered to hear the girl reply. Indeed, I clutched at Ben's arm and was glad of the additional support of Mrs. Malloy's sturdy presence behind me. "Daddy!" A breeze, absent until now, fanned my cheeks and fluttered my skirts. It was caused by Ariel's sobbing breath. She raced around me, hands extended, spectacles askew, and limp hair flying. "Please, please don't be cross. I've got the loveliest surprise planned."

Tom's smile had the look of a false mustache that could be taken off and hurriedly slipped into his pocket if it didn't meet with his wife's approval.

"Get indoors this minute, Ariel!" Betty's rigidity suggested an outraged Barbie doll. So far she had not deigned to glance at Mrs. Malloy, Ben, or me. Neither, for that matter, had Tom.

"Oh, but not before I tell you about the surprise!" Ariel flung herself at her stepmother. "This morning I had the brilliant idea to phone a—"

"I'm not interested. You've caused no end of an upset at a time when your father and I have other things to worry about. Tell her, Tom."

The recipient of a jab from an undoubtedly sharp elbow cleared his throat. "You shouldn't have done it, Ariel. We've been worried sick about you, and I'm sure you've put Cousin Ben and his wife to a lot of bother." He finally looked our way. "Whatever made you take off like that?"

"And why to them?" Betty's tone said it all.

"I couldn't think of anyone else. Ellie had been kind, sending those books to me." This was uttered in a broken little voice. "We don't have many relatives and none that we ever see, now that Grandma Hopkins is dead. I've been so mixed up and miserable. Everything changed after the lottery. People talking about us. Moving to this house. Being frightened that you're right, Betty, about Lady Fiona murdering her husband and burying him out here where we could be stepping on him every day and disturbing his eternal rest. I can't sleep at night because I'm so scared of waking up to see his ghost."

"Clever little whatsit!" Mrs. Malloy muttered from behind me, and Ben murmured agreement.

"Ariel, you know that murder business is nonsense," said Tom.

What was there that Betty could say? She stood looking furiously flummoxed, and Ariel nimbly seized the moment.

"You're right, Dad, I did put Ben and Ellie to a lot of trouble. But they were wonderful. And so was Mrs. Malloy, who works for them. It was mostly her who made me see what a silly girl I'd been, not talking my fears over with you instead of running away. We have to find a way of making it up to them, don't we?" She turned and beckoned to us, her smile one of timid optimism.

The scene had come more broadly to life. There was concerted movement now. The Hopkinses were moving toward us, Ariel with the prancing gait of an exuberant six-year-old, Betty with a visible lack of enthusiasm, and Tom looking uncertain as to whether or not he should take his smile out of his pocket and stick it back on his face. I let Ben and Mrs. Malloy go ahead of me. While they were being greeted, I focused my attention on the stark edifice that was Cragstone House.

It lacked a north tower, or the remnants of an ancient keep, so beloved of my heart in fiction. But in other ways it was splendidly suggestive of dark doings, fueled by unbridled passion, being conducted within. It was many times the width of Merlin's Court, its rugged gray stone walls rising three stories to a jagged roof as black as a night sky, with chimney pots too many to count. I could picture it gobbling up normal-sized houses for breakfast and, like Oliver Twist, asking for more: just one small cottage . . . or maybe two . . . to keep things going until lunch. There was a furtive aspect to the tall narrow windows, which when combined with the grappling ivy and the shadowy passageway separating the ground floor of the main structure from the west wing, produced the requisite shivers to be experienced by the hapless governess or the unwanted visitor about to enter the premises. Yes, I could see why Ariel had nicknamed it Withering Heights.

Ariel appeared at my side to grab my hand and propel me forward, whispering to me as I put one faltering foot in front of another, "Dad seems pleased to see Ben, and Betty is thawing, so now it's up to you not to ruin everything. Act humble and impressed."

"That shouldn't be difficult." I was the governess clad in a stiff black gown with the demurest hint of a white collar. My bonnet was serviceable, my boots sturdy and well polished. Poverty had not defeated my attempts to present myself tidily to an uncaring world.

"Betty, darling!" Ariel, still clutching my hand, was jumping up and down in a way that Tam and Abbey at seven had outgrown and even five-year-old Rose didn't do much anymore. "Here's Ellie. Oh, I do know the two of you are going to be great friends! I can feel the emanations!"

Did we have here a budding Madam LaGrange?

Betty extended a miniature hand, which I took gingerly, for fear it would break off in my grasp and Tom would have to put the Barbie doll back in the purchase box and return it to the manufacturer for a refund. That would solve my problem of trying to get on her good side in hope of being asked to spend a few days at Cragstone.

"As Tom has been saying to your husband, we appreciate your bringing Ariel home and sorry her acting out had to involve you. It's embarrassing for us and awkward for you." Her voice was stiff and jerky, causing me to wonder if the wrong mechanism had been installed or she had been played with more than recommended.

"She's at a difficult age."

"You can say that again. Sometimes I think she hates me." Emotion showed fleetingly on Betty's face.

"It's a stage. We all went through it."

"I'm not sure I've outgrown mine," she said surprisingly. "Let's go inside, shall we? You must be ready for a cup of tea."

"Thank you, that sounds wonderful." We followed in the

wake of the others, Tom and Ben going up the stairs ahead of Ariel and Mrs. Malloy.

"Your cleaning woman seems brighter than most." Betty pointed a finger at the purple taffeta figure now entering the house. "She's come to see her sister, she said."

I had to stop grinding my teeth to reply. "That's right, Melody Tabby. She's secretary to a Mr. Scrimshank."

"We went to him for some advice about the money we . . . came into. But he won't be handling our investments." Betty stepped through the open front door. "We feel quite capable of doing that ourselves."

"Do accountants often perform that service?"

"He did for the Gallaghers who owned this house. But that may have been because they were friends. Perhaps Ariel told you"—she gave me a speculative look—"that Mr. Gallagher disappeared, just upped and vanished, about a year and a half ago. And no sign of him since."

I hedged. "I heard what she said to you and her father, about a murder and a ghost."

"All these months I've thought she, like Tom, didn't believe me."

"The police?"

She shrugged, a gesture so akin to Ariel's it might have been genetic if they had been blood relatives. The hall in which we stood was vast and thick with shadow. Given the lack of light, it could have been any time of day—from early afternoon, which was the case, to dead of night. The vast chandelier was unlit and too closely resembled the branches of a gallows tree to suit my sensibilities as a designer. The window high on the staircase wall resembled a leper's squint. The rest of the group, though standing just a few feet away from us, were mere silhouettes in monkish robes. Ever since picking up my first gothic romance, I had yearned to enter a house such as this.

The sensation I had experienced when looking at the exterior was now heightened. The dark wainscoting, somber furniture, and looming paintings in heavy frames issued a hushed warning that Death could be lurking behind a door or crouched down on some hidden step. I shivered, despite a muggy warmth that was oppressive in itself.

Betty flicked a switch and the chandelier burst into light. No longer did it look like a gibbet. It glinted with gold and sparkled with crystal. The paneling was revealed as a richly mellow walnut, the staircase a graceful curve of banisters and broad steps, exquisite in its simplicity. Regency, I thought. Or more likely Queen Anne, my favorite period. There was an Aubusson carpet underfoot, its colors faded by time to possibly even greater beauty than originally present. A grouping of Empire chairs with black gilded frames and yellow silk seats occupied one corner, along with bronze-topped tables. To my right stood a magnificent long case clock of Beuel design and on my left a Chinese chest whose period I could not even begin to guess at.

My foolish panic evaporated. Perversely, I found myself wishing for a more Tudor atmosphere: dark oil portraits of Elizabethans in ruffs staring censoriously down at me, pewter tankards on a trestle table, rush mats on the floor. This was all very lovely but too suggestive of an ultra-expensive hotel.

"I don't know why you don't leave that light on, Tom," Betty called across to him. "It's not like we have to worry these days about meeting the electricity bill."

Had things been tight for them financially before the big win? Had the stress of pinching pennies made her snippy? I paused in the general movement toward an arched doorway to glance sideways at an assortment of porcelain snuffboxes on the Chinese chest. A cobalt blue and gold one caught my eye. It was a lovely thing with birds delicately painted on the lid.

But it would not do to dally. As it was, I made up the rear in entering a drawing room that possessed two superb marble fireplaces.

Although the leaded front windows did not admit an abundance of light, this was more than compensated for by wall-to-wall glass doors at the rear, leading into what appeared to be a conservatory. The furnishings were an elegant eclectic mix of antiques and the contemporary. There were groupings of gold damask sofas and chairs covered in black and cream toile. I spotted an art deco table, a William and Mary secretary desk, and two Venetian glass lamps by an artisan whose name was currently being spoken with awe. The artwork was an interesting juxtaposition of abstracts and meticulously detailed etchings. I gave the Hopkinses' decorator top marks. A major name, I supposed, from a London firm. I couldn't have come up with anything this good.

"What a wonderful room," I told Betty.

"That's a real compliment, seeing you're in that field. Tom's mother mentioned it. We were very close." She ushered me toward a chair positioned across from the front fireplace and took the one beside it. The others were already seated and engaged in conversation, save for Mrs. Malloy, who, with her handbag on her lap, appeared to be soaking up her surroundings, the better to report back to her chums in the Chitterton Fells Charwomen's Society. It would be something to fall back on if she returned with her tail between her legs after a failed reunion with Melody. "I had a friend help me with the details," Betty continued. "Well, not a friend exactly, more of an acquaintance living at the Dower House. Val gave up her job at a travel agency in London to come and look after her great-aunt, Miss Pierce, who was once Mr. Gallagher's nanny."

"What a good niece. She's obviously enormously talented."

"Never took a decorating class in her life." Although she

70

was perched on the very edge of her chair, Betty's feet didn't touch the floor. "It's just something Val's interested in. We were talking one day and she made a couple of suggestions that sounded all right. Tom didn't offer any opinions. That's how he is, but I knew he liked yellow." She looked to where he was sitting with Ben on one of the gold damask sofas. "We tried to get Val to let us pay her, but she wouldn't hear of it. I'll have to come up with an idea for a present. I thought of flowers, but it doesn't seem enough. She's certainly been a big help."

That was apparent. I looked around the room that had been brought to life and beauty by an amateur and felt more than a twinge of envy. I was not a nice person. Hadn't I all too readily bought into Ariel's negative opinion of Betty? Looking at her now, I saw that the pale blue of her designer suit might be to blame for her plastic appearance. She needed warmer colors, softer lines and subtler makeup than the dark eyeliner and cherry lipstick that clashed with her red hair. What a pity the otherwise helpful Val hadn't offered these suggestions—and allowed Betty and Tom to infuse something of their own personalities into the house. There I went again! My nasty side creeping in.

"Lucky for us Val came to look after her great-aunt," said Betty.

"She could be hoping to inherit the old lady's money," Ariel responded direly.

"Who's Val?" Ben inquired sleepily from his chair.

"You'll meet her. She's always here."

"I don't think she's out for what she can get from Miss Pierce," protested Tom mildly.

"She's not always here!" Betty shot back at Ariel. "Sometimes we don't see her for days on end."

Hardly surprising if Val was poring over decorating books,

along with taking care of Auntie, whom I was picturing as partially bedridden and in need of nourishing little meals on trays and lengthy talks about what Mr. Gallagher was like as a small boy. Such a one for objecting to wearing his neddy when taken for a walk in the grounds! And, oh, the naughty fuss he made about eating his tapioca pudding! All highly entertaining, no doubt, but time consuming.

"Life do get so busy," Mrs. Malloy remarked, in the plummy tones befitting a woman who had twice been chairwoman of the Chitterton Fells Charwomen's Association. "I can state without a word of a lie that I work me fingers to the bone at Merlin's Court. I'd expect me head to land on the chopping block if the kitchen wasn't shipshape when Mr. H gets to trying out one of his fancy recipes." She patted her two-tone hair and inflated her bosom, I hoped without a poke from a dislodged underwire.

Betty eyed her narrowly before looking at Ben. "I'd forgotten you're a professional chef."

"It's work I enjoy." He smiled at her, and she turned her attention back to Mrs. Malloy.

"Mavis, our daily woman, is pretty much useless."

"I wouldn't go that far, Betty." Tom bestirred himself to remonstrate. "Lady Fiona seemed to think she was okay."

"That doesn't mean anything, coming from someone as vague as she is."

"I thought you'd decided that was just an act, to cover up the fact that she's a ruthless killer." Ariel kicked the legs of her chair.

Betty flared back at her. "Don't stick your nose into the conversation. You should be locked in your room, hoping we'll let you eat again."

"I'm already starving."

"Don't talk back, dear." Tom got to his feet. "I'll go down to the kitchen and ask Mrs. Cake to rustle up some lunch."

This sounded good to me. It seemed an age since Betty had made the welcome offer of a cup of tea.

"And how's she going to manage that, stuck in a chair as she is with her sprained ankle propped up on a stool?" Betty inquired sarcastically.

"I'd forgotten."

"The best she can do is sit with a bowl in her lap shelling peas."

"Perhaps she could whisk up some eggs instead."

"And sit with the toaster on her lap, popping up slices of bread?"

Ariel looked from me to Ben and Mrs. Malloy. "Mrs. Cake's a wonderful cook when she can be on her feet." Sentimental sigh. "She makes the loveliest scones and things. Although not as good as that chocolate cake of yours, Ben."

Life has its lively twists and turns. Heroes have a way of popping up when least expected. From the expression on Betty's face, it was clear our visit was no longer entirely unwelcome. Ben was offering to accompany his cousin into the kitchen and prepare a meal, if that would be helpful.

"We don't like to impose, do we, Tom?"

"No, dear."

"If you're sure, Ben?"

"It will be my pleasure." His smile was directed at Betty, but I knew with secret wifely knowledge that it was meant for me.

Betty practically sparkled. "Thank you, and take Ariel with you. Put her to use with the washing up."

This produced the requisite scowl in return.

"Now, then, no need to bother the child. Surely that's what I'm here for." Beaming fatuously at one and all, Mrs. Malloy converted instantly into trusted family servitor. "Got me pinny right here. Never without it in case it's needed." She opened her handbag and withdrew a scrap of white nylon trimmed with lace. To my knowledge it had never put in an appearance at Merlin's Court, but the washing up there is not very grand on a daily basis. Our humble soup bowls, earthenware casserole dishes, and stainless steel cutlery deserve no more than a tea towel tucked in at the waist. Here, if Val's revamping included the kitchen, it would be a different matter.

"Ariel!" Betty pointed a finger.

"Don't you want me to stay and tell you about the lovely surprise?"

"I told you I'm not interested." The green eyes flashed. "Something has to be done about your escapade, but I can't concentrate on that now, or even Mr. Gallagher's murder. I've a huge calamity on my hands."

"I'm sorry," I said, as Ariel pirouetted out the door. "And here you are with three extra people on your hands."

"I've been frantic." Betty gripped her tiny hands. "My first social engagement as lady of the manor is coming up, and I was sure it was doomed! But perhaps there is a way to salvage the situation if Ben and Mrs. Malloy would agree to help me out." She eyed me with the desperate appeal of a woman trapped on a cliff ledge in a storm equal to the one we'd had yesterday. "It seems a lot to ask, Ellie, because it would mean your all staying on here for a few days."

5

❦

"I told Ellie about the awful fix we're in regarding our up-coming social engagement," Betty informed Tom a half hour later.

Our merry bunch was in the dining room, grouped around a large, beautifully polished oval table set with Royal Der-byshire china, sterling silver, and sparkling crystal, all a delight to the eye. The wallpaper was a watered raspberry silk, the car-pet centered on the parquet floor a prize from the Orient, the chandelier dazzling, the William and Mary display cabinets a repository of treasures. Val of the Dower House had again performed her magic. I could only wonder if the Hopkinses had stretched their multimillions too thin, forcing them to cut down on milk and eggs in the coming weeks.

So far there seemed to be no shortage of provisions. Ben, with some assistance one presumed from Tom, Ariel, and Mrs.

Malloy, had produced a sumptuous feast, making it hard for me to decide what to dig into first. The spinach salad with cilantro, garlic shrimp, and toasted pecans, the golden-crusted French onion quiche, or the little sausages simmered in a Bordeaux sauce?

"You told Ellie what, Betty?" Tom scrunched in his fair eyebrows and focused his protuberant blue eyes on his wife. Mrs. Malloy and Ariel picked up their knives and forks. Ben passed me a silver basket lined with white damask. Admiring the artfully arranged slices of crusty French bread, I wondered if it would appear piggish to take two.

"Come on, Tom, you know what I'm talking about!" snapped Betty.

Puzzlement faded; light dawned. "You mean the vicar, Mr. Hardcastle, bringing a retired clergyman over for Sunday tea tomorrow? Something about the old chap having visited Cragstone as a boy and wanting the see the place again before he cops it. And here we are with Mrs. Cake off her feet and no possibility of putting on a decent spread." Apparently satisfied that he'd answered well enough to avoid being sent to his room, Tom applied himself in an absent manner to the quiche on his plate.

"That's not it." Betty set down her water glass with a bang that would do little for its longevity. An hour earlier I would have dismissed this as outraged Barbie behavior. Our brief talk, however, had brought her into better focus. I wasn't sure whether or not I liked her, but she was no longer a plastic doll. For better or worse she was flesh and blood. There was a spot on the lapel of her blue suit and several chips in her nail polish.

"Then if it's not the tea party . . . ?" Mrs. Malloy was well on her way to being admitted into the CPC (clean plates club), an honor unequal to that of being a lifelong member of the

CFCWA (Chitterton Fells Charwomen's Association) but nonetheless nice to have on one's résumé.

"It's the big swank that's set for Thursday afternoon," said Ariel, her mouth full.

Betty ignored the curled lip. "The Milton Moor annual garden party. As I told Ellie, hosting it here has been a tradition. Reverend Hardcastle's predecessor suggested it to the Gallaghers as a treat for the village children. It was arranged that it be held on the Thursday closest to the middle of July, children to be accompanied by at least one parent. Over the years the event expanded to include any of the local people who wished to attend. We weren't here for any of the previous ones. But there are games for the children, three-legged and egg-and-spoon races, that sort of thing. Lady Fiona asked if we'd keep the tradition going after we moved in. She made quite a point of saying how much her husband had enjoyed it."

Rather sweet of her, one would think, fondly sentimental, and yet Betty somehow succeeded in making her ladyship's request sound sinister. An opportunity to enjoy the delightful sight of laughing, squealing children and thumping adults dancing on her husband's grave?

"They didn't entertain much otherwise." Tom, having finished his quiche, made this contribution without prompting. "Very likely they couldn't afford to splash about with the fizzy drinks. Apparently they've been short of funds for some time now."

"Think that's why Mr. Gallagher performed his disappearing act?" Ben raised an inquiring eyebrow.

"She was the one with the money and the house when they married." Betty's expression made its point: Lady Fiona, having discovered that her husband had squandered her inheritance, had lost her temper, slapped him with a shovel, and popped him in the wheelbarrow for future planting. "But to get back to the garden party. A couple of hundred people usually show up. Tents and chairs have to be set out, but that can be managed. The huge problem is the food. The Gallaghers, despite any financial difficulties, always put on quite a spread: catered of course, by an exclusive firm. She gave me the name, so that's who I phoned, weeks ago. But late yesterday afternoon, when I rang to check that they had everything down pat, this nasty male voice 'reminded' me"—Betty clenched her hands—"that I'd phoned a couple of days ago to cancel."

"Did you?" Ariel displayed wide-eyed interest.

"Of course not!"

"Well, I never!" Mrs. Malloy looked suitably shocked.

"I said there'd been a mistake, some sort of mix-up, but there was no getting through to that wretched voice. He kept going like a recording, saying it was too late to set things back up; another job had been accepted for that date. And when I really got exasperated and may even have yelled a bit, he said in a horridly haughty manner that I was wasting my breath and his time."

I sat puzzling over the matter. If there hadn't been a mix-up—as in the caterer having confused one client with another—who had made that cancellation phone call and why? Was there any reason to look further than the thirteen-year-old girl now neatly arranging her knife and fork on her empty plate?

"Did you ask him if the voice sounded like yours?" Mrs. Malloy was teetering around the table on her high heels, pouring coffee from a silver pot into fluted rimmed cups, a paragon of helpfulness in her nylon and lace pinny.

"I didn't think. I was too shocked."

"Darling Betty!" Ariel sympathized. "You must have been ready to chew glass."

"And then to find out you'd run off!"

"Upsetting," agreed Tom.

"Think of the talk—lottery winners too stingy to put on a decent spread! I was on the phone all morning before you arrived." Betty's gaze circled the table and fixed on Ben. "First one catering firm, then the next, but no luck. Every one of them was booked solid for this coming Thursday. But now you're here, and you *are* Tom's cousin, and"—her laugh was giddily nervous—"as the saying goes, family is family."

"Blood's thicker than water," Ariel chanted.

"I think what Betty is trying to say"—Tom twiddled with his coffee spoon, set it down, then picked it up again—"well, to put it in a nutshell, Ben, it's like this. If you and Ellie would consider staying on here for a few days—that's if you can spare the time and don't need to rush back home—we'd be no end appreciative of your help in getting us out of this fix."

Ben's eyes glinted with amusement. "I think we can manage that, don't you, Ellie? It'll be like the old days at Uncle Sol's. Those were some good times."

"I suppose they were." Tom looked awkward. "Working that old-fashioned cash register. Perhaps I didn't get as much out of it as I should." This not sounding quite right, his fair skin reddened. "What I mean to say is, I don't think I was cut out to be behind the till."

"We should have stayed in touch," said Ben.

"It's been a lot of years."

"Tom! Do stop twiddling!" Betty scolded.

"Sorry." Tom dropped his coffee spoon with a silvery clatter into his saucer.

Betty turned to me. "You said Ben would agree. Some women do know their husbands. Can you persuade him to also work his magic for tomorrow's afternoon tea?"

"A mini trial run, what could be better? But I'll need my

support team." His smile took in Tom and Ariel but lingered on Mrs. Malloy, who was looking seriously put out.

"Well, I don't know as I can say what'll I'll be doing or where I'll be tomorrow afternoon, Mr. H," she responded huffily. "It could be my sister will beg me to stay with her. Then again, maybe she won't and I'll find meself a nice hotel with one of them services offering back massages and facials."

"Oh, don't do that," cried Betty in alarm. "I meant for you to stay on here as well; I assumed that would be understood. We want you to feel like one of the family, just as you do at Merlin's Court."

"I'll need time away to see me sister," Mrs. Malloy said firmly.

"Her employer, Mr. Scrimshank, is invited to tomorrow's tea." Betty inspected chipped nail polish. "It seemed a good idea, considering his friendship with Lady Fiona."

"In that case it's good I'll be here to meet him."

"Lady Fiona is also invited. Mr. Scrimshank claims to have received a phone call from Mr. Gallagher after his disappearance. It was then the police decided there was no further need to investigate."

"Yes, do stay, Mrs. Malloy! You're such fun!" Ariel's eyes sparkled, and again I noticed some pink in her cheeks. Perhaps she would turn into a pretty young woman. But would she be a nice one? That was the question. Was there any point in asking her if it was she who had canceled the caterer?

"Fun? Not when I'm working, I'm not. Can't be any frolicking about when there's important jobs to be done. That's spelled out in the charter of the CFCWA."

"A local business organization of which Mrs. Malloy is a founding member and two-time chairwoman," I explained, for the benefit of Tom and Betty's blank looks.

"The Chitterton Fells Charwomen's Association." Mrs. M's posture merited her royal purple ensemble. The turn of her head suggested the necessity of keeping a crown on straight. As chairwoman she wore one when presiding at annual meetings, and doubtless the memory lingered. "We have strict rules, Mrs. Hopkins, about honing in on another professional's territory. I wouldn't want to go upsetting Mrs. Cake by taking over her sink and cupboards like they was me own. She seemed a nice person. Sad to see her sitting with her foot up on a cushion while we was getting lunch. Had to make her feel out of things. Spoke to me very nice, she did. Told me where to find the washing-up liquid."

"I'm sure Mrs. Cake will appreciate your pitching in for a few days." Ben attempted to speed things along, and Tom agreed.

"Well, I wouldn't want her forced back on her feet before she's ready." Mrs. Malloy adjusted her crown. "And I could be a big help getting some of the regular meals, along with keeping things straight while Mr. H is hard at it."

"Then that's settled!" Having done battle, Betty sat back.

"Not so fast. There's the woman that comes in to do the cleaning: Mavis, I think you said her name was. I can't be treading on her toes neither. It wouldn't be right. And you'd be in a worse pickle, Mrs. Hopkins, if she was to take umbrage and walk out."

"She'll probably do that anyway. I had a set-to with her yesterday afternoon. It wouldn't surprise me if she doesn't show up for work on Monday, let alone come in for a couple of hours to help with the tea tomorrow. Like she'd agreed to do."

"I heard you going at her from three rooms away." Tom showed emotion beyond his general awkwardness. He looked seriously upset. "It was embarrassing, especially with Val there.

She'd just come in with a wallpaper book you had asked her to bring. Needless to say, there was no lingering; she got out the door fast."

"People will say lottery winners forget how to treat the unfortunates of this world." Ariel dropped her face in her hands, peeping through her fingers at me.

"Stop talking like you're the conscience of the nation!" Betty looked ready to explode. "I had every reason to be furious. Mavis was nowhere to be found when I went looking for her. Probably outside smoking a cigarette or however she chooses to kill time. Then she had the nerve to ask me yet again if she could bring her little boy to work with her, because she can't find anyone to watch him during the school holidays. When I repeated what I've said previously, that other women manage, especially ones with husbands sitting at home because they're too lazy to work, it was Mavis who went off on me, saying she wouldn't have brought the matter up if Mrs. Cake hadn't told her she should. And then she flung a dirty dishcloth. She claimed she was aiming for the sink, but it got me smack in the face."

Ariel giggled through her pried-apart fingers.

"I don't see why she shouldn't bring the little boy with her," Tom said.

"And have him tear up the house!"

"Somebody for me to play with," Ariel sobered sufficiently to suggest.

"He's seven! And an absolute brat, from everything I've heard."

"Lady Fiona let him come." Tom leaned back in his chair, looking tired.

"Oh, that woman's so vague." Betty waved a dismissive hand. "She wouldn't have noticed if he'd brought the place down around her. Or that's the impression she gives. Besides, she didn't have much left of value sitting around to get smashed. Most of it had gone to the sale room, remember?"

"It does become clear that I am needed here." Mrs. Malloy assumed the burden with the graciousness befitting a monarch. "And"—her crown slipping just a bit—"it would be interesting to meet Mr. Scrimshank tomorrow afternoon in a social setting. Size him up, so to speak, on me sister's behalf; see if he's the gentleman she says he is. Melody don't understand men, never did. And I wouldn't want him taking advantage of her, on account of having misread the signals. Like I used to tell her, the way she types, pouring all her repressed passion into pounding them keys, could give any man the idea she'd be all fire and fury if he could get her to stop and take off her glasses and look at him. The London Philharmonic never sounded so good."

"Prelude on the piano in C minor for the typewriter." Ben's amusement wrapped itself around me, drawing me close even though we were seated apart from each other. "Sounds like heady stuff."

"They've worked together for a long time," I pointed out.

"In every man's life there is one of those moments when his life flashes before him and he realizes what he has been missing." Was he remembering the day, the hour, the minute when we met? "Should we all rush over and rescue Mr. Scrimshank before he is swept away on a torrent of thundering chords and forgets he's a gentleman and an accountant?"

"It's Saturday. His office will be closed." Suddenly struck by this realization, I looked at Mrs. Malloy. "This means you'll have to go to your sister's home and hope to catch her in."

"I don't have the address; she always listed the business one. But it's no problem; Melody will be working today. It's Fridays they take off. She'll be there till five-thirty. She always makes mention of it in her Christmas cards, to fill in the space, I suppose, there not being a lot else for her to say. Not much going on in her private life is my guess."

"Making it all the nicer she gets to play the typewriter keyboard at work. Maybe she can make a recording sometime." Ben laughed.

"I hope she has a sense of humor and would be amused by these quips at her expense. Don't you think you should be setting off, Mrs. Malloy?" I looked at my watch. "It's after three now."

"You said you'd come with me." She got to her feet to a chorus of scraping chairs. "I'll be needing a lift."

"There's a bus you can catch just along the road," said Betty. "You can see the stop clearly from the bottom of the drive. Old Nanny Pierce still takes the number ninety-four into the village every Wednesday. She says she doesn't like to put Val to the trouble of taking her, but I expect she likes having her weekly outing to herself and not being tied to a time for getting back."

"Or I could drive you," Tom offered.

"Thank you." Mrs. Malloy inclined her royal head and adjusted her robes. "But if it's all the same with everyone we'll leave things as planned. Suit you, Mrs. H?"

I told her I was ready when she was, to which she replied that first she needed to find her handbag. When this turned up alongside her chair, after being stepped on and subsequently picked up by Tom, she whispered in my ear that she could do with going to the lav before setting off. In fact, it would be a real treat. Betty, who obviously had good ears, encouraged her to go and freshen up. There were two powder rooms off the hall, she told us.

Lovely as these were likely to be, we were not destined to use them at that time. Ariel insisted on escorting us to our assigned bedrooms, each of which had its adjoining bathroom.

Betty disappeared to have a word with Mrs. Cake. Ben and Tom went companionably outside to bring in the luggage from the Land Rover. And Ariel led Mrs. Malloy and me up the lovely curve of staircase, in the manner of a tour guide in the employment of the National Trust.

Looking at her prim self-important back, I took in the magnitude of what had happened to her. The sudden wealth, the move to splendid surroundings: yes, it all sounded wonderfully exciting in theory. But to suddenly find herself a rich kid without having been brought up to it, her former life swept away as if rolled up in newspaper and put out in the dustbin, people treating her differently . . . it had to be overwhelming and possibly frightening.

We've all heard of people whose lives have been ruined by too much money and insufficient guidance to keep them anchored to reality. Then again, might their problems also be blamed on personality flaws? Was there something fundamentally malicious about Ariel's peeking glances and frequently voiced dislike of Betty? Should I feel sorry for her or be warily on my guard against her schemes? Both, I determined, thinking about my own children and how I always needed to keep one step ahead of them, however dear their little faces and sweet their voices.

We were now walking down a long gallery with the banister railing to our left overlooking the great chandelier-lit pool of the hall below. There were doors to our right, interspersed with portraits and gilded electric lamps on the wall. At a word from Ariel, Mrs. Malloy scuttled into the room that was to be hers, heading directly for the lav, tossing the information over her shoulder that she would wait for me at the top of the stairs, but I wasn't to rush because she planned on enjoying the moment.

Sincerely hoping she would find the lav provided a throne

worthy of her, I followed Ariel past two more doors until she came to one she opened for me. But we didn't go inside immediately. I had halted before a portrait. Given the subject's hairstyle, it would appear to have been painted some thirty or forty years previously. It was of a lovely young woman, seated at a small table, looking out a window. Winsome, I thought; that was the word for her: fine-boned, shadowy-eyed, and graceful, even captured as she was in immobility. The turn of her head, the pensive gaze, conveyed a quiet sorrow.

"She looks like she's watching for someone, hoping he'll come." Ariel's voice made me jump. "Well, it has to be the boyfriend, doesn't it?"

"You think so?"

"She wouldn't have that dippy look on her face if it was the milkman or just any old person, would she? I suppose you've guessed who she is."

"Lady Fiona?"

"She asked if she could leave the portrait here until she finds somewhere permanent to live. I must say she's not bad-looking even now. Her hair's still fair, not much gray at all really. Betty thinks she's too skinny for her height and age, but she would; she wants everybody to be fatter than she is. That's why she's always trying to get me to stuff myself with food. Especially things I hate, like tapioca and rice puddings."

I let this pass. "You think her ladyship is looking out that window, hoping to see Mr. Gallagher come riding up on his white horse?"

"No, I think it was the other one."

"Who?"

"The man she was madly in love with, the man her parents wouldn't let her marry because he was too common. Mrs. Cake told me about him. She's a great one for reminiscing about the past: quite fun, really. She said the two of them met on the sly

86

down by the old mill and used to hide love letters in a hollow tree, just like in a book. Only to be really exciting, they'd have had to run off and get married and then been found out and dragged home—"

"By her hard-hearted parents, blast their interference!" I thought of Tom's parents, who had objected to his first love on religious grounds.

"And he'd have been murdered by them." Ariel was warming to her theme.

"Or the jealous rival. That would be Mr. Gallagher. Oh, the horror of it!" Obviously, I was also getting caught up in the story.

"Lady Fiona would never have recovered from the tragedy." Ariel reclaimed her narrative.

"Whatever really happened she appears to have done so, at least sufficiently to marry Mr. Gallagher."

"That would have been on the rebound. Mrs. Cake says that one person who didn't attend the wedding was Miss Pierce—"

"Nanny?"

"That's right. She claimed to have the flu, but I bet that was an act. I think she hates Lady Fiona. You can see it in her eyes, even when she's pretending to talk nicely about her. She didn't think her good enough for her Nigel. Mrs. Cake says the title and the fortune didn't cut any ice with Nanny. Only a princess would have been up to scratch, and there'd probably have been something wrong with *her*."

"Maybe what Nanny wanted was to keep Nigel all to herself in the nursery."

"Ugh!" Ariel pulled a face. "That's really creepy."

As was the idea of Lady Fiona murdering her husband. I kept this thought to myself while continuing to look at the face in the portrait. Surely it was a travesty to imagine that lovely girl committing so monstrous an act later in life. Giving myself a mental shake, I said cheerfully that Mrs. Cake sounded like a great conversationalist.

"Having lived in Milton Moor her whole life, she knows everyone in the area."

"That helps."

"She does know stuff. Like Sergeant Walters being too busy knitting to get married. And the butcher being a closet vegetarian. Anyway, I find it interesting. And there's no one else for me to talk to around here. Mavis hardly ever looks up from her work."

"There has to be an enormous amount for her to do."

"Yes. It isn't fair for Betty to say she's useless."

I kept my mouth shut. In former times a place of this size would have employed dozens of servants. Housekeeper, butler, footmen, upstairs and downstairs maids, boot boys . . . the list went on. Finding people eager to do that sort of work these days probably wasn't easy. But that should have led Betty to value Mavis more highly. Were she and Tom reluctant to spend their newfound money on sufficient hired help? They'd managed to avoid paying for an interior designer, hadn't they?

Ariel read my mind. "We do have a team of cleaners come in every other week for three days. They go through the whole place, except for the west wing; it's shut off and there's hardly anything in there. On the off week, it's the gardening people. Betty didn't want a lot of people underfoot all the time. Mavis is all right. I don't see what's wrong with her, except she's so quiet. But Mrs. Cake is better. She says she has a soft heart and a fondness for romance, but she knows when it's important to keep her mouth shut."

"I hope she won't feel that way when talking to me and Mrs. Malloy. Speaking of whom"—I reluctantly withdrew my gaze from the portrait—"it won't do to keep her waiting when she's eager to set off to see her sister."

Ariel followed me into the bedroom that would be Ben's and mine during our stay at Cragstone House. "Can I come, Ellie? I could show you where Mr. Scrimshank has his office; that would save you time."

"That's awfully nice of you, but better not."

"Then I won't tell you my surprise." She sat down with a thump on the dressing-table stool.

This was another lovely room: luxury converted into cozy comfort. The wallpaper was striped green and white; the daffodil-yellow curtains matched the slipcovers on the two easy chairs by the fireplace. The bleached pine of the four-poster bed and armoire, the perfect placement of the lamps, the velvety sage carpet underfoot: all whispered of relaxation and ease. Ariel sat raking a tortoiseshell comb through her lank hair as I nipped into the bathroom with its tasteful appointments to freshen up, to use Betty's phrase rather than Mrs. Malloy's more blunt talk of going to the lav.

Betty's words were far more suitable, given that the toilet handle, as well as the taps for the shell-shaped sink, looked as though they'd been hand-picked for Versailles by Marie Antoinette, with a little help from the royal decorator. (Somehow, I doubted that that soon-to-be-headless wonder had made do with the suggestions of an amateur.) Looking up from washing my hands with rose soap from a crystal dish, I searched my reflection in the mirror. Was I jealous of the yet unseen Val's accomplishments throughout the house? Or merely amazed that according to Betty she was untrained?

I frequently advise my clients that an excess of perfection can be not only monotonous but stressful. You can't wear the wrong clothes without the fear of failing your surroundings.

Something always needs to be just a little off: a picture looking as though it has been randomly chosen, a mismatched cup and saucer placed where they seem to be left out by mistake, a brass or silver candlestick in need of polishing. It was advice I had received from a guru designer, a former teacher and now friend of mine, who knew everyone in the business and, in my opinion, more than all of them combined. But getting things too right wasn't the kind of mistake likely to be made by even the most gifted nonprofessional. The risks of such a person's efforts looking more like a five-star hotel than a home were minimal.

The chances were good I'd meet the woman behind the enigma, I told my reflection as I toweled off my face. No point in dredging up excuses for disliking her unseen. So what if I hadn't slept well the night before, was missing the children, had got drawn into another family's problems. Laying down the monogrammed hand towel and sticking a smile on in lieu of lipstick, I went back into the bedroom and said to Ariel, still seated on the dressing-table stool, that we should go and look for Mrs. Malloy.

"She just popped her head around the door to say she'd like another ten minutes to finish her makeup."

"Then we might as well stay put until we hear her coming." I perched on the side of the bed. "There's never any missing the sound of her high heels clicking down a wooden floor."

I pictured Mrs. Malloy in her bathroom, mixing one facial cream with another, intent on concocting an instant rejuvenating formula of the sort that had eluded scientists for the last fifty years. I doubted we would hear her high heels tapping along the gallery very soon, which was all to the good, seeing that there was a matter I wished to broach to Ariel without seeming to pounce.

"What a lovely room. Ben and I will be really comfortable here," I said from the bed.

"Yes, I suppose Val didn't do a bad job. Better anyway than Betty's attempts. She kept ordering furniture that she didn't like when it showed up in the van. Poor Dad; she made him move it from place to place before sending it back. He'd get fed up, but most of the time he didn't say anything, because she goes off at the drop of a hat, just like she did at Mavis."

"We all lose our tempers from time to time."

"Not the way she does."

"Let's discuss why she was on edge." I shifted farther around to face her squarely.

"Why?"

"That business about the phone call to the catering firm. The one Betty said she didn't make, canceling the arrangements for the garden party on Thursday."

"What about it?" Ariel was now scraping the tortoiseshell comb along the edge of the dressing table.

"Who would have made that call?"

"How would I know? She should have kept her temper when she rang yesterday and got the news, but no! She had to go into one of her screaming rages. I'll bet she was the one who threw the dishcloth at Mavis."

"And now she's been forced to invite us to stay so Ben can take on the catering."

"Well, I didn't set that up, but only because I didn't think of it," Ariel replied defiantly. "Maybe it was Mavis, out to get back at Betty for not letting her bring her son to work. That's pretty scummy, don't you think?"

"Not if he's as destructive as she said."

"Oh, I might have known she'd get you on her side!"

I looked at her, still fiddling with the comb, and, despite the rudeness, felt a pang of pity. Why wasn't something done about her hair? A more attractive cut and frequent washing could make all the difference. And then there were the over-sized spectacles and the clothes, which did nothing to give her life and color. I had been far from a childhood beauty, but my parents—my mother in particular—had always boosted me up, pointed out my good points, made sure that what I wore suited me and helped me feel good about myself. And they hadn't had the money that was now at the Hopkinses' disposal. Again I was making judgments. Suggestions, especially if coming from Betty, were apt to be summarily spurned by Ariel.

"I'm not on anyone's side," I said gently, "but I don't think you should criticize your stepmother to me. Last night was a little different; you had to give me your account of why you ran away. Now I'm a guest in her home. Isn't there someone else you can talk to about your feelings?"

"Such as a psychiatrist?" She pounced to her feet to stand glaring at me, skinny arms folded. "You're saying I'm crazy, aren't you?"

It was too much . . . the scared look in her eyes, the quiver of her lips before she tightened them; the sight tore at my heart. I could have been looking at one of my own children, but I didn't dare go over and put my arms around her. She would have pushed me away, become even more upset. Her pride was something she held on to grimly. I understood. I'd been there. And my childhood had been a day at the seaside compared to hers. No devastating loss of a parent in a tragic accident.

"That's not it at all," I said crisply, setting my mood to hers. "We all need to get things off our chests from time to time. Have someone really listen to us. What about one of your teachers at school?"

Ariel hunched a shoulder.

"What about your church?" I asked.

"What about it?"

"Is there anyone there you could talk to? The vicar's wife, for instance?"

"We go to the Catholic church, remember? And Mr. Hardcastle, the Anglican vicar who's coming to tea tomorrow, doesn't have a wife. She ran off with one of the altar boys."

"No!" I stalled on my way to the door, having heard Mrs. Malloy's heels clicking down the gallery.

"You're right." Ariel trailed after me. "I remember now; it was one of the vergers. Okay! I'm kidding. Mr. Hardcastle hasn't ever been married. Mrs. Cake says many a woman has pricked her little fingers to the bone embroidering altar cloths and kneelers, but it hasn't got them measuring for curtains at the vicarage. She said he's a confirmed bachelor. And I told her he should be. A bad example if he wasn't *confirmed*. It was a joke, but I don't think she got it. She spent twenty minutes explaining she meant he's happy as he is."

"That's nice." I opened the door carefully, not wanting Mrs. Malloy to have a black eye on meeting her sister. "We'll have another talk later, if you like, Ariel."

"I asked Mrs. Cake if Mr. Hardcastle knits like Seargent Walters does. She said it wouldn't surprise her, seeing it's getting popular again with both women and men. She prefers a night out at the Bingo hall."

"Bingo?" Mrs. Malloy uttered the word in throbbing accents. She stood facing us at the top of the stairs, but had she been in Angola she would have overheard just as well. Not only is Bingo one of her consuming passions, she obviously grasped the implications of Mrs. Cake's being a fellow enthusiast. A way had been provided to open up a conversation that would weave its way to the recent unsettling events at Cragstone.

"Oh, no!" Ariel exclaimed as we rounded the final curve of

the staircase and saw the group below us in the hall. "It's them!"

"Who?" I lowered my voice, hoping she would take the hint and do likewise. Alongside Tom and Betty I saw two people, neither of whom was Ben. Mrs. Malloy, equally interested, strained to see over my shoulder. We must have looked like those ghouls who stop to stare at an accident: for the thrill, not to offer assistance.

"The Edmondses. Frances and her husband, Stan."

"What's wrong with them?" Mrs. Malloy asked, out the side of her mouth.

"Frances steals stuff; she's a klepto. Stan's a weasel. Ugh! Just look at him hugging and kissing Betty. It's not like he's even keen on her. No chance of *them* being desperate for each other. He's like that with everyone. All smoochy-woochy." Ariel's whisper turned into a giggle. "Old Slop Face! Doesn't he make you want to throw your shoes at him and hit him on the head?"

That would have been extreme in my case; so far I'd only seen a squidge of profile and an ear. Tom was blocking most of the view, preventing a full sight of Frances as well. But when Mrs. Malloy and I reached the hall, Ariel having ducked back upstairs, he stepped aside and beckoned us forward.

"Come and meet our friends the Edmondses." He might have been telling us that the doctor had arrived to take out his tonsils.

Stan, who did look like a weasel, stopped squeezing Betty's hand to flash a sharp-toothed grin and wave a paw. His slicked-back brown hair and small darting eyes were enough to make me hope he wouldn't decide to hasten over and kiss me. His wife made a better picture. True, she had a lumpish figure, her complexion wasn't great, and her hair too brassily blond, but there was something appealing about her bright eyes and broad smile.

I didn't look at Mrs. Malloy to try to assess her opinion of the Edmondses. We needed to get off to see Melody and perhaps even get a glimpse of Mr. Scrimshank. Betty explained that she and Tom had lived next door but one to the Edmondses in London. Stan poked Tom playfully in the ribs, saying some got lucky after playing the lottery only once, while their friends who played every week never won a bean.

Just as I was starting to miss Ben, he came into the hall from the other end of the house, which made for another buzz of greetings and a flurry of handshaking. I wove my way toward him, intent on telling him that Mrs. Malloy and I were heading out the door. He looked up from listening to something Frances Edmonds was telling him, but he didn't catch my eye.

The front door had opened, a woman came into the hall, and all conversation and movement stopped. It would have been impolite to go on talking. But there was more to it. Any entrance by this woman would have had a similar impact. Impossible for all eyes not to be drawn to her. She was wearing a peasant skirt, which swirled softly with each step, and an off-the-shoulder lawn blouse. Her legs were bare, and she was wearing a pair of high-heeled shoes with narrow crisscrossed straps. I knew they had a gold-leaf design on the back, because Mrs. Malloy had a pair exactly like them. My cousin Vanessa is a fashion model and stunning, but I didn't think I'd ever seen anyone this lovely. Hair the color and shine of blackberries, skin like cream, eyes bluer than any sky, and cheeks brushed with rose. The ideal of Irish beauty proclaimed in soulful ballads.

"Hello, Val." Tom shifted his gaze between Mrs. Malloy and me. More introductions, he had to be thinking.

"Have I come at a bad time?" The voice had the slightest of lilts. Betty said something, I didn't catch what, because Ben brushed past me without a glance. It seemed to me that what happened next did so in slow motion. I saw him take hold of the woman's hands, heard the surprised query in his voice.

"Valeria? How do you come to be here?"

"Ben?" I could hear her intake of breath. "It can't be! We're imagining this, aren't we?" She leaned into him, her face hidden on his shoulder. The smallest sound—a shifting foot, Tom's hand smoothing down the lapel of his sports jacket—became magnified. The ticking of the long case clock seemed to be coming from inside me. In a moment it would explode. I saw Val—Valeria—draw back from my husband as if it required all the strength at her disposal to do so. She was still holding his hands. *They* were holding hands. At last she spoke, in a voice between a sob and a laugh.

"Betty, Tom . . . however did this happen? Ben and I know each other! We met when I was training in the travel agency and he was working in his uncle's restaurant."

There was nothing to disturb me in this disclosure. Old friends meeting again; what could be nicer? The way Ben avoided looking at me when going up to her had been bothersome. But that was nothing compared to the shuttered expression on his face when his eyes finally met mine.

6

I don't know as I like to bring it up," Mrs. Malloy said in a deplorably smug voice, as I drove past the Dower House and turned onto the road in the direction of Milton's Moor's business area.

"Then don't." My voice was tart, and I didn't regret it.

"All right. Keep your hair on, Mrs. H!"

She should have said chauffeur's cap. I was proud of my professional handling of the car. My hands were steady on the wheel, my nose pointed in the right direction. I wasn't blubbering, begging for the loan of a hanky, or leaning my head on her shoulder, any of which many a woman would have done under the circumstances. *She* was the one looking as if she had been struck a mortal blow.

"I'm sorry for snapping. Please go ahead with what you wanted to say," I told her. We were passing the man with the

97

sheepdog I had noticed on our arrival. I no longer cared about their romantic appearance. I hated romance. It was the root of all evil. From now on I would read only nonfiction. My favorites would be appliance manuals.

"I expect you're missing the children," Mrs. Malloy answered forgivingly, "but don't you worry. They'll be having the time of their lives with their grandparents and that dear little dog, Sweetie, to play with. That is, if he hasn't come down with rabies; he looked like he might be doing that the last time I saw him. But as I said to you then, very likely that breed always foams at the mouth."

"Say what it is you don't want to say."

"It seems silly."

"Please!" I was tempted to bury my face in my hands, if it wouldn't have made for irresponsible driving.

"Well, it's about her shoes. They was the same as mine."

"Whose shoes?" As if I didn't know.

"Val's. Or Valeria, as Mr. H called her."

"It's a lovely name. Therefore, perfect for her." I continued driving at a steady speed; my foot did not vibrate on the pedal; I did not roll down the window, stick my head out, and shout something nasty at a passing clump of trees.

"Yes, well. . . ." Without looking at her, I knew Mrs. Malloy was pursing her lips and looking judicious. "I suppose there's bound to be some as would say she's not bad-looking, but I don't think she'd win a prize for her legs. Which is why I feel I can say, without boasting, that them shoes didn't look near as good on her as they do on me."

"I didn't realize you had them on." I involuntarily glanced down as she nudged a foot in my direction.

"I changed from what I *was* wearing when I went upstairs. Have to put me best feet forward for Melody."

"Some can wear shoes and some can't." My eyes were again

riveted on the road. But in my opinion Val's—Valeria's—legs were as great as the rest of her.

We were now passing the house with the BED AND BREAKFAST sign on the gatepost, but this time there was no woman with orange hair on display.

"According to Betty, we should turn right at the next corner and then shortly make another right in order to reach the part of the high street where Mr. Scrimshank has his office." I hoped Mrs. Malloy would concentrate either on coming face-to-face with her sister Melody or on admiring her footwear.

"What was it," she said, as I knew she would, "that made you snap at me just now, Mrs. H? And you always so even-tempered." She did know when to lay it on thick. There never was any keeping things from her when I was seized by a desperate need to pour my heart out.

"I was afraid you'd bring up Madam LaGrange and her predictions, in particular the one about a woman having problems when her husband's old girlfriend showed up."

"Oh, that!" Mrs. Malloy chuckled unconvincingly. "The way I remember it, we agreed she was spouting off nonsense. I've even stopped worrying about that bus-stop business. Of course," she could not resist adding, "you could say as how the part about me traveling to foreign parts has come true, seeing as Yorkshire isn't England as we know it down south and the people do talk with a funny accent. Not Tom and Betty and Ariel, of course, but Mrs. Cake's speech is quite broad. But"—backtracking hastily—"that was probably just a lucky guess on Madam's part. I don't think you need to worry about Mr. H and . . . her."

"You don't?"

" 'Course not! If there ever was something between them, it came to nothing, didn't it."

"There could have been reasons."

"Well, let's just say, to make you happy, that once upon a time they was all hot and bothered about each other. That's in the past. You can't reheat a week-old stew and make it worth eating. Besides, it goes against the laws of nature."

"What does?"

"Them being physically attracted to each other. They've both got black hair and blue eyes—well, maybe Mr. H's are more green. Still, it comes to the same thing. In the sort of books you and me like to read, the hero and heroine are always opposites when it comes to coloring, him usually being the one that's dark. I should have realized that when I got the wind up about me third husband having a thing for the woman next door. They both had hair as red as fire. It was her *hubby* mine was after. Ran off together, they did, and they've been happy as larks ever since. And who can begrudge them, seeing as they were a miserable pair of buggers before?"

"There's sometimes a killjoy."

"The difference is, Mr. H is happy. He's daft about you. Nothing's going to change that. You and the children—and his pots and pans—are his whole world."

"He didn't even see me after she walked in. At least that's how it was at first. When he realized I wasn't the long case clock, it was as though he shut the connecting door between us."

"And hung up the NO ADMITTANCE sign? Now you just stop this, Mrs. H!" Mrs. Malloy rounded on me, nearly elbowing the steering wheel out of my hands. "Working yourself up over nothing, when we should be asking ourselves why Mr. Gallagher did a bunk. Jealousy's an ugly thing! If you let it get hold of you, it won't let go. That was the root of the trouble between Melody and me. Always out to put a spoke in one of me wheels, she was, because I was better at leapfrog and could do the cat's cradle without looking."

I felt myself relax. I had worked myself into a state over

nothing. My wretched insecurities! Before setting eyes on Val I'd felt absurdly threatened by her talents in what was supposed to be my field. When would I grow up? So she was beautiful! Had I ever in all the years of our marriage feared that Ben was pining for a long-lost love? Never! Suddenly I felt like singing, but this was hardly the time. We were now in the high street, making it even more important to concentrate on my driving. There was quite a lot of traffic. This being a Saturday, pedestrians bustled along the pavement, many of them loaded down with shopping bags. Mrs. Malloy peered out her window, looking at the street numbers on the buildings.

"There's Barclay's Bank," she pointed out, "and the bus stop, a bit farther down. Remember, Betty said it's right outside the office. Slow down, we turn here into the alleyway. She said it was a good place to park without a meter. There. Pull up alongside that car."

I did as I was told, turned off the engine, and stepped out. Upon seeing that Mrs. Malloy had done likewise, I locked up and put the keys in my pocket. The sun was shining as brightly as it had done earlier in the day, but as far as I was concerned it had just come out. My world was back to rights. On our return I would laugh with Ben over my silliness about Val. Or maybe I wouldn't say anything. It was that unimportant.

Facing us in a brick wall was a glass door inscribed with the name ARCHIBALD SCRIMSHANK and, beneath it, CHARTERED PUBLIC ACCOUNTANT.

"Should we just walk in?" Mrs. Malloy was tugging at her dress, fussing with her hair, shifting her handbag from one arm to the other. By way of answer I tried the doorknob.

"It's locked."

"Better ring." Nothing like pointing out the obvious but it was my turn to boost her flagging confidence, so, telling her that was a great idea, I pressed the bell. While we waited she told me haltingly that perhaps it hadn't been kind of her to mention Melody's not being good at leapfrog or doing the cat's cradle while not pointing out that she'd been unbeatable at the egg-and-spoon race.

"Concentration, that's what did it for her. It couldn't be said she was a fast runner, but—"

"Relax, Mrs. Malloy. You're not here to be measured for your coffin."

"Very funny!" She was now the one to snap.

There was no time for more; the door opened. A querulous voice bade us enter, and we stepped into a hall. It was not quite as gloomy as the hall in Cragstone House had been before the lights were turned on. Even so, its dimness required me to blink several times before deciding that the person regarding us with extreme pessimism couldn't be Melody. Not unless she wore gray pin-striped suits and had a domed bald head and a sizable Adam's apple. Mrs. Malloy was no help, having turned into a pillar of salt.

"Mr. Scrimshank?" I produced my best boarding-school smile.

"Yes?" His voice was as thin and reedy as the rest of him. My eyesight having adjusted, I decided he was wise not to subject himself to strong light. A candle held too close might have caused him to crumble to dust.

Returning to life, Mrs. Malloy edged around me to stand admiring a closed door to our left. Given the choice it was better than looking at his long poky nose. "Pleased to meet you, I'm sure." Her smile was better than mine, having the benefit of purple lipstick. She even achieved a modest fluttering of the eyelashes. "I'm here, if it's all right with you, to see Melody, Mr. S." Such familiarity! Nerves, of course. For a ghastly moment I feared she would elbow him in the ribs and announce with a coy chuckle that she'd always found accountants irresistible and was he up for an evening of Bingo?

He looked perplexed. Understandably so, it seeming unlikely he had ever previously had his name abridged in such a way. Very likely his own mother had addressed him as Mr. Scrimshank from the time he could sit up. "There is no Melody here."

"Miss Tabby."

"Good gracious! I had no idea. Are you sure?" He appeared to be in shock. Had there been a chair handy, I would have urged him to sit down and place his head between his knees. "Such an odd name for her. I suppose she must have written it on her application for employment, but that was a great many years ago."

"She's me sister." Mrs. Malloy looked ever more robust as he faded into the paintwork.

"I didn't know she had one. Not that I don't believe you. But again, it does seem odd, her having any sort of family. I've always thought of her as having been, one might say . . . manufactured."

The bobbing Adam's apple was having a hypnotic effect on me. I heard him say, in a voice sufficiently recovered to sound reproving, that we had come to the wrong door, the one reserved for deliveries. In future, should we have reason to return (not sounding particularly enthusiastic about this), we should do so by way of the front entrance, which did not require ringing the bell.

Pinching my cheeks hard in an attempt to bring myself back to sharper focus, I realized Mr. Scrimshank was leading us down the hall and around a dusky corner to a door, which he opened, before stepping back to allow Mrs. Malloy and me to precede him.

The room we entered was the size of a pantry, made even smaller by the number of filing cabinets crowded into it. They allowed little room for the utility-styled desk, behind which a woman sat typing away with incredible staccato speed on a manual typewriter. The window was partially blocked by a blind pulled three quarters of the way down, providing only a narrow view of the street and cutting off people standing at the bus stop at the knees. One thing the room did not lack was light. It glared down from a high-wattage ceiling fixture like a baleful one-eyed god who hadn't yet had his sacrificial virgin for breakfast. But given that Melody Tabby had not bothered to look up at this invasion of her sanctum, it was impossible to assess her appearance beyond a bent frowsy head—and the flying fingers, of which she seemed to have more than the standard ten. I stared in awe. Mrs. Malloy opened and closed her handbag. And Mr. Scrimshank exuded an eagerness to escape to his adding machines and ledgers.

"Miss Tabby, there are two women here to see you."

"Thank you, Mr. Scrimshank. Please send them away. They will be the pair that came a week ago last Thursday. That would be"—a glance at the desk calendar, with no diminishment of speeding fingers—"the thirtieth of June. They attempted to sell me bottles of paper ink. I told them I had no use for such stuff, having not made a typing mistake in thirty-seven years."

"These women come on a different matter."

"Even more reason, Mr. Scrimshank, to get rid of them. They will be the ones handing out religious pamphlets. Kindly tell them I already have one. It's called the Bible."

"Let me have those letters by five-thirty, Miss Tabby."

"They will be on your desk, Mr. Scrimshank"—another sideways glance, this time at the desk clock—"by sixteen minutes to five. That will be in one half hour precisely."

He made what I considered an ignoble retreat.

"You haven't changed a bit, Melody Tabby." Having rolled her eyes at me, Mrs. Malloy stalked toward the desk. "I could smack you for breathing, if I hadn't needed to be the grown-up since the day you was born."

"So it's you, Roxanne Malloy." If the fingers slackened, it was imperceptible. "And who is it you've brought with you?"

"Mrs. Haskell, if it wouldn't kill you to take a look. You'll remember, seeing as you've never forgotten a blooming thing in your entire life, that I've mentioned her in me Christmas cards. Among other things, we're partners in the detective business."

An exaggeration, but I made allowances.

"Good afternoon, Mrs. Haskell."

Her right hand may have hesitated for the barest second before zapping the carriage return. "Sorry I can't ask you to sit down, mine being the only chair."

"Don't mind that, she'll perch on one of them filing cabinets." Mrs. Malloy's voice was ripe with sarcasm. "Mrs. H is related to the new people at Cragstone House. The ones that won the lottery."

"Thank you, Roxanne. Mr. Scrimshank had me note the day they bought the place on his calendar. I also copied it onto mine. In addition to being the former owners' accountant, he has long been personally acquainted with them. Indeed, he provided helpful information to the police"—again that minute hesitation—"as to a phone message he received at four-thirty P.M., three days after Mr. Gallagher's disappearance on the evening of the sixteenth of January, the year before last." Another whap of the carriage return. "Are you and Mrs. Haskell in Yorkshire to determine his present whereabouts?"

"I'm not saying as that's the case, nor that it isn't." Mrs. Malloy looked furiously down at the bent head. "I've been invited to stay at Cragstone for several days, along of Mrs. H and her husband. Tomorrow afternoon there's to be a tea party, and Mr. Scrimshank and Lady Fiona are both going to be there, along with some other people."

"So I am aware."

"I've been hoping to see something of you while I'm here. If the idea isn't too hard for you to swallow, I think we should try and patch things up."

"And why would you want to do that?" The fingers slowed on the keyboard. I shifted back toward the door, indicating to Mrs. Malloy with silently mouthed words and sideways jerks that I'd go and wait in the hall. She responded with an adamant shake of her head.

"Because, like it or lump it, Miss Melodymatic, we're sisters. And"—purple taffeta bosom heaving—"forty years is too long even for you, that never forgets a blooming thing, to bear a grudge. Perhaps it wasn't nice, me making eyes at your boyfriend, even if you didn't want him. Which gives us at least one thing in common, because the minute he tried putting his hand up me skirt I didn't want him neither."

"It was him breathing through his mouth I couldn't abide." Melody kept her head down but did remove her hands from the typewriter keys. I pretended to be a filing cabinet.

"Adenoids," heaved Mrs. M. "There never has been and never will be nothing romantic about adenoids."

"They say it's not catching." Melody finally looked up. "Not that I ever believed it. But I still tend to worry whenever I catch myself talking through my nose."

"Doctors don't know everything. Outside of books, that is, when you don't mind because they usually have a silver-gray Rolls-Royce and a thrilling foreign accent."

I moved to the window and watched feet lining up at the stump that comprised all I could see of the bus stop. My hands itched to raise the blind. Ben is claustrophobic and I've become more so since being married to him. Perhaps that's something else that's catching, despite medical views to the contrary.

"Books!" Melody repeated. "I haven't read a novel since putting down *Jane Eyre* for the last time."

"So that's it!" From the corners of my eyes I beheld Mrs. Malloy doing a tiger stalk in front of the desk. "I thought as you was looking downright peaky. Frightened me, it did. That's why I wanted Mrs. H to stay, on the off chance I should pass out and need her to catch me as I fell. But now I know all that's needed to buck you up is for me to take you down to reapply for your library card, I feel better. Me heart's not hammering so bad. Maybe I won't need to take one of me tablets."

What tablets? They were news to me. I looked from one sister to the other. Despite Melody's washed-out coloring, there was a strong resemblance between them, not only in body build and facial features but also in the set of the jaw and the tilt of the head.

"You've got heart trouble, Roxanne?"

Mrs. Malloy avoided an outright lie. "Wonky tickers run in our family, Melody."

"Mine's all right."

"Yes, but then you're younger than me. Always have been and always will be." The nobility of this admission almost brought me to tears. But then she lapsed. " 'Course, people do say as I don't look a day over forty. Still"—her halo, or it could have been her royal crown, reemerged—"I can't claim to look a slip of a girl the way you do, Melody."

"Really?" Another of those sideways glances, but this time not at the desk calendar. Did Melody hope to see a mirror magically appear on the wall?

"I like that new way you're doing your hair."

"You do?" Fingers poked at the shapeless frizz.

"And your figure! You've lost your puppy fat. Must be from keeping yourself so active at the typewriter. I've never seen the like of the way you go! How many words can you do a minute?"

"Only three hundred and twenty-two as of nine-thirty-seven this morning. I've fallen off a bit since a week last Tuesday. That would be—"

"Yes, so it would," said Mrs. Malloy. "You'll pick up your speed again, Melody, once you get that library card. By the way, did you ever get over Mr. R?"

"Thirty-six years ago today."

"Well, happy anniversary."

"I woke up at six-thirty-one and thought, Let Edward Fairfax Rochester have his Jane Eyre. And then it came to me. It was just a book! Quite a nice little story, not badly written, but that's all there was to it. Fiction has its place; I can admit that now. I should have renewed my library card. But I have my living to earn." Melody was now dusting between the keys with a cotton swab. "And in the evenings and on my days off I have other claims on my time. There's my small flat to clean, and—"

"A gentleman friend?" Mrs. Malloy inquired coyly.

No response.

"Not"—Mrs. M's smile vanished—"Mr. Scrimshank?"

"I did have a glimmer of hope twenty-two and a half years ago as of last Saturday that something might be developing between us, but it flickered out before he finished that morning's dictation. And subsequent events, coupled with certain doubts"—she was now digging even more assiduously between the typewriter keys—"have led me to believe that Mother was right in saying very few men are what they appear to be. And the worst are the kind who look like they'd never do an underhanded thing in their lives, let alone something criminal."

Mrs. Malloy and I exchanged startled looks.

"What doubts?" Mrs. M asked sharply.

"I can't get into that now. I have a dozen letters to finish in seventeen and three-quarter minutes if I'm to get out of here by five-thirty." Melody rammed a sheet of paper into the typewriter. "So if you and Mrs. Haskell will excuse me, we'll have to talk about this another time."

"This evening, then."

"Thank you." Melody's fingers were poised above the keys. "But I have a prior engagement. I always spend Saturday evenings with a friend."

"Male or female?" Mrs. Malloy was instantly sidetracked.

"A person who, like myself, is a keen knitter. It makes for quite an intense bond. The hours fly by. Sometimes we hardly talk. There's no need. Our knitting pins do the communicating for us."

"I never saw you so much as cast on a row of stitches!"

"My life has gone in new directions. We have a very active knitting circle in Milton Moor. Some noteworthy people belong."

"Well, if that isn't wonderful! It makes me feel a lot better knowing as how you've at least been reading patterns for jumpers and cardigans instead of giving yourself over body and soul to the telly. But you can't go leaving Mrs. Haskell and me in suspense over what you was saying about Mr. Scrimshank."

Melody merely compressed her lips. They weren't purple but might just as well have been. It was an expression I knew well. Neither did Mrs. Malloy's response differ from what might be expected.

"If I walk out of here not knowing, I'll be up all night with palpitations and a doctor will have to be sent for, unless I'm rushed off to hospital with an oxygen mask stuck to me, which is something I'm sure wouldn't suit the shape of me face. Is that something you really want to happen, when we've just had this nice reconciliation after forty years?"

Melody appeared to think this over. She got up, opened the door, looked outside, and returned to her seat. "I had to make sure he wasn't listening." She lowered her voice. "It all connects up to Mr. Gallagher's disappearance. There's nothing concrete, just these uneasy thoughts that might mean something and might not. My . . . knitting friend says they don't amount to anything that Mr. Scrimshank couldn't easily explain away. Suspicion isn't evidence."

"Start from when you first became concerned," I suggested.

"I always thought it curious that he kept the Gallaghers' records in the safe in his office, rather than giving them to me to file, and that he took to sending me off on some trumpery errand when her ladyship and her husband came in to talk to him."

"Why do you think that was, Miss Tabby?"

"It started a couple of years ago. Mr. Gallagher came on his own one Monday morning at—"

"No need for the twiddly bits, Mel."

"You're right, I need to hurry this up." She looked nervously toward the door. "He could come in for those letters. I've never been a second later than promised when putting them on his desk. On that occasion Mr. Gallagher did something most unusual. He came in here to talk to me about being surprised that what should have been sound investments had done so poorly over the last few years."

"Did he sound suspicious that Mr. Scrimshank had mishandled the funds?"

"He talked about the country going downhill, blamed the economy on the present government, all that sort of thing. Then Mr. Scrimshank walked in, looking rattled. The door was ajar and he could have heard. My knitting friend says it's understandable Mr. Scrimshank wouldn't appreciate Mr. Gallagher discussing his financial affairs with me. And that it's not strange about those records being in the safe when there was a friendship as well as a business relationship."

"True." Mrs. Malloy pursed her lips.

"There's more." Melody's voice dropped lower and she spoke faster. "It has to do with the woman who came in to clean at night, after the office was closed."

"What about her?" Mrs. Malloy and I asked as one.

"Mr. Scrimshank sacked her. He said she had been stealing. Small things: paperweights off his desk, a little box for holding paper clips. I'm sure she did it, because my coffee cup went missing, and of course I hadn't moved it. Like everything else on my desk it had its precise spot, never a half inch to the right or left. Even so, I felt sorry for her." Melody paused to glance again at the door. "She seemed a pleasant enough woman. Of course, I didn't approve of the way she bleached her hair. Mother would have described her as blowzy. Her name's Frances Edmonds and—"

"We've met her and the husband. Just as we was leaving to come here." Mrs. Malloy turned to me. "Who'd have thought! Betty Hopkins with her nose for crime is all pally and free as a breeze with a kleptomaniac."

"Ariel told me Frances stole things," I said, "but it seemed best to take some of what she says with a grain of salt."

Melody, her fingers scratching at the typewriter keys, continued hastily. "I came into work one Friday, which I don't do as a rule because the office is closed. Naturally, I have a record of the time and date, but . . . anyway, there was some filing I wanted to get done. What surprised me was seeing Mr. Scrimshank's hat and coat on the hall tree in the alcove by the side entrance. So I went down the hall to his office to let him know I was there. The door was open and I could hear his voice. Frances Edmonds was with him. Mr. Scrimshank wasn't shouting or going off the deep end. He was speaking in a low calm voice, but I could hear every word. She was crying buckets and begging him not to turn her over to the authorities. I froze where I was, afraid to move because . . . well, whatever she'd done, I didn't want her to know that I'd heard."

"You always were a softie, Mel." Mrs. Malloy sniffed audibly. "It's the reason people like meself got to walk all over you when we was younger."

"He said the alternative to criminal proceedings was for her to write a signed confession that he'd keep in his safe. She said she would, crying even harder, thanking him over and over . . . groveling. That was when I got myself together and crept back down the hall. I didn't stay to do the filing. There'd been something about the way he'd looked at her, like he knew he'd got her in his pocket. I tried to forget about it, but of course you know that's an impossibility for me, Roxanne."

"It's the way you was made. I can see now, as it was wrong of me to find it irritating. 'Course there was that time you had to go and remind me in front of Mother that I'd broken her George VI coronation mug, but never mind that."

"There's more, isn't there?" I said.

Melody nodded. "I came here another time when Mr. Scrimshank wasn't expecting me. Again some filing I wanted to get a head start on. That was the evening after Mr. Gallagher disappeared. And"—she paused—"it was like turning on the television and seeing the exact same program you've already watched. As before, Mr. Scrimshank's door was open, not all the way but enough for me to see that he was again with Frances Edmonds. He was saying that he wanted her to phone him from a public box."

"And?" I asked.

"That was all I heard. I was quicker off my feet that time

and didn't stay to do the filing. But I didn't dwell on it, not until it came out in the newspaper that Mr. Scrimshank had received a phone call from Mr. Gallagher. Then it crept into my mind that Frances Edmonds's signed confession had put her under his thumb. The police might check where the call had come from. He couldn't risk them simply taking his word that he'd heard from Mr. Gallagher."

"It wouldn't matter what Frances said when she rang." I looked at both sisters. "She could have recited a poem or read him her shopping list. The important thing was to establish that Mr. Gallagher was alive and well."

"Instead of dead and buried on account of finding out Mr. Scrimshank had been embezzling Lady Fiona's money." Mrs. Malloy sucked in an outraged breath. "Blooming hypocrite! Scaring that poor Frances into thinking she could be going to prison for life if she didn't knuckle under and do as he said. It looks as how Betty Hopkins is right about there having been a murder, only she had it that the wife did it. But then, to be fair, she doesn't have the experience in solving murders as do me and you, Mrs. H!"

How true! We had guessed right off the bat, before setting eyes on him, that Mr. Scrimshank was the culprit. He must have been in a state when Lady Fiona sold Cragstone, if that's where he had disposed of the body.

"My knitting friend said there could be any number of reasons Mr. Scrimshank wanted Frances Edmonds to phone him. And I should try talking to her. But I can't risk Mr. Scrimshank's finding out. What if she told him and he gave me the sack . . . or worse? I've never shared a bed with a man, let alone a grave with one. It doesn't seem fair to the wife. In addition to the fact I'd prefer to stay alive."

"I don't like the idea of you still working here," said Mrs. Malloy, in a scolding older-sister voice.

Melody squared her shoulders and elevated her chin. "I have no choice. Somehow, someday, I'll succeed in getting into that safe. I have never seen Mr. Scrimshank open or close it, although I have been constantly on the alert during the last year and a half. When I think he might be going to do it, he always closes his door. On every opportunity provided by his absence, I go into his office to try out various sequences of numbers, all of which I have recorded so as not to duplicate them."

"Melody, be careful!"

"Don't alarm yourself, Roxanne. I take the notebook home at night. There being a finite number of mathematical possibilities, I am confident that given time I shall succeed. And once I get my hands on the Gallaghers' financial records and make copies, I will quickly discover how Mr. Scrimshank managed to pull the wool over their eyes for as long as he did. And now if you and Mrs. Haskell will excuse me, I must type these letters. As it is"—eyeing the clock—"I shall be thirteen and a half minutes putting them on his desk."

"I'm staying." Mrs. Malloy addressed her bent head. "I'm going home with you when you leave. You'll just have to cancel your friend's coming over."

"I suppose I could." Melody returned to her typing. "But you'll have to wait outside until it's time for me to leave. It will put Mr. Scrimshank in one of his moods if he walks in and thinks you're going to keep me from finishing on time. Oh, and Roxanne?"

"Yes, Mel?" Mrs. Malloy had joined me at the door.

"It will be good to pour my heart out. An answer to prayer. A miracle, really. I feel I can go forward now"—a hand reached for a tissue and a nose was blown—"in getting my typing back up to speed and . . . all the rest of it."

I eased out into the hall on the assumption that the sisters would share an emotional embrace, even though they would be seeing each other again within the hour. There could be tearful murmurs of affection, regret voiced over the wasted years, and promises made never to be nasty to each other again. Not a moment for onlookers. I expected to stand looking at the blank walls for several minutes, thinking up schemes for unmasking Mr. Scrimshank, not only as a murderer but also as the evil prankster at Cragstone. But Mrs. Malloy followed me promptly. And before I could think further than how unlikely it was that our selected villain would look much different in prison gray than in his pin-striped suit, we were in the parking lot.

"I wanted to give Melody a hug, Mrs. H! But I knew we'd both break down, and that wasn't worth risking. It would never do for that man to suspect her of being human, with the eyes and ears to go with it. It's safer for the poor little cabbage"— more vigorous application of the hanky—"for him to go on seeing her as a robot incapable of absorbing information beyond what's been programmed into her for the job. Let him keep thinking she exists for no other reason than to pound that typewriter. Remember what he said to us about his having thought she'd been manufactured? Hateful, sneering thing to say!"

"I'm glad she agreed to spend time with you this evening," I said. "Perhaps she'll ask you to stay the night."

"Well, I can't do that, can I? The Hopkinses would worry that I won't be back to help with the tea tomorrow. And you and me has to have a confab about what Melody's been telling us. Now off you go, Mrs. H, I'd like to be alone till she comes out. Get me thoughts in order. I'll take a taxi back." She patted the Land Rover's side as if it were a horse eager for a gallop.

7

Getting into the driver's seat, I nosed my way out of the alleyway into the high street, which was even heavier with traffic than it had been earlier. But at least I now had my bearings, making it unlikely I would take a wrong turn on my way back to Cragstone House.

Why hadn't I spotted Mr. Scrimshank as a murderer the moment he opened the door? It was there in his eyes, that nasty dull brown color, with no eyelashes to speak of. I pictured him seated at his desk thinking up his next move, instead of doodling like a normal person. Though Betty might have been wrong about Lady Fiona's being the one who did away with her husband, I now thought it sadly likely the man was dead.

But always the silver lining. I was no longer fixated on Val and whether Ben was one of the rare people ever to call her

Valeria, or why after all these years she'd remembered that the uncle he'd worked for in London had been named Sol. People don't need to be in a relationship of a lifetime to remember such details. What did keep popping into my head was the thought of Mrs. Malloy's bag of toffees. I was starving. But there was no hope of her having left them on the backseat. They would be on her bedside table, along with a framed photo of herself, adding a personal touch to her room away from home, as advised by her favorite travel magazine.

Slowing my driving to a crawl, I focused on Mr. Gallagher's demise. Could it be that her ladyship and Mr. Scrimshank had been partners in bringing it about? One thing seemed clear. The Gallagher money had been severely depleted. Tom and Betty had said so, and in addition Lady Fiona had sold her ancestral home.

What if she'd found out her husband had squandered her fortune through bad investments or riotous living? Maybe he'd had a gambling problem or bought racehorses that went lame. She could have lost her head and decided he had to go. What if Mr. Scrimshank's offense was not embezzlement but covering up the losses on paper in an attempt to rid her ladyship of a motive for murder? Had he really been desperately in love with her for years? It was hard to imagine, given his desiccated appearance, but let's not forget old Lord Snearsby's searing passion for his forty-year-old female ward in *The Faulty Fortress*.

My mind went to the portrait of her ladyship as a young woman. She was beautiful and, according to Ariel, in love with a man her parents considered unworthy. What if that were because he was a mere accountant, rather than a member of the gentry? What if that man were Mr. Scrimshank, and despite the passage of time he'd continued to worship her, so that when she went to him begging for his help in concealing up the murder, he'd agreed to make up that story of a phone call? Far more convincing to the police than her ladyship saying she had heard from her husband. Had Betty thought along those lines? Was that her reason for inviting Mr. Scrimshank to tea tomorrow afternoon, to see if he and Lady Fiona avoided eye contact when Mr. Gallagher's name was mentioned?

I had arrived back at Cragstone. Having driven through the gateway, I was about to pass the Dower House when someone stepped almost in my path. Fortunately, I was driving so slowly a three-year-old on a tricycle could have zapped past me, or I might have knocked the person down. But I had applied the brakes in the nick of time, and when a face appeared at my window, I quickly rolled it down.

"I'm sorry," said a quavering voice. "I thought you were Val, but I see you're not. On you go, I won't keep you!" I was looking at a very old, much wrinkled lady with scant white hair twisted into a knot on top of her head. Her surprisingly sharp eyes were sufficiently dark as to be almost black.

"Are you Miss Pierce?" I asked her.

"That's me, and you'll be one of the guests of the new owners at Cragstone. I remember this car now; I saw you arrive earlier."

"We brought Ariel home after an overnight stay with us."

"Oh, yes! I heard by way of Mrs. Cake." The black eyes gleamed. "The things children get up to these days. What is the world coming to? My Mr. Nigel would never have pulled such a stunt. You'll know I was his nanny?"

"Yes."

Miss Pierce continued to hover at the car window. "I came with Mr. Nigel when he married; nothing—certainly not his bride—could have persuaded him to leave me behind. Such a nice house his people had in Staffordshire. He never had any reason to run away when he was a little boy." Her voice cracked, but she went gallantly on. "It's some comfort now, when I find myself wondering when I'll see his precious wee face again, to remember that his was a happy childhood."

"Of course."

"I saw to that. His parents were so supportive and sensible, never any interference on how I brought him up."

"Really?"

"Extremely well bred, both of them." Miss Pierce might have been discussing a pair of cocker spaniels that had done well at Cruft's. "They stayed in the background, as is best. Always concerned for his welfare, always pleased when I brought him down to the drawing room for half an hour after tea. They did enjoy hearing him recite his little poems."

"It must have made their day."

"Very proud they were of his stout little legs. 'Legs,' his mother used to say, 'are very important. His will stand him in good stead throughout life.' And so they have, with all the walking he does on his travels. But she and her husband understood that it's confusing for young ones to be thrust into family life too soon. It's Nanny they want until they're older." Miss Pierce's face was like an apple that has been stored too long in a dark cellar. At her age it was understandable that she clung to her memories.

"We've heard that Mr. Gallagher . . . went away." I floundered.

"It was something in him, the need to answer the call of nature. Bless him!" The dark eyes gleamed with pride. "He never needed to tell Nanny when he had to go; I knew the signs by the way he'd stand, getting fidgety all of a sudden. And there would be that mournful look in his eyes."

"Really?" What were we talking about?

"Her ladyship was never quick to see what was happening," Miss Pierce lamented. "But I will admit she never did get annoyed afterward. It'll all come out in the wash, seemed to be her attitude. Every other time, she carried on just as usual. But this time, when Mr. Nigel went, she phoned the police."

This was interesting. "Was there something different on this occasion?"

The white head nodded. "He'd forgotten his walking stick. I suppose she thought they might be able to advise her on how to have it sent to him. He goes to quite remote places. Once he felt compelled to go to the Amazon, and a few years later it was the Himalayas . . . or was it Honduras? Off he'd go, without saying a word beforehand."

"So as not to upset Lady Fiona ahead of time?"

"It was me he worried about. And he was always a touch absentminded, even when he wasn't thinking about Brazilian butterflies or arctic sunrises. It really wasn't kind of Lady Fiona to put the wind up me this time with her imaginings, silly as they were. It placed a cloud over things, and now I have this premonition that I won't be here to greet dear Mr. Nigel when he returns from his happy wanderings."

The wind did not moan, nor the skies darken ominously at her words, but she looked a very old lady in her gray skirt, prim white blouse, and hand-knitted cardigan.

"Would you like me to walk you back to your house?" I asked.

"That would be kind. I came outdoors looking for Val, my great-niece. I can't think what can be keeping her! I've had dinner waiting this past half hour."

"She was at Cragstone House when we left." I got out of the car.

"I don't understand that—her wanting to get in thick with people who don't now and never will really belong there. I know you and your husband are friends of theirs"—Miss Pierce caught herself—"but I'm sure you can understand my feelings."

"You've had a long relationship with the Gallaghers," I said, offering her my arm. The early evening air was heady with the scent of roses that cascaded in pink and yellow exuberance over the low brick wall that separated the Dower House from the rest of the property. A yew arch provided entry onto a path that curved its way across a velvet spread of lawn to a white door with black iron hinges and knocker.

Miss Pierce sat down on a garden bench. "Val came back here this afternoon looking emotional. Maybe those Hopkinses didn't get excited about her latest choice for wallpaper. Then she went off in her car. Some errand, she said. I don't pry. She and her brother, Simon, who's two years older, came to stay at Cragstone one summer when they were children. It was the best their parents could do for them by way of a holiday. Mr. Gallagher didn't mind my having them. I was still living in my rooms in the west wing in those days. And I am happy to say they didn't disturb him. Naturally, I made sure they behaved well and entertained themselves quietly. Not that Lady Fiona would have noticed if they'd fallen on her from the ceiling. Poor Mr. Nigel, she didn't know he was alive half the time."

"Oh, dear!"

"But, bless his sweet face, he never complained, not even to me, the one person in the world he could always trust, even when others let him down."

Miss Pierce got up and opened her front door. I followed her down a cream-painted hall, with an ebony floor and staircase banisters, into an equally bright sitting room arranged with some handsome wood pieces and a comfortable-looking slip-covered sofa and easy chairs. Looking worn out, either from her evening constitutional or the emotional upheaval of talking about her absent pride and joy, she accepted my help in getting seated.

"May I get you a cup of tea?" I asked.

"No, thank you."

I hesitated, wanting to get back to Cragstone. It wasn't fair to keep the others from sitting down to dinner, but I didn't want to appear too eager to get away.

"There's my Mr. Nigel." Miss Pierce pointed to the mantel-piece and I duly admired the photo of a blank-faced man in his sixties. "I wish I could show you one of my great-nephew Simon, but it's not in its usual place. Val must have moved it. She will touch things and then say I've forgotten where I put them."

"I misplace things all the time."

"Simon is very good-looking—as you can imagine, having seen his sister—or he was when I last saw him, twenty years ago at least. Of course it was a great pity about his ears. My heart would have broken if it had been Mr. Nigel. But his were perfect little shells from the day he was born." Her voice broke and I said that must be a great comfort. "Val occasionally kept in touch with me. It was different with Simon. He's living in Ireland . . . or would it be Scotland? He married a woman from whichever it was. Not at all suitable, from what I gathered. Something about a brush with the law, or was it selling vacuum cleaners door-to-door? The best of men behave foolishly when a woman is determined to haul him to the altar like a sacrificial lamb." Miss Pierce's eyes searched the bookcase next to the fireplace. "Where *is* Simon's photo? It was always next to that little bud vase. Perhaps I *am* getting forgetful; dear Mr. Nigel would worry," she was saying, when Val came into the room like a breath of rose-scented air.

"Hello again," I said, feeling my petals droop.

"What a good thing you're back," said the vision of loveliness. "You're wanted up at the main house."

"Oh, dear, I must have held up dinner!"

"I don't know about that. It's what else is planned for this evening that had Betty all excited. That's all I can say without spoiling what Ariel called her big surprise."

"I suppose this means you have to leave." Miss Pierce looked at me as though she'd had her rice pudding taken away. "And just as I was about to tell you about the day Mr. Nigel—"

"Perhaps another time," said Val.

Promising to come again and receiving no further protests, I scooted out of the house and into the Land Rover. During the minute it took to reach the end of the drive, I congratulated myself on a successful second meeting with the woman from Ben's past. She hadn't insulted me with a gushing greeting, and I hadn't ripped off her eyelashes. All very civilized. I parked and went up the steps to Cragstone's front door, eager to know the nature of the surprise in store.

I wasn't to be kept wondering. Ariel pounced on me as I stepped over the threshold.

"Here you are, Ellie!" She grabbed my arm. "But where's Mrs. Malloy?"

"Spending the evening with her sister."

"Oh, no! She can't possibly. We'll have to rush over and kidnap her!"

"Ariel? What's going on?"

"If you'd listened when I tried to tell you earlier, you'd know all about it! And nothing would have kept Mrs. Malloy from being here." She stepped back to glare at me, through the typically askew spectacles. "Madam LaGrange is what's happening."

"Say that again?"

"When Mrs. Malloy told me about her, last night, and said Madam's new specialty is conducting séances, I knew I had to get her to perform one here because it would please Betty so much she might ask you and Ben and Mrs. Malloy to stay.

Well, that all worked out anyway. But phoning Madam La-Grange this morning at Merlin's Court, and arranging for her to come by train and take a taxi here, isn't a wasted effort on my part. A séance will be enormous fun. Of course I had to promise she'd be paid triple her usual rate in addition to traveling expenses, but I knew that even if Dad threw a fit Betty wouldn't begrudge the money if she could have a revealing chat with Mr. Gallagher."

"Did you get Madam LaGrange's phone number from Mrs. Malloy?" I asked, through my own trance.

"No. I looked it up in the phone book. If Mrs. Malloy had any idea, do you think she'd still be with her boring old sister?"

"Probably not." My lips moved, but was the voice coming out of my mouth my own?

"I suppose it's too late to go and get her now. Madam La-Grange will be here in ten minutes if she takes the train I told her to. Luckily I still had the timetable I'd used to get to your place." Ariel scowled ferociously. "Oh, I do hate families!"

"So I've noticed." Betty appeared out of nowhere. "Go upstairs and at least comb your hair if you insist on being at the séance."

"Why shouldn't I be? I'd think you'd want me there in case you get frightened when Mr. Gallagher asks you to join him for an evening in the grave. Dad won't be any use; he'll be asleep."

"Go!"

Ariel scampered and Betty turned to me. "Tom went against me as usual and said I should appreciate the effort she'd made for me and let her be there. I suppose it was sweet of her, but I can't help wondering what she's got up her sleeve. If you're hungry, Ellie, there's the quiche we had for lunch and some sandwiches Ben made. After Ariel dropped her bombshell, it seemed best to let everyone forage for themselves instead of having a sit-down dinner."

"Where is Ben?"

"Somewhere. Probably with Tom having a scoffing session about the séance. Men just don't get these things." Betty pressed tiny fingers to her brow. "I do hope I'm not getting a headache. It was stressful having Ariel make her announcement with the Edmondses and Val present. It seemed ungracious not to ask them to participate, but I really didn't want them. From what I've heard, Nigel Gallagher didn't enjoy large gatherings. And it would be so disappointing if the numbers kept him away."

"What makes you so sure he was murdered?" I asked her.

"Besides the inexplicable events that Ariel is bound to have told you about, it's a feeling deep inside." Betty gave up on her brow and moved her hand to her breast. "I think I've always been a little psychic, and now this house has brought it to the fore. Finally I have a talent for something. . . . It's rather nice."

"I can see that." If it were real, and not the wishful thinking of a woman who suddenly found herself with too much time on her hands and an emotional void to fill.

Betty had started to say something else as the doorbell rang. "That will be her!" She hurried forward. "I do hope she's not too theatrical; Tom will hate that. But it'll be a letdown for me if she looks as if she should be pushing a grocery cart around Tesco's."

The hall filled with people. Tom and Ben came out of the dining room. Ariel raced down the stairs. She didn't appear to have combed her hair, but she had added a string of red beads to her ensemble. Madam LaGrange couldn't reasonably complain about the welcoming party. And I decided upon her entrance that she looked just as a psychic should, meaning she conformed to the image I had formed in my mind when Mrs. Malloy talked about her: reasonably tall, sturdily built, and dressed all in black from the silk scarf wound around her head to her flowing skirt. There might be a touch too much fringe and red lipstick for Tom's taste and not quite enough for Ariel's, but Betty looked suitably impressed.

"It's so good of you to come, Madam LaGrange," she said.

"The girl's phone call impelled me to do so. At the first sound of her voice, I felt the overshadowing of a soul trapped in the timeless warp between this world and the next. In almost all cases this happens when a death is violent, and there is a need to communicate with someone." Madam LaGrange had a suitably throaty, hypnotic voice. I enjoyed listening; it kept me from continually glancing at Ben to see if he still had that shuttered look on his face. But Tom cut her off.

"Shall we go into the drawing room?" he suggested brusquely.

"Have you felt a presence in there?"

"No."

"Yes," said Betty.

With this we made the move. I'd have liked a sandwich in my hand for additional company, but with luck Betty or Tom would offer Madam LaGrange refreshments and I could take a bite off her plate.

She swept into the center of the room, spread out her arms, and turned in a circle, adding the possibility that she would trip on the hem of her long skirt to the mounting sense of expectancy.

"Nothing," she announced, on ceasing to revolve. "This room has recently been redecorated? That could be the reason the departed does not feel comfortable joining us in here. Is there a room that is much as he left it?" Pausing, she held up a hand. "No one speak yet. I am seeing a study . . . dark paneling, a Jacobean oak table, leather chairs."

Ariel giggled, nervously, I thought.

Ben stood with his hands in his trouser pockets, looking inscrutable. I wished desperately for the comfort of Mrs. Malloy's presence. She would be so sorry to have missed this.

"Is there a room such as I describe?" Madam LaGrange swiveled to glance at the assemblage.

Tom looked askance at the invitation to speak in his own home, but Betty did so eagerly. "Mr. Gallagher's study. According to Mrs. Cake, the cook, he spent most of each day there. And the furniture is the same. We bought those pieces with the house, because Tom liked them."

"And he has to have his own way sometimes," chipped in Ariel, who was standing on one foot.

Betty didn't waste time glaring at her. She was leading the way to a door next to the dining room; we all swarmed in after her. Madam LaGrange had described the study accurately—little surprise there, considering it was typical of its kind, but she looked pleased with herself.

"Yes, this is where he wants us to be. I can feel his presence strongly. He is eager to get through, but sometimes there are difficulties . . . other entities trying to make contact. I never promise anything, but if someone will draw the curtains to block out most of the light, I suggest we seat ourselves around the table."

Tom saw to the curtains while the rest of us positioned the necessary six chairs. A hush filtered into the room as we took our places. It was still possible to see one another's faces, but the shadowed effect blurred some contours and sharpened others, so that the known became unknown. I shivered despite my conviction that Madam LaGrange was a fraud and

Mr. Gallagher was no more likely to join us than the man in the moon.

"Let us hold hands to form the life circle." Madam La-Grange closed her eyes.

"Aren't we supposed to light a candle?" Ariel muttered from my right.

"Unnecessary. The strength of our belief is the beacon that will light the uncertain passage that leads from their world to ours. There must be no doubters here."

Tom gave a snort, which he converted into a cough.

Ben cleared his throat. I knew he was trying not to laugh.

"Then we begin." Madam LaGrange's hand tightened on mine. I had the privilege of being seated to her right. She began to hum, a low deep unmelodious sound that thickened to a rasp . . . then to a growl. I bit my lip and stared straight ahead to prevent myself from shaking with rude mirth. My brief unease gone, I was ready to enjoy the show: sedately, if possible. Madam's grip slackened; I felt her body sag. The growling ceased. All was silent. A shaft of light slid through the narrow gap between the curtains, making for a nice visual effect. Betty squealed. Ariel giggled. Someone said *shush*. Silence again. The tension mounted nicely; a maestro couldn't have orchestrated it better. Then came the voice, and despite myself I jumped. Earlier in the hall I had wondered if the one coming out of my mouth was my own. Did Madam LaGrange find herself in a similar situation?

"Hold your horses!" thundered the voice. "Who wants me?"

"Are you Nigel Gallagher?"

"Bill Johnson . . . used to deliver the milk."

"Another time, perhaps. This evening it's Nigel we need."

"Bugger!"

I had to admit Madam LaGrange was doing a good job of

switching voices. As herself, she sounded drained of energy. She now jerked and strained upward in her chair.

"Nigel?"

"Yes. It is I!" This male voice was lower, more cultivated.

"Would you prefer that I address you as Mr. Gallagher?"

"Doesn't matter. Have to hurry! Others pushing me aside, mustn't lose the connection." Did he think he was on the phone? "Must talk to the woman who bought the house."

"She's in the room, Nigel."

"Yes, I'm right here," said Betty steadily.

"Elizabeth. . . ."

"No one ever calls me that."

"Beautiful name . . . suits you."

"Thank you." Would she begin to believe he'd fallen in love with her from beyond?

"Right for Cragstone. The west wing . . . Elizabethan. Other tragedies over the years . . . papist priest met the same end as I."

I could almost hear Betty thinking, My darling, I think only of you! "Tell me how I can help you," she urged tearily.

"Know you care, felt it from the first. Tried to get through . . . sent indicators."

I heard Tom snort and agreed wholeheartedly. A funeral wreath and some dead birds as love tokens? I scoffed inwardly. But then men always say they never know what to send.

"How can I bring your murderer to justice, Nigel?"

"You will know when the moment comes . . . soon. Very soon. Don't . . . tell anyone what you are about to do. Might try to stop you. . . . Go alone. Promise me, Elizabeth."

"I do."

"Can't stay . . . have to leave."

"Must you?"

"Until . . . we meet . . . again."

A depleted sigh issued from Madam LaGrange's lips. She had done such an admirable job of conjuring up Nigel Gallagher that I missed him deeply until I came to my senses. Nobody spoke for several minutes.

"Did he come through?" she finally asked in her own voice.

Betty's was thick with emotion. "Oh, yes!"

"I can never be sure. We need no longer hold hands."

"I don't know how to thank you, Madam LaGrange."

"We can pay her the fee Ariel promised her." Tom sounded understandably sullen. He'd been forced to witness his wife throwing herself at a ghost. Who better than I to appreciate his feeling, having watched Val do the same thing with Ben? Or hadn't that been the other way round? I suddenly felt as worn out as Madam LaGrange was pretending to be. When Betty excused herself and rushed from the room, I was tempted to follow suit.

"I never accept any payment in situations that involve murder. My gift is meant to help make the world a better and safer one," Madam was telling Tom when we heard Betty talking to someone in the hall. She did not return. It was Miss Pierce who hobbled quickly into the study.

"Where is he?" she quavered.

"Who?" Ariel pranced toward her as Tom and Ben got to their feet and Madam LaGrange fiddled with the fringe on her sleeve.

"My Mr. Nigel. I woke up to hear Val telling me he was home where he belongs, but when I sat up in bed she said I'd been dreaming and cried out in my sleep."

"That's what happened." Her great-niece was suddenly at her side. "Aunt, you shouldn't have come up here."

"I've got a coat over my nightgown. I wouldn't let Mr. Nigel see me not properly dressed."

"I know; you look entirely presentable. But he isn't here and you've interrupted the Hopkinses' evening with their guests." Val looked apologetically at Tom, but was it the sight of Ben looking at her intently that brought the lovely flush to her cheeks?

"Miss Pierce, Mr. Gallagher hasn't come home," Tom told the old lady, with a kindness that surprised me.

"He did pay a fleeting visit"—Ariel began, then checked herself—"to Istanbul, Mrs. Cake told me."

"He never went there," Nanny Pierce replied crossly. "He went to Constantinople, somewhere quite different. Oh, I am disappointed that I don't get to make Mr. Nigel a welcome-home cup of cocoa."

"Someday soon." Val put an arm around her, to have it shoved away.

"No need to coddle me like I'm demented. I'm as sharp as I ever was. None of that forgetting names and faces for me."

Madam LaGrange pushed up her sleeve to look at her watch. "I'd better go out to wait for my taxi. I booked it with the man who brought me here, for ten minutes from now. But he's going to be early."

"It must be marvelous to know things ahead of time." Ben smiled at her. He had stopped looking at Val.

"Yes, there is that." Madam glided into the hall with Tom following like a bridesmaid. After they left, Nanny sat down in the nearest chair and began reminiscing about her Mr. Nigel. Val looked embarrassed. Ben didn't look any way at all. And Ariel asked me if I'd enjoyed her surprise.

"Betty did. I don't know if that's good or bad." Suddenly I couldn't stand the constraint between Ben and myself a moment longer. Without bothering to excuse myself as Betty had done, I hurried into the hall. Deciding that wasn't far enough away, I opened the front door and headed down the stone steps in time to see Madam LaGrange get into her taxi. It was still quite light.

"Who's that?" Mrs. Malloy popped up at my side and pointed a finger at the departing guest.

"Is your eyesight failing?"

"What's that supposed to mean?"

"That you should recognize Madam LaGrange."

"But that wasn't her."

"Are you sure?" We stood staring at each other.

"'Course I am. Madam LaGrange is a slip of a girl, not much taller than Ariel and no more than eighteen years old."

"Then who was that woman?"

8

When I related to Mrs. Malloy what had transpired at the séance, one thing became clear: someone, for whatever dubious reason, wanted to confirm Betty's belief that Mr. Gallagher had been murdered. The real Madam LaGrange might not have produced Nigel at all, let alone have him play so effectively on Betty's emotions; therefore the switch. We agreed not to say anything to the Hopkinses for the time being. Better, Mrs. Malloy and I decided, to let the devious plot unfold.

Upon our return to the house, she immediately phoned the real Madam LaGrange and got her voice mail. Not thinking it wise to leave a message that might result in Madam's phoning back and talking with one of the Hopkinses, Mrs. Malloy told me she would ring back the next morning.

She and I also talked about Miss Pierce: my visit to the Dower House and her arrival at Cragstone following the séance. Was there anything to Mrs. Malloy's suggestion that Val might have had mercenary reasons for keeping in touch with the old lady over the years and then had jumped at the chance to move in with her? A practical move, Mrs. M had pointed out, if the old lady's gratitude was demonstrated by making Val her sole heir: ousting the brother who had bunked off to Ireland or possibly Scotland, made an unfortunate marriage, and forgotten all about the great-aunt. But was there an inheritance worth bothering about? The fact that Lady Fiona had not taken up residence at the Dower House merely suggested an unwillingness to turn out an elderly person who might have nowhere else to go. It was far too big a leap to assume that a grateful Mr. Gallagher had persuaded his wife to gift the Dower House to his devoted former nanny.

I was proud of having introduced this caveat. It was good to know I had not succumbed to unkindness as a result of petty and completely unfounded jealousy toward the beautiful woman who had stood that afternoon with my husband in a tableau that excluded everyone else present, clinging to his hands, gazing deeply into his eyes. What else should be expected from two people who come unexpectedly upon each other after a long interval of time? Our vicar would be proud of me. His wife might go so far as to offer me the lead in her next play, *The Merry Wives of Chitterton Fells*.

The rest of the evening was such that Ben and I were never alone until we came upstairs, at which time we were occupied with the necessary unpacking. I whisked into the bathroom, not to avoid conversation but because I like concentrated time with my teeth. It is a source of some pride to me that I have never had a cavity, something most women in their thirties cannot claim. Val must be about my age, I thought, as I hung up the dainty hand towel. Whether she looked younger might be in the eye of the one doing the beholding. The mirror informed me that I could shed a few years by unplaiting my hair and shaking it loose down my back. True, in the morning I'd look as though I had escaped from an attic, but so what? Then again, maybe what Ben needed at this time was a wife with whom he could converse without visible distraction. There had to be so much he was aching to tell me: what he had thought of the séance, how it felt to be reunited with Tom, his impression of Betty, and what he was planning for the tea tomorrow and the catering for Thursday.

I left my hair in its plait and smoothed the demure collar of my nightgown before leaving the bathroom and making my way to the four-poster bed where Ben awaited me under the covers.

"Sleepy, darling?" I asked, settling back against the comfy down pillows.

"Yes, but not too tired to talk." His hand reached for mine but instantly let it go, as he lay in a straight line on his back, arms at his side, eyes on the ceiling.

I resisted the urge to rearrange him like a piece of furniture that needed to be set at an angle. Instead, I switched off my bedside lamp and watched him subside into shadow. Nice, I told myself: peaceful contentment at the end of a long day. No need to talk. Everything that had occurred since our arrival at Cragstone House could wait till morning to be discussed. Of course he must be tired, after the early start and the drive to Yorkshire.

"How was Mrs. Malloy's reunion with her sister?" he asked, across the great divide that can happen in beds designed for families of six.

"Interesting."

"In what way?" Ben inquired of the ceiling.

"We met Mr. Archibald Scrimshank. He looks like an Archibald. Melody had some pertinent things to say about him and his relationship with the Gallaghers." I went on to explain, speaking faster as the feeling increased that he was only half listening. When I petered out, it was several moments before he answered. I wondered if he'd fallen asleep.

"Do the sisters resemble each other?"

So much for depicting Mr. Scrimshank as the pin-striped villain of the piece and exciting Ben's interest in ways to prove him guilty of embezzlement and murder.

"Looking at Melody was like catching Mrs. Malloy on the hop without any makeup or hair dye. I felt I ought to apologize and back out the door, promising not to breathe a word to anyone that I'd seen her naked."

Another silence, during which Ben compressed his arms even closer to his sides. I waited for one of us to start humming as the faux Madam LaGrange had done earlier. When that didn't happen, I brought up the visit to the Dower House. Finally, in a giddy attempt at providing him with a clearer visual image of the scene, I mentioned Val's arrival.

"She'd brighten the dullest room, wouldn't she?" I said.

"You think?"

"Oh, yes! I don't know when I've met anyone so lovely." Now I was the one making a confidant of the ceiling.

"Ellie. . . ."

"You must have been stunned to see her walk into the hall this afternoon." It was said at last. Now he would explain what she had or had not meant to him once upon a time. I would pose gentle questions and receive all the right answers. I would confess to having felt just the tiniest bit threatened until Mrs. Malloy had talked sense into me on the drive to see Melody. He would take me in his arms and tell me tenderly that I was the only woman he had ever loved, and the bed would shrink to its proper size with only room for the two of us.

That was what should have happened. Instead, his response increased the distance between us.

"She was someone I knew."

"And?"

"It was a surprise to see her walk in."

"You didn't know that she had a great-aunt living in this part of the world?"

"Ellie." He reached again for my hand and this time held on to it. "There's a lot I didn't know about Valeria Pierce. We crossed paths. . . . Can we leave it at that for the time being?"

"Absolutely."

"No probing questions? No digging up the past?"

"You were ships passing in the night." I squeezed his hand, to let him know I understood, before turning over and pressing my quivering lips against the pillow. So silly to react in such a way! But why was he reluctant to talk about the woman if meeting her again had not reawakened regrets for what might have been? I was convinced I wouldn't be able to fall asleep with Ben lying beside me like a block of wood and unanswerable questions hammering away in my head. But misery provides its own stupor, and I found myself dragged down into a bog that suffocated thought.

No unhappy dreams disturbed my slumber. I awoke to sunlight blasting through the windows, bouncing on and off the furniture and spray-painting the walls with gold. Mother Nature is not always the most sensitive of souls, and at first I recoiled. Let the birds chirp their little hearts out, let the sky be the color of bluebells, I would not be coerced into a more cheerful frame of mind. I would burrow deep into my Slough of Despond, put a pillow over my face, and refuse to set foot out of bed. But then pride had to go and rear its ugly head. Ben was already up. Did I really want the entire household, of which Val seemed to be an integral part, to know I was sulking? My mind said it didn't matter. The rest of me collaborated in getting out from under the covers. Despicable, how we can turn against ourselves at crucial moments.

But once up I felt marginally better. It was a relief that Ben had stolen a march on me and did not have to be faced immediately. A steaming hot shower further improved matters. Indeed, I found myself wondering if I hadn't blown our bedtime chat out of all proportion. So he hadn't wanted to talk about Val. What man would want to rehash a past relationship with his wife? Maybe she had dumped him in a way he found embarrassing to remember, or he was the one who had broken things off and he still felt somewhat guilty. By the time I had finished coiling my hair into its chignon, I was convinced I had upset myself over nothing. It also came to me that Val reminded me of Bridie O'Donnell, the girl in my class at school whose dark curls and blue eyes had made me feel so hopelessly inferior.

I drifted downstairs renewed in spirit. On hearing voices emanating from the far end of the hall, I went through the open kitchen door to find a beehive of activity. Ben was making toast and Mrs. Malloy was handing around cups of coffee. Ariel was jabbering about not wanting to go to church. Betty, wearing a green polished cotton suit two sizes too big for her, was insisting that Ariel was going, like it or lump it. Tom, in yesterday's country squire's outfit, seemed to be working on being invisible. Nobody mentioned the séance.

Smiles here and there wafted my way as I sat down at the large table in the center of the room. A coffee cup and plate of toast magically appeared in front of me, followed by a butter dish and marmalade pot.

"How are you this morning?" Ben asked, his face a breath away from mine. The world righted itself completely.

"Awake, which you know is amazing, since I'm not a morning person." I hoped he'd read between the lines and realize I was telling him I now saw things more clearly. His hand touched my hair and Val's specter drifted away to the funeral heap of what might have been but wasn't.

The kitchen, despite its being in need of refurbishing, was meant for cheerful occupancy. In time, I thought without a pang, the present-day Val would bring new life to its old-world charm with new cabinets, countertops, and appliances. The floor perhaps she would leave; I liked the honey-colored stone. It would be good to find a modern replica of the large country sink and 1920s cooker, but my opinion was not what counted. Chance had given the Hopkinses their decorator, a friend who only a few short months before had been a stranger to them both. A happy outcome among neighbors.

Regrettably, Ariel was not happy. Her face was marred by the fiercest of scowls as she stood with her hands on her hips, squaring off at her stepmother. "If I have to go to church, why can't it be to St. Cuthbert's? Their service is shorter."

"Because it's Church of England and we're Catholic?" Betty looked ready to sling a slice of toast at anyone who moved.

"Then why have their vicar for tea?"

"You know the reason. Mr. Hardcastle has an old clergy-man friend staying with him who remembers Cragstone House fondly and wants to see it one more time before he kicks the bucket. Tom"—rounding on him—"say something to your daughter or I'll run screaming from this house."

"Ariel—"

"Oh, please!" Betty screeched. "Not in that wimpy voice!"

"Aren't we a lovely family?" The wretched child flung her arms wide and beamed a smile around the room. While I looked at Ben, hoping for inspiration as to what to say, Mrs. Malloy, disporting herself in emerald taffeta this morning and wearing more than her usual amount of rouge and incandescent eye shadow, announced that she had sometimes rather fancied becoming a Roman Catholic.

"Trouble is, me doctor advised against it. Bad for the knees, he said, all that bobbing up and down in the pews. A shame, really, because I've always liked their views on Bingo. Protestants have never taken to it the same way. To be fair, there's nothing in the Bible that says anything about it one way or another." She returned to pouring coffee.

"Ariel." Tom made another attempt at being the heavy-handed father. "Go upstairs this minute and wash your hair. You can't go to church looking like that."

"Why?"

"It's"—he struggled to come up with a word—"greasy. I don't know why nothing is ever done about it."

"Meaning I'm supposed to introduce her to a bottle of shampoo, tell her what it does, and point the way to the nearest tap?" Betty grew a full inch with rage.

"No." Tom hastily retrieved the look he had darted at her. "But other girls her age don't go around looking like she does."

"If I do wash my hair," said Ariel smugly, "I'll be too late for church."

"Suit yourself." Betty marched toward the hall door with Tom following at a snail's pace behind. "Anyone else want to come?" she asked belatedly and, receiving responses in the negative, she and Tom departed.

"I think having afternoon tea with two vicars is enough spirituality for me on any given Sunday," Ben confided, into the hush that followed.

"We'll go twice next week." I buttered another slice of toast.

"I tried making that phone call just now—you know the one I mean, Mrs. H—and again got no reply." Mrs. Malloy winked at me before skewering Ariel with a neon-lidded look. "You, missy, has to be one of the rudest children I've ever laid eyes on. Was it me in charge, you'd spend the rest of the day in your room, tied to the frigging bedpost."

Before Ariel could respond, a door to the left of the pantry opened and a woman emerged, carrying a bucket and mop. She looked to be in her late twenties: slim, with chin-length mousy hair and a tight-lipped nondescript face. Her floral apron was faded, her shoes serviceable lace-ups, her gaze indifferent.

"I thought the kitchen would be clear by now," she said, to no one in particular. "But then I'm not used to coming on Sundays. I guess I can get started somewhere else. Makes me no mind."

"Please don't let us upset your routine," I said quickly, and Ben agreed that we would instantly get out from underfoot.

"I'm guessing you're Mavis." Mrs. M eyed her in a comradely sort of way. "I'm Roxie Malloy from the Chitterton Fells Charwomen's Association. I'm staying here with Mr. and Mrs. H, who are cousins of the Hopkinses."

"Is that right?"

Ben and I smiled and said yes.

"The way things has worked out," Mrs. M continued, "you and me'll be working together for the best part of this week. You won't find me interfering."

Did she have her fingers crossed behind her back? Mavis, still holding the bucket and mop, was not moved to reply, let alone register any noticeable interest.

"Mrs. Cake seems to think we'll get on like a house afire."

"Is that so?"

"Mr. H, who's a proper chef, will be doing the cooking for her while she's laid up. A real shame, her taking that fall downstairs."

"Wasn't it?" Mavis walked over to the sink, to stand with

her back to us while turning on the tap and sticking the bucket under it. A gurgle, a sputter, and then a full rush of water put up a barrier of sound that Ariel ignored.

"How's your little boy?" she swallowed a mouthful of toast to ask.

"Why do you want to know?"

"Just wondering. I think it's sad you can't bring him to work with you."

"Yes, well, that's not on, is it?"

"What's his name?"

"Eddie." Mavis turned off the tap. The bucket was full. "So do I start in here or don't I?"

The rest of us cleared out of the kitchen in a swoop, to stand in the hall and ponder our immediate future. Ben said he would go and have a word with Mrs. Cake, whom he had seen earlier hobbling into the sitting room next to the conservatory. I would have to delay talking to her in an attempt to discover what she could tell us about the Gallaghers. Ariel wandered away, hopefully to go upstairs and wash her hair. Mrs. M, after remarking that Mavis was a rare ray of sunshine who had cheered her up no end, headed upstairs to give herself a manicure.

I found the phone and rang Ben's parents to see how the children were doing and spoke to all three in turn. It was lovely hearing their little voices, and great to know they were having such a wonderful time with Grandma and Grandpa. Feeling dial-happy, I tried my own number in hope of getting Freddy and asking if all was well with him and Tobias, but the voice mail came on instead. Either he was at Abigail's or still in bed. I was thinking of following Mrs. Malloy's example and doing my nails on the off chance that one of the vicars would be of the courtly hand-kissing sort when Ariel materialized beside me, still with hair needing shampoo, to ask if I would like to go exploring.

"Where?" It was another lovely day and I enjoyed a walk.

"Here in the house. Would you like to see the west wing?"

"Very much." Indeed, I thrilled to the prospect of taking on the role of intrepid governess venturing into murky chambers haunted by history.

"It's the part of the house that dates back to Elizabethan times."

"So Madam LaGrange, as Nigel, made mention."

"You can get to it only from inside on the upper floors. It's separated on ground level by the exterior arched passageway constructed at the time of the Georgian addition." Ariel was in her best tour-guide mode. "There's an outside door, but nobody ever uses it," she explained, while leading me along the gallery past the portraits on the wall, including the one of Lady Fiona as a young woman. "Mrs. Cake says that door has never been locked for as long as she can remember. If there's a key, no one knows where it is. Isn't it fun to realize that anyone could break in at any time?"

"I prefer the idea of a new lock."

"So does Dad, but Betty's dead set against it. She's hoping Lady Fiona will break in to retrieve some vital piece of evidence that would prove she murdered her husband. What did you think of the séance? Dad and Betty won't talk about it."

"I wonder why?"

"Didn't Madam LaGrange do a super job?"

"Marvelous."

"You'd think Betty would stay grateful instead of going on about my hair."

"It could do with a wash." I followed her around a corner and up a short flight of steps.

"Ellie, you're supposed to be unraveling the mystery of who's been pulling the spook stunts."

"Someone who's staked Betty out, either because she's the most susceptible or on account of a grudge against her?"

"Maybe. I thought we were going to be a team."

"Are you worried or just out to amuse yourself?"

"I told you: it's like being in a book. Last night made a really good chapter. But I wrote that one, so it really doesn't count in getting us to the revealing conclusion. Why won't you tell me what you're thinking?"

"Because I haven't had time to think."

"We are now entering the west wing." Ariel opened a door at the end of a short shadowy passage. "Careful, we go down a couple of steps. Hold on to me if you like; I'll find the light switch. Oh, good! Here it is. Okay?"

"Fine," I said, appreciative of her solicitude. We were in a wainscoted hall, vast enough to have been used in bygone days as a ballroom. In addition to the electric wall sconces, mullioned windows brought sunlight flooding in like golden waterfalls rippling across the time-polished floor. The furniture was limited to an armoire taking up one corner, which looked as though it had been designed for the gentleman whose wife insisted he hang up his suit of armor before getting into bed, and a couple of thronelike chairs with tapestry seats. Easy to picture Sir Walter Raleigh sitting in one of them, ruminating on whether or not to take his cloak to the dry cleaners—the one he no longer felt quite so sentimental about Queen Bess having walked on, now that she had decided to chop off his head. It was not a particularly grim thought. Indeed, there was nothing in the space to re-create the feeling of gloom I had experienced on entering Cragstone House yesterday before Betty turned on the hall lights. There was no rotting bride's veil of cobwebs, no reek of despoiled antiquity, no stealthy scratching behind the paneling to suggest an infestation of rodents. Even so, had I in truth been a Victorian heroine intent upon meeting up with unkindly fate in the form of a skeleton wearing only the remnants of his ruff, I would have preferred to do so somewhere else—the British museum being my first choice. They have curators eager for that sort of thing to happen, who would insist on having first dibs on Mr. Bones Jangles and palm me off with a nice cup of tea.

"Why are you looking nervous?" Ariel wanted to know.

"I didn't like the way that door groaned shut behind us."

"It's a very heavy door." Did she say that with unnecessary relish?

"Good for keeping drafts out." I shivered nevertheless.

"I expect we could scream our heads off and no one would ever hear."

"Probably. Did you hear that creaking sound?"

"No. When Betty's being particularly hateful I think about her being stuck up here and wailing uselessly for someone to come and rescue her. Oh, don't look so shocked!" She danced down the center of the hall and spun back to face me. "I wouldn't lure her here and run away. There wouldn't be any point. There's no lock on the door. Besides, well . . . I just wouldn't."

"I should hope not."

"You don't think she's vile, do you?"

"No one's perfect."

Ariel gave me one of her disgusted looks before flouncing down onto one of the throne chairs. "Do you want to know why she won't let Mavis bring her little boy with her? It's because she thinks anyone who can afford to drive to work should be able to pay for child care."

"What about his being a difficult child?"

"That too." Ariel sat, rhythmically kicking the legs of her chair. "But it's more about Mavis having a car. Anyone would think it was a Rolls-Royce instead of an old rattletrap. Now we're rich, Betty wants everyone else to be poor. And she's wrong about Mavis's husband sitting around all day being lazy. Mrs. Cake says the firm he worked for moved to Sheffield and

145

he decided to set up a home office on his own. He's a locksmith. And the kid gets sick if he has to drive around too long in the van. Eddie." Ariel turned the name around in her mouth. "Imagine being a little boy with a name like that these days!"

"Perhaps he's named for his father," I suggested, "or another family member."

"Like Valeria-rhymes-with-malaria. After you and Mrs. Malloy escaped yesterday afternoon, I asked her how she got stuck with that name, and she said it was after her great-aunt, Nanny Pierce. Wouldn't that be enough to make her want to bump the old lady off?"

"What a bloodthirsty child you are." I moved to inspect a portion of wainscoting. "Old-fashioned names are popular again. My older daughter Abbey's full name is Abigail, after a long-ago relative whose portrait hangs above our fireplace."

"I remember. She looked quite nice."

"So does Valeria." I studied a section of the carved oak trim that divided the wainscoting into squares.

"Yes, but to get stuck with a name that sounds like a disease! No wonder she shortened it."

"Anyone would say she's beautiful."

"Not Dad; I asked him and he said he hadn't noticed. Maybe she only lets very special people call her Valeria, the way Ben did. Probably they were really good friends at one time." Ariel stopped kicking the legs of her chair. "But you know, Ellie, I don't think you should be upset about that or the way they were looking into each other's eyes like they were drowning. It must have been the surprise. I think you're every bit as lovely as she is, in a different way. But better safe than sorry."

"Meaning?"

Ariel got up and came to stand beside me. "I'm not sure, really. I guess it's that I don't see why she has to be so friendly. Taking over the decorating like it's her own house. Advising

Betty on what clothes to wear. Maybe she likes to borrow husbands like they're cups of sugar."

I laughed because it made a good solid sound. "Mrs. Malloy borrowed her sister's boyfriend, and it led to a forty-year rift."

"So that's what did it." Ariel surprised me by not following up on this. "At least with Betty you know where you stand."

"And quite possibly you're not being fair to Val."

"I suppose." She gave one of her shrugs. "The trouble is that when I'm bad I'm very, very bad and when I'm good I'm still horrid."

"Rubbish! You just need to be a little less hard on yourself and other people." I reached out to touch her but she edged away to point a grubby fingernail at the carving I had been examining.

"Are these Tudor roses, Ellie?"

"Probably."

"There's an *E* above that doorway." Ariel stalked ahead of me down the length of the room, and I admired the carving before asking what lay beyond.

"Rooms. They're all empty, except for the one Nanny Pierce used before moving to the Dower House."

"I wonder why she slept in this wing rather than the main house?"

"To keep her out of the way as much as possible? That would be my guess. I expect Lady Fiona found her a real pain. Always fussing over Mr. Gallagher like he was still her sweetie-weetie baby boykins. You won't believe how nutty she was about him till I show you."

"What exactly?"

"This." Ariel stopped in the middle of a sizable hallway to push open a door and beckon me into a room with a bed, a narrow wardrobe, and a great deal of shelving filled with the paraphernalia of a boy's childhood. Books, butterfly nets, magnets and magnifying glasses, microscopes and telescopes, several Noah's arks, and a regiment of toy soldiers. It was impossible to take them all in at once. Each object lovingly, laboriously arranged: row upon row of what would now be desirable collectibles to the antique toy connoisseur. I sat down on the bed, the better to feast my eyes, and hastily jumped back up, having been poked by a sharp object that proved to be a guardsman with a bayonet. On the floor beside my foot I spotted another one, and next to it a miniature horse and rider.

Ariel watched me as I gathered them up. "Dad was up here last week fixing some of the doors because they stuck. I expect his banging about made things fall off the shelves. Don't you think it's creepy, Nanny Pierce keeping all this stuff in her room? And there's more in what was her sitting room."

"The question is, why didn't she take them with her to the Dower House?"

"She didn't move down there until after Mr. Gallagher went away. Mrs. Cake says Nanny wants him to find this room just as it's always been when he comes back—apart from her photos of him, which she took with her. Can't bear to go to sleep at night without kissing his little face a dozen times over."

"Ariel." I put the misplaced items back on a shelf. "Miss Pierce is a very old lady."

"Okay, but whose fault is that? I'll bet she was always weird, and Lady Fiona was thrilled to finally get away from her, even if it meant she has to be the one staying in a hotel. No moving in together, you notice. Now that you've met Nanny Pierce, don't you think she could be one who's been trying to frighten us away from Cragstone, either with Val's help or on her own? That tottery business could be an act."

"Ariel, a woman of over eighty is entitled to totter."

"Come on, I'll show you the other rooms up here."

I looked at my watch. "Let's do that another time. Your parents could be back from church by now and looking for you."

"I keep telling you, Betty's not my mother."

There being no answer to this that would have gone down well, I made my way back to what I thought of as the ballroom with Ariel trailing behind. Would I now be given the silent treatment? It was a relief when we exited the west wing and the heavy door groaned shut behind us, blocking off the sense of unease. Was I yet another Madam LaGrange, I thought testily, dredging up impressions from past lives? And what had become of my oft-vouched enthusiasm for the foreboding?

"We'll go down the back way." Ariel scampered ahead of me through an archway and down a flight of linoleum-covered steps. "These were for the servants. They're the ones Mrs. Cake fell down. Her bedroom is along there." She stopped on a small landing branching off to our right. "Poor old thing, I really like her and her homemade toffee. I'm very keen on toffee. I wonder if Mrs. Malloy still has some of the ones she had in the car?"

"In her bedroom. She put the bag out as a decoration." I wasn't sure if Ariel had heard me; she had whisked ahead, a straggly-haired wraith in spectacles. Moments later our descent brought us to a second landing, this one with a narrow rectangle of window to our left.

"It overlooks the passageway separating the two parts of the house." Ariel swiveled around on one foot to point. "If you squint, you'll get a view of Mavis's car and see what I mean about it being a rattletrap."

I did see it—I've always been a good squinter—and I also got a partial view of the Dower House and someone walking away from it.

"It's Ben." Ariel peered over my shoulder, adding, just a little too quickly, "I expect he had an uncontrollable urge to bond with Nanny Pierce. Val probably isn't even there; she's been going for a lot of walks lately. Keeping in shape, I expect. Mrs. Cake says you don't get a figure like that by sitting on it."

"And right she is. Lead on, Macduff!" I followed her down the rest of the steps, determined that the one thing I would not exercise was my imagination. Ben could have gone to the Dower House for a variety of perfectly innocent reasons, including the wish to see Val. They were old friends. They had years to catch up on. Really, it was heartwarming to think of them chatting about the past. How they had danced the night away in each other's arms, night after wretched night. I discovered I was grinding my teeth. This was not good. It might well lead to cavities, of which I had none and hoped Val had a great many. I wished Mrs. Malloy were with me so I could lay my head on her robust shoulder and weep copious tears down her taffeta bosom.

Blessed relief! There she was, in the passageway, when Ariel and I came to the door that had lost its key and welcomed burglars.

"A fine time I've had, Mrs. H, looking all over for you," she announced, as Ariel faded away in the direction of the main house. "I want you to hear me recite the poem I've written for Melody."

"That would be nice," I said, hoping she would notice I sounded wan and would usher me indoors where I could sit on her knee and tell her I was being spiteful and petty again and ask if she knew of something I could take for it.

"Nice to hear you sound so encouraging, Mrs. H. Now hold on a minute, let me get posed just right." She squared her shoulders, drew in her elbows, and clasped her hands over her middle. This not being quite what she was after, she made some adjustments. One hand went to her bosom and then down to her side. "Don't rush me, Mrs. H!"

I thought of Mr. Gallagher's parents, who had, according to Miss Pierce, doted on his teatime recitations. Perhaps my failure to get into the poetry mood was because there were no little sandwiches and fancy iced cakes on a table in the passageway. Despair tends to make me hungry; it had to be time for elevenses, if not for lunch. Sausages would be nice and perhaps some bubble and squeak. Ben made wonderful hubble-bubble, as we called it. Quite possibly it would be the thing I would miss most about him when he was gone.

Glancing over my shoulder, I saw him walking toward us, dark head bent, seemingly intent on counting every piece of gravel on the path.

"Here goes, then! Tell me if the words' gas meter, or whatever they call it, is all right." Mrs. Malloy cleared her throat before beginning:

> " 'Tis forty years since last we met,
> And I am filled with deep regret,
> That I didn't see your point of view,
> Like an older sister's meant to do.
> But now it's time to start again,
> May lessons learned not be in vain."

"Very poignant," I said, with what I hoped was a noticeable glow of enthusiasm. Ben had looked up and seen us. He had a piece of paper in his hand, which he now waved.

"I'm not finished." Mrs. Malloy rebuked me. "I did seven more verses. I got so carried away I forgot to give meself a manicure."

"Then you'd better go in and do it before I rope you in to help with lunch." Ben drew up in front of us and flashed her a smile. "Escape while there's still time."

"I don't see as it would hurt Betty to get one meal. It's not like she's always been a lady of leisure. Too much time on the hands all of a sudden isn't good for nobody. Probably bored out of her

151

mind and picking holes in Tom and Ariel for something to do. But I'll leave you two together," said Mrs. M magnanimously, before teetering down the passageway on her high heels— different shoes from the ones she and Val had in common. I looked at Ben, seeing the flecks of gold in his eyes before he lowered his head, again concentrating on the gravel as he slid an arm around my shoulders and we walked toward the kitchen door.

"When I was talking to Mrs. Cake, she suggested I go down and ask Miss Pierce for her recipe for currant scones." He folded the piece of paper and put it in his trouser pocket. "She said it's a good one and the old lady would be pleased."

"Thoughtful of Mrs. Cake to suggest it," I told his shoes, "and nice of you to take her up on the idea. You've nothing to learn when it comes to making scones."

"I thought it was my hubble-bubble you were particularly fond of." I could hear the smile in his voice.

"Funny you should mention it. I was just pining for some."

"Two hearts that beat as one." His arm drew me closer. I should have brimmed over with happiness. I was happy. There had been a perfectly reasonable explanation for his visit to the Dower House.

"Will Miss Pierce and Val—Valeria—be at the tea?"

"Of course." It was said lightly, but I felt I'd stepped on his toes. Had I sounded like the jealous wife in *Master of Darkwood Manor*? Would it not be wise to reflect that she had not lived happily ever after?

9

A back door to the main house opened and Betty stuck out her head. "Hello there. Tom and I just got back from church."

"Good sermon?" Ben asked.

"I couldn't concentrate. Tom said he felt wonky in the middle of it and went out to sit on a bench."

"Is he feeling better?" I inquired of her back, as we went inside.

"Who knows? He's been out of sorts ever since you arrived." Betty made up for this tactless observation by saying the magic words. "I'll get coffee and biscuits, if you like. I really was fairly domesticated, before there no longer seemed any point. Or would we do better having an early lunch, as we'll be having the tea at three? Anyway, come into the kitchen and we'll sort it out."

We found Tom slumped in a chair at the table and Ariel staring moodily into space. The wall clock showed that it was almost noon, so we agreed on lunch, which I offered to get, but Ben said he would handle it and there was no need for the rest of us to clear out because he worked well with an audience.

"I'll applaud like mad if you hit Dad over the head with a frying pan," said Little Miss Sunshine. "Okay"—holding up her hands—"I just meant he needs waking up."

"Sorry." Tom got to his feet and asked Ben, without looking at him, whether he required help finding things.

"No, thanks, I've learned my way around."

"Up early this morning, weren't you? Hope it wasn't because you didn't sleep well."

"Never better. I wanted to get organized for the tea. All that's left on that score is to make Miss Pierce's scones that Mrs. Cake recommends so highly." Ben was cracking eggs into a bowl. "Mushroom omelets agreeable to everyone?"

"Aren't we all having the loveliest time?" said Ariel, getting in his way. "Smile, Betty! You look almost as sour as Dad. Didn't church agree with you either?"

"Will you ever learn to zip your mouth? It wasn't church, it was bumping into Frances Edmonds afterward and being forced to invite her to tea this afternoon. I thought I had put her off yesterday, by saying we'd have her and Stan on their own next Sunday. But this morning she kept pressing, saying she was dying to meet Lady Fiona, and finally she came out with it."

"Out with what?" I asked, because nobody else did.

"That I didn't want my old friends around my posh new ones. That I've turned into a raging snob and forgotten that until a few months ago, I lived in a small semi-detached and stood on my feet all day long hairdressing and went home at night to bang plates of baked beans on toast on the table and call it dinner."

I hadn't known she was a hairdresser. It explained why Tom thought she could have done something about Ariel's greasy locks and why the little minx was so intent on not letting her. One more small rebellion for mankind.

"All that pent-up jealousy! It came pouring out of Frances's mouth. How she and Stan have played the lottery faithfully ever since it started, and we'd bought one bloody ticket and won the jackpot. And how if we'd been any kind of friends, we'd at the very least have paid off their mortgage and bought them a new car, and if we'd been *really* decent we would have insisted on giving them half of what we won."

"Oh, God!" Tom paced around the table. "I did say to you, Betty, that that's what we should do. They'd have split with us. We've known them for years. They've been like family: Christmas and birthdays celebrated together. And with my mother gone, neither you nor I have any relations we're close to."

That put Ben and me in our place. Fortunately, it didn't have any impact on his ability to slice mushrooms at lightning speed. I managed my discomfort by getting down plates and setting out cutlery.

"And I told you, Tom," snapped Betty, "that we need to take our time deciding what we should do for other people. We've both heard the horror stories of what can happen when even the postman thinks he's entitled to his cut."

"I understand exercising caution, but not when it comes to the Edmondses. They're the salt of the earth."

"So Frances steals things!" Ariel gave one of her irritating giggles.

"Not from us." Betty, looking suddenly deflated, sank down on the chair Tom had previously occupied. "Not once. Never! At other times, with other people, she can't seem to help herself. It's Frances's particular quirk. We all have them." She seemed pathetically small in the oversized green suit. Even her red hair looked too big. "Stop panicking, Tom. I got Frances calmed down by saying that of course she was welcome at the tea. I'd been concerned she'd find the rest of the company boring."

"Does that include Ellie and Ben?" asked Ariel, through another giggle.

"Don't be silly! Why have you still not washed your hair? The real reason I didn't want them today is I'm afraid they'll start telling their dirty jokes, and I can't see that being our two vicars' cups of tea."

"Why does that matter if we're in that disgusting room, with all those naked people on the ceiling?" All merriment had left Ariel's face. She was back to her most disgruntled self.

"She's speaking of the conservatory," Tom said, catching my eye. "I don't understand either. It's like being in the Sistine Chapel."

"Mrs. Cake says it was Lady Fiona's favorite place to sit," Betty responded.

"Then she's disgusting," blared Ariel.

"Her grandfather had that ceiling painted by a famous artist." Betty pressed a hand to her brow. "When she married Mr. Gallagher, he thought it needed a little cloud cover, so she had that done. It's a terrible shame there've been leaks from the bathroom above; we'll need to get a plumber in to take a look, although Mrs. Cake thinks the damage may have been caused by one or the other of the Gallaghers allowing the bath to overflow."

Betty stood up at the moment Mrs. Malloy came though the door to announce that her poem had ended up being twelve verses long. Did we all want to hear it from start to finish? Fortunately we were spared the solemn responsibility required of critics. Ben said that if there could be an exodus to the dining room he would bring in the food.

Lunch was, as expected, delicious. In addition to the

omelets and my desired hubble-bubble, we had tomato basil soup and a spinach salad, followed by a luscious lemon soufflé. Would tea that afternoon be an anticlimax? I offered to help with the washing up, but Betty insisted on taking that job. Ariel was given final marching orders to go and wash her hair. Mrs. Malloy, having put on her nylon and lace pinny, asked where she would find the paper doilies. Ben handed them to her. Tom wandered away like Mr. Gallagher's ghost returning to the place where his body had been buried. I found myself remembering my unease in the west wing, as I crossed the hall to go upstairs and encountered Mavis coming down them with the bucket and mop.

"Hello," I said, feeling a complete sloth. "Do you get to go home now and enjoy what's left of Sunday with your family?"

She didn't return my smile. "My husband's a locksmith; he gets called out a lot on weekends. It's always the time when people get stuck out of their houses and cars." She didn't add *silly fools*, but her expression made it clear.

"They must be relieved when he gets there. Are there any doors he can't open?"

"Not Ed." She thawed minimally. "I tell him he must have been a safecracker in a former life, or else it was in this one and he didn't tell me. But no need to bother about any of that around here. You can walk in for the looking. I hope Ed"—her face closed down as she shifted the bucket from one hand to the other—"I hope my husband isn't home wanting his dinner. Anyway, I'm ready to leave." She came down the last of the stairs and brushed past me without answering my good-bye, and I went up to my room.

It was my intention to lie down on the bed for five minutes and think over the morning. But I fell almost instantly asleep and woke to find Ben bending over me, rubbing my shoulder and telling me it was gone two o'clock. Whereupon I staggered up, felt my way into the bathroom with my eyes half closed, and proceeded to splash my face with cold water. By the time I had pulled on a more afternoon sort of dress and redone my make-up and hair, he was gone. Would it be like this all week, I asked my face in the mirror, each of us playing musical rooms so we were rarely alone for any space of time? Was that how we both wanted it for the time being, while we each had other claims on our attention?

In the gallery I met up with Mrs. Malloy, looking resplendent as always, but I focused on the white lace-trimmed pinny.

"You don't plan on wearing that at tea, I hope?" I said.

"'Course I do."

"You don't work for Tom and Betty. Admittedly, you've agreed to help out, as Ben has done, but to all intents and purposes he's a guest and so are you."

"No need to get on your high horse for me, Mrs. H! I know where you and me stand, but it strikes me I'll get to do a lot more eavesdropping going around the room with a tray than sitting down next to one person."

"You could be right, although I doubt you'll get to hear Mr. Scrimshank confide to Lady Fiona that he's embezzled her money and capped it off by murdering her husband when he became suspicious. That's not exactly cucumber-sandwich conversation."

"Well, there's no telling what little nuggets I'll pick up. By the way, have you been helping yourself to my toffees?"

"I haven't been inside your bedroom."

"Somebody has. The bed looked as though it had been bounced on, and that bag of toffees is half gone. Ariel, I suppose. And her talking about Frances Edmonds being a kleptomaniac. The child needs a good old-fashioned spanking. Still," she mused soulfully, "like the poet says, a sweet's a sweet for all that!" Concerned that this was a precursor to her asking if I'd like to hear her "Ode to Melody" in its entirety, I said we should get downstairs. To which she replied she'd take another scoot back to her room to make sure her eyebrows were on straight.

The long case clock was striking three as I reached the hall and came face-to-face with Lady Fiona. Having seen her portrait, there was no mistaking her. She had aged, as is said, gracefully. I explained who I was, and she said I could call her Fiona if I wished. She was very much the way I had imagined she would be at her present stage of life: tall and thin, with good bones, fine eyes, and a vague, drifting way of moving. I sensed that even when talking or listening, she would always be somewhat removed from the scene.

"The little girl opened the door for me and then vanished, saying she had to wash her hair before Mrs. Hopkins chopped off her head and it didn't matter anymore. Family life is different today, isn't it? In Nanny Pierce's opinion, our parents had the sense to keep out of the way until they could make some useful contribution."

"She said something like that to me yesterday."

"I really must do something for her, take her out to luncheon this Wednesday; yes, I will mention it to her. I suppose she'll be here?" Before I could answer she glided down the hall. "Really, I have neglected her sadly in recent months, but I hear she has some young woman living with her now at the Dower House."

"Her great-niece."

"I seem to remember there was one—and, I think, a brother. Didn't turn out well. Gambled or drank to excess. Went to live in Ireland—or am I thinking of another family? The Bledstowes, from Cambridge . . . yes, I think now it was they. They had a dog that could play the piano." She was now looking through the open drawing-room door.

"Will we be having tea in here?"

"In the conservatory. Betty thought you would like that."

"Who? Oh, yes, that will be the new maid. The people who bought Cragstone came into money from an aunt in New Zealand, I believe it was. They'll be able to take on plenty of help. I do hope they kept Mavis on. She hasn't had an easy time. I seem to remember she grew up in an orphanage and had to sort rags in order to buy stockings."

Before she could say that maybe she was thinking of a book she had read—I was pretty sure I knew the one—she drifted on down the hall and I entered the conservatory behind her. There was no one else there as yet, so we had our choice of sofas and chairs.

"I miss Cragstone," she said. "Particularly this room."

It *was* attractive, with its abundance of plants on stands and tables. The glass walls provided a sweeping panorama of the grounds, but I was preoccupied with adjusting my nose to the smell of earth and mold, which is not one of my particular favorites. Then I looked up at the ceiling. It was indeed something to behold. A celestial nudist colony! Patriarchal males, all of whom looked as though they were named Zeus, disported themselves on cloud sofas. Women with crimped gold tresses and rounded bellies cavorted in streams of sunlight. The Sistine Chapel it wasn't. Religious, no; ribald, yes. What it had been like before Mr. Gallagher's request for more cloud cover I did not care to imagine. My heart went out to the cherubs, who looked more shocked than soulful. For the first time since meeting her I found myself in complete agreement with Ariel. That ceiling needed a speedy coat of whitewash.

Presumably inured to its impact, Lady Fiona sat down on a sofa and asked how I liked England and if I found it cold after living abroad so long. "How is your aunt in Jamaica doing, Mrs. Honeywood?"

I was about to remind her my name was Haskell, and say I didn't have any aunts, when Mrs. Malloy came into the conservatory with a plate of dainty sandwiches. I got up to make the introductions. Mrs. M, who has an intense aversion to mold, pressed a handkerchief over her face, which made her look like a bank robber waiting for the bank to open.

"And what of your cousin's little boy?" Lady Fiona asked me. "The one who accidentally swallowed his goldfish and insisted on having his stomach pumped, so it could be taken out alive. You do believe it to have been an accident?" She took a sandwich from the silver tray Mrs. M proffered. "Such a worry for his parents if he did it on purpose."

While I was avoiding Mrs. Malloy's eyes, Betty and Tom came into the room with Mr. Scrimshank, whose looks had not improved since yesterday. If anything, he looked even more like someone who has been brought back to life after being badly embalmed. When I went over to him, he gave no sign of remembering who I was. And even when Mrs. M removed her mask and asked if he'd like cucumber or cheese and tomato, the doggy brown eyes in his white face looked none the wiser.

"We were at your office yesterday, to see me sister, Melody," she told him, "and you was nice enough to point out we'd come in the wrong door."

"Ah!" Light had dawned. "Miss Tabby. Yes, yes! She was late getting those letters on my desk. Never happened before in nearly forty years. I do hope she's not cracking up. I've wondered about that possibility recently, ever since I heard she'd taken up knitting. These enthusiasms can take a terrible hold on a woman of her advanced age."

Mrs. Malloy raised her eyebrows at me in both outrage and inquiry. Luckily for him, Mr. Scrimshank left us without another word to sit beside Lady Fiona.

"Ah, Fiona!" He intoned the name through his nose. "Any further word from Nigel?"

"None. It was a relief to hear that he rang you that once, Archibald. It set my mind at ease that nothing untoward had happened to him. Preferable perhaps if he had got in touch with me instead, but I understand his reasoning. He would have worried that Miss Pierce would get on the line and keep talking, making it seem it would be forever before he could get back to exploring the Amazon or wherever he is. Devoted as he has always been to Nanny, Nigel has intimated that there have been occasions when he found her constant fussing over him irksome. He didn't mind so much while he was still in his forties, but . . . I say no more. It will please him on his return to find her settled in the Dower House. I acted in accordance with what I knew would be his wishes. Somebody was just telling me"—she looked vaguely around the room—"that Nanny has some friend or relation living with her. I hope it works out until the time she finally hangs up her butterfly net, to use Nigel's phrase."

The expression did seem preferable to *kick the bucket*. But before I could murmur this opinion to Mrs. Malloy, who was setting out more trays of perfectly presented sandwiches, delectable-looking iced fancies, and fruit tartlets and currant scones, our eyes were drawn to the door where Frances Edmonds cowered against her husband's shoulder.

"Oh, whatever's wrong with her now?" Betty brushed past Tom to draw the peeping twosome back into the hall. Remembering that someone, possibly me, needed to start handing round cups and saucers, I moved to the buffet table, where if I strained my ears sufficiently I could hear voices and hiccuping sobs.

"For goodness' sake, Frances! Why would I think to mention Mr. Scrimshank would be here? It was Lady Fiona you were so keen to see. How could I know he sacked you for not cleaning behind the radiators and you never want to see him again? Stan, get her to stop crying. Oh, come on, both of you, let's go into the kitchen so you can both have a cup of tea before slipping out the back door, if that's what you want to do. I wonder what's been keeping Ben from joining us in the conservatory?" Betty's voice faded away, along with the dwindling footsteps.

"Now you take that look of your face, Mrs. H," whispered Mrs. Malloy, "like you're sure he's in the pantry canoodling with that Val. Miss Pierce felt a bit faint after the walk up here and he had her sit down in the kitchen and found her a glass of brandy. They'll all be in soon. I wonder what's keeping them two vicars?"

Right on cue, in they came. The one who had to be Mr. Hardcastle was handsomely middle-aged, with kind eyes and a pleasant smile. Clutching at his arm, and also wearing a clerical collar, was a frail little man with wispy white hair and a face that had shriveled to the point of being all nose. With luck, his infirmities would prevent him from ever looking at the ceiling.

"Mr. Hardcastle." Tom roused himself out of whatever doleful thoughts had been claiming him to hasten across the room.

"No formality, please; call me Jim." It was a nice voice, hinting at humor and the ability to pour the right amount of oil on troubled waters.

"Let me help you get your friend—"

"Simeon Tribble," piped up a reedy but cheerful voice.

"A pleasure to meet you, sir," responded Tom, moving with more speed than usual to help the ancient gentleman to a chair. While this was being accomplished with a great deal of tottering and some false lowerings, Betty returned without the Edmondses and took over the general introductions. As she was finishing up, it became necessary to start again. Val, Miss Pierce, and Ben had entered the room.

Mr. Scrimshank left Lady Fiona to direct his attention to a feathery fern in a container the size of a dustbin, so I again sat down beside her.

"I understand that you are related to a family of the same name in Chichester, Mrs. Honeywood," she said.

Taking the easiest course, I invited her to call me by my first name.

"Ellie? I had thought you were Edith. Then you're the one with an aunt in Gibraltar, not Jamaica."

"That's right." I let my mind stray. Val was wearing rose pink and looked even lovelier than yesterday. Blackberry curls, creamy skin, those deep blue eyes, she was a rare flower, worthy of Kew Gardens, let alone this conservatory. What a picture she made, standing with her hand on Ben's arm, smiling up at him. Would it be described in books, I wondered with a numbed detachment, as a tremulous smile? I could hear what she was saying; she was thanking him for being kind and giving her great-aunt the brandy and waiting to make sure she was feeling better. All very prosaic, but I saw Tom looking at them in stark surprise, before turning to ask Betty if she knew where Ariel was to be found.

"No idea," Betty said, before asking Mr. Tribble how he was enjoying his stay at the vicarage.

"Very much," he replied in his trembly voice. He poked inside his clerical collar, perhaps in hope of finding that a fifty-pence piece had dropped in when the collection plate was passed. "Jim's father and I were great friends. He brought me here once when I was a young man."

"Nice for you to have the chance to come back." Mrs. Malloy, standing with a plate of sandwiches, eyed him with concern. "Maybe you should sit back on that chair. Looks to me like you're about to fall off."

Mr. Hardcastle prevented this by making the necessary adjustment. I wished Mr. Tribble had a seat belt. Interestingly, the old man did not appear nervous. Maybe he had jumped out of airplanes as a lad and still enjoyed living dangerously. He certainly displayed a spirit of adventure by holding his own cup and saucer while peering with interest at Lady Fiona, who was now asking if I painted in oils, as my mother had done, or preferred watercolors, as did the aunt in Gibraltar.

"Mrs. H does lovely with both." Mrs. Malloy gamely got aboard the ship bound for nowhere, enabling me to bite into a scone.

"The Chichester Honeywoods collect sculptures." Lady Fiona accepted a refill of her teacup from Betty, who then went to attend to Mr. Scrimshank, apparently not having seen him empty his cup into a flowerpot. "Are those two young people recently married?" Her ladyship gestured with her teaspoon. The good-looking dark-haired couple. Standing next to Nanny Pierce."

"Why do you ask, your ladyship?" That scone might have been made from a marvelous recipe, but it left the taste of ashes in my mouth.

"They have that look of belonging together. The similar coloring."

"I see what you mean." So much for Mrs. Malloy's belief that like didn't respond to like, but having retreated to pour herself a cup of tea she didn't get to state her case.

"One remembers what it is like to be desperately, one might say foolishly, in love." Lady Fiona gazed reflectively at a standing potted plant.

"Actually," I heard myself say, as if from a vast distance, "Ben is my husband and the woman standing with him and Miss Pierce is the great-niece. The one staying at the Dower House."

"Is she?" Her ladyship drifted a look at Val. "Yes, I seem to place her now. She was an extremely pretty child when she and her brother spent that summer at Cragstone. Never having had children of my own, I had concerns. But they were no trouble. I only remember Nanny Pierce mentioning one upset. She would have thought it unconscionable to withhold such information. A betrayal of her duty to Nigel."

"I see."

"It involved the boy's locating the priest hole in the west wing and refusing to tell his sister how to open the panel. Nanny said Nigel would never have behaved in such a way. She assured him neither child would go near that secret room again, which relieved him greatly. He didn't at all like the idea of them getting shut in and being unable to find the release catch in the dark."

"What a horrible thought." I held on to it, while not looking at Ben and Val. I also focused on the rhythmic spatter of water landing on my head. Betty had talked about a leak from the bathroom above. Lady Fiona showed no sign of noticing that it was beginning to rain indoors. "According to family legend a priest did get trapped in that priest hole during Tudor times. Or would it have been Jacobean? Sadly, he wasn't brought out until it was too late; he had suffocated. But perhaps that was a blessing. They did have that nasty tendency to hang, draw, and quarter people in those days." Lady Fiona sipped her tea. "How long have you and your husband been married, Elsie?"

"Nearly nine years." It was now sprinkling quite heavily over our sofa, but the rest of the room remained under clear skies.

Our conversation caught Mr. Tribble's attention, sending him off on a tangent. "Did I marry you, Lady Fiona?" He might have leaned too far forward if Ben hadn't darted forward to reposition him.

"I do tend to be somewhat absentminded," responded her

ladyship serenely, "but I think I would have remembered had you ever been my husband."

"What Mr. Tribble means is did he perform the wedding service," said Mr. Hardcastle, with his nice smile. "No, Simeon, you didn't. I was a guest at Lady Fiona's marriage to Nigel Gallagher. It was Howard Miles, not you, who officiated."

"I could have sworn—" A few drops of water landed on Mr. Tribble's head.

"No, you wouldn't." His friend laughed heartily. "Swearwords are not in your vocabulary. Or mine, although I sometimes come close when I drop a stitch in my knitting—I trust I may count on your discretion not to spread word of my new hobby around in clerical circles. I happen to find it relaxing when I'm thinking through an upcoming sermon. And I'm not the only man in these parts to have taken it up. There's the Barclay's Bank manager, the village school headmaster, Police Sergeant Walters, and—"

"I still feel sure"—Mr. Tribble continued to peer at Lady Fiona—"it would have been, now let me think . . . what year was it? Never mind! It will come back to me. These things always do."

Other conversations flowed around me. Tom talked to Mr. Scrimshank, Betty said something to Nanny Pierce, and Val joined in, while her eyes followed Ben's every movement. Mrs. Malloy continued handing out replenishments of sandwiches, cakes, and scones. Still no Ariel!

Lady Fiona left the sofa, saying she must talk to Nanny Pierce about taking her to lunch on Wednesday. Feeling abandoned, I stared into my teacup. There was something floating in it. Something shaped like a leaf. But not a tea leaf; it was too big and too white! It could only be. . . . I looked up at the ceiling, to behold an extremely well-endowed Zeus now absent a very necessary part of his cloud cover.

Finally, others noticed it was raining.

Betty yanked at Tom's arm. "Ariel must have left the water running after washing her hair. Run and turn it off! Ben, will you go with him and help mop up?"

"Of course."

"And I'll go and look for Ariel, if you like," said Mrs. Malloy.

Out the three of them went, and Val, whose hair of course was curling even more beautifully in the damp, adjusted her great-aunt's cardigan and put an arm around her shoulders.

"Dear me," said Mr. Tribble, as more drops landed on his head, "I'm afraid we came without our umbrellas, Jim."

"Oh, I expect it's only a summer shower," Mr. Hardcastle reassured him gamely. "No need for us to race for cover, Mrs. Hopkins. I'm sure it will pass over very quickly."

"We could go into the drawing room." Betty stood, twisting her hands.

"Not on my account, dear lady." Mr. Tribble made the understandable mistake of looking up at the ceiling. Instantly, it became apparent that whatever else might be failing, his eyesight was not. If ever a man goggled, he did. "Oh, my!" His voice creaked. "Whatever next!"

The answer was a significant piece of cloud landing in his teacup. Betty hurriedly produced a new one for him and then looked distractedly around for the milk jug and teapot.

"I wonder if he might prefer a glass of brandy." Lady Fiona lifted a decanter from a table.

"Indeed, that would be welcome!" Mr. Tribble held out his cup. "Just pour it in here, no need to trouble yourself fetching a glass. Yes, right to the middle." Her ladyship had wafted to his side. "That will do very nicely. Thank you."

"My dear Simeon," Mr. Hardcastle protested. "I think that may be too much."

"No, no. I would say the amount is exactly right. Or

maybe"—peeking up at Lady Fiona—"you would kindly pour in just an inch or two more. . . . Perfect, thank you." He smiled up at her. "May I say you have changed remarkably little over the years. It is now coming back to me. It wasn't a big wedding, just the two of you . . . and both so young. Ah, well! Time marches on! Is anyone else going to indulge?"

"Perhaps a very small cup," said Mrs. Malloy, who had returned to the room with Ariel. Whatever the resulting problems, the girl had finally washed her hair.

"I didn't even go into that bathroom," she muttered to Betty. "I used the kitchen sink. Whoever left the water running, it wasn't me. Maybe it was the spirit who visited last night."

"Yes!" Betty's face glowed. "The poor dar—man has such limited means of letting me know he's counting on me to act when the moment is right."

Ariel sat down beside me. "Maybe," she whispered, "Nanny Pierce went upstairs to fill the bath for her precious Nigel and then forgot about it. Or acted out of clear-headed malice."

Had the old lady left the conservatory? I didn't remember. I'd been preoccupied. Could Ariel be lying through her teeth about not having caused the deluge?

Mr. Tribble raised his cup. "To everyone's good health, mine included."

Lady Fiona came up to me after returning the decanter to the table. "I do hope he's not the sort to drink and drive."

"I'm sure it will be Mr. Hardcastle behind the wheel," I said.

"That does relieve my mind, Mrs. Honeywood . . . Elsie. Neither Nigel nor I ever learned to drive. Nanny would have worried too much in his case. She was ill for a week when he got his first tricycle."

And how old would he have been at that time, fifty? I was looking at Betty, thinking how pretty she was with that dreamy smile on her face. What would she think of the living Nigel Gallagher, were he to show up? I retained some hope that he would do so.

"In the end his tricycle had to be given away to a needy child. But he did enjoy operating the vacuum cleaner; he loved the sound of the motor and pressing the pedal to make it stop. I imagine it was one of those man things." Her ladyship paused to stare across the room. "Oh, dear, Mr. Tribble has dropped his teacup and is falling off his chair."

Mr. Hardcastle bent over the crumpled figure. The rest of us, apart from Mr. Scrimshank, who remained rooted near his fern, went over to help. It was Mrs. Malloy who got there first. "He hasn't just fallen off his chair!" Her eyes met mine. "He's dropped off the twig!"

10

Dreadful as it sounds, Mr. Tribble's shocking demise had the advantage of taking my mind off Val's blatant attempts at resurrecting a relationship with Ben and his failure to give her the cold shoulder. I'd like to say it was the reminder that there are real sorrows in this world on a daily basis that brought me up short. Mr. Hardcastle had seemed very fond of the old gentleman and there would doubtless be others to miss him, but I didn't think about that at the time. It was more a matter of the practicalities taking over.

Betty made the necessary phone calls. Mr. Scrimshank offered to drive Lady Fiona back to her hotel, a good move on his part or the undertaker might have mistaken him for the corpse. Miss Pierce, after tut-tutting about the evils of brandy served in a teacup, something Mr. Nigel's parents would never have countenanced, appeared energized by the excitement. It took some persuasion on Val's part to get her to return to the Dower House. She was talking volubly as they left and I would have liked to hear what she was saying, but while Tom and Ben sat with Mr. Hardcastle, I helped Mrs. Malloy to clear away the tea things. Ariel trailed after us into the kitchen, and a moment later Betty hurried in, all agog.

"Didn't I tell you that woman's a killer?"

"What woman?" Ariel peeked up from the chair where she now sat hunched. If ever a child looked as though she needed a cat on her lap, she was it. And no wonder! She might talk glibly about death, but having been in the room with it was something else. I placed a hand on her shoulder, but she shook it off.

"Oh, don't be dense!" Betty did not bother to look at her. "Lady Fiona! Who else would I mean? She's struck again!"

Mrs. Malloy handed Ariel a cucumber sandwich. "Get that down you. Having something inside will help settle your nerves. Works wonders every time."

"Surely, Betty," I said, "you don't think her ladyship killed Mr. Tribble?"

"Certainly I do. She must have slipped something, a tablet or a little packet of powder, into his teacup when she poured him the brandy."

"How did she do it without anyone's noticing?" Ariel bit into the sandwich as if it also might be poisoned.

"Sleight of hand. Those fluttering gauzy sleeves of hers. She could have had whatever it was in her skirt pocket."

"She just happened to have the stuff on her, like it was a lipstick?" Mrs. Malloy elbowed me aside to get to the sink and deposit more plates.

"It could have been some medication she keeps with her at all times." Betty poked at her red hair as she scanned the room in search of believers. "Or something she brought along for the specific purpose of killing him."

"Why?" Ariel demanded.

"She must have recognized his name when I mentioned he would be one of the guests. Her need to shut him up has to connect in some way to her motive for murdering dear . . . her husband. Remember how Mr. Tribble kept going on about being sure he'd performed her wedding ceremony?"

"Do we look gormless?" Mrs. M might have her hands in the sink, but she remained quite clear about her true position in this household. "Of course we remember, and I'm sure the same thought occurred to Mrs. H as did to me: that her ladyship was married to someone else before she tied the knot with Mr. Gallagher, and he found out about it, right before he disappeared."

"There *was* that other man you told me about, Ariel," I said.

She gave one of her characteristic shrugs. "Betty would know about him too, if she'd ever bothered to talk to Mrs. Cake."

"Oh, please! Just for five minutes can I not be the wicked stepmother?"

"The first marriage could have took place on the sly if her ladyship's family was against it." Mrs. Malloy handed me a tea towel to dry the cups and saucers. "Sounded that way, from how Mr. Tribble talked about its just being the bridal couple. There'd have been witnesses, of course, but they could have been anyone: people off the street. Yes," Mrs. M mused, "it should have been easy to hush things up when the marriage turned out to be a mistake. Better to do nothing perhaps than bother with a divorce, as would have got in the papers."

"There you are!" Betty drew in a breath. "When Nigel discovered he'd married a bigamist, he must have been so outraged he threatened to go to the police and press criminal charges."

"Perhaps he said he would keep quiet only if she signed the house and all the money over to him—what was left of it." I looked at Mrs. Malloy. Did the possibility ripen that Mr. Scrimshank and Lady Fiona had joined forces in murdering the man everyone assumed to be her husband? Had they each seen themselves facing imprisonment for different reasons if Mr. Gallagher remained on the scene? The likelihood of Lady Fiona's being slammed up for bigamy struck me as slim, but she might have panicked or, even more, disliked the thought of being embroiled in a scandal. Mr. Scrimshank's situation was more dire. If her ladyship had discovered he'd embezzled her money, agreeing to help her out of her difficulties by way of recompense might have struck him as a good alternative to the realistic prospect of spending a considerable portion of his declining years behind bars. What was one small murder between friends? Now, if Mrs. Malloy and I were to believe Betty, there had been a second.

"Before we convict Lady Fiona in absentia"—I dried the last of the cups—"we need to find out if indeed there was a prior marriage and, if so, whether or not it was legally terminated."

"And how do we go about that?" Removing Ariel's half-chewed sandwich, Betty tossed it in the trash bin.

"Well, what I'm thinking," said Mrs. Malloy, "is that tomorrow morning me or Mrs. H should phone Milk Jugg and ask him to see what he can track down."

"Who's he?"

"A private investigator we know. Its being Sunday, he won't be in his office today, but I'm sure we can talk him into lending a hand, seeing as we did him a favor recently and got no thanks in return."

I wasn't convinced that Milk would be ready to forgive our interference in one of his cases, but Mrs. M knows far more about the male psyche than I do.

"That sounds like a good idea," Betty said, after a moment's thought. "I only hope it's what Nigel would want."

"Can't you stop talking about him?" Ariel pounced up from

her chair. "I've never seen you go all silly about Dad. I wish I had run away for good."

"Oh, Ariel, I *am* sorry," Betty said surprisingly, as the doorbell rang.

"Why don't I get that?" I hurried out into the hall, but Tom was there ahead of me to let the doctor or the undertaker, whoever he was, into the house. They disappeared into the drawing room and I stood thinking about what had transpired in the kitchen. Poor Ariel! Had motherhood taught me nothing? The focus should have been on her reaction to Mr. Tribble's death, rather than a discussion of matters better left until she was not present. Guest in her house be blowed, I ought to have cut Betty off when she got started. How likely was it anyway that Lady Fiona was responsible for the old gentleman's dropping so abruptly off the twig, to use Mrs. Malloy's phrase? Betty had talked glibly about sleight of hand, but her ladyship, so far as I knew, was not a professional magician. What would she know about misdirecting the eyes of her onlookers? Or had she got lucky in that regard with the water dripping from the ceiling? Could it be Lady Fiona who had crept upstairs earlier after Ariel admitted her to the house and subsequently left her alone? Had she entered the bathroom above the conservatory, put the plug in the basin sink, turned on the taps, and left it to overflow? Someone had done this, and Ariel had been vehement in her denials. Who better than her ladyship would know how to make Cragstone a conspirator? And yet somehow, I couldn't see it. Perhaps I didn't want the lovely young woman in the portrait transformed into a demon.

There was something else I couldn't see as I remained in the hall, looking down at the Chinese chest with its exquisite display of snuffboxes on top. The cobalt blue and gold one I had particularly admired on first entering the house was missing. Had it been stolen or merely moved to another location? According to Betty and Tom, their kleptomaniac friend Frances Edmonds had never helped herself to any of their possessions. But the relationship had altered. The Hopkinses were now filthy rich and hadn't rushed to be generous. Had an already resentful Frances snapped this afternoon after discovering that Mr. Scrimshank was one of the guests for tea? Had she, however unreasonably, considered this another act of betrayal on Betty's part and taken the snuffbox in retaliation?

"What are you thinking about?" Ben came up beside me.

"This and that." I continued to stare at the chest.

"You look troubled." His gaze was intent.

"A man dropped dead less than an hour ago."

"It was sad and startling, but—"

"Betty thinks Lady Fiona poisoned his brandy."

"Don't tell me you believe her? Mr. Hardcastle was just saying that the poor old gentleman was well over ninety, making it unlikely he had the heart of a twenty-year-old. His doctor is amazed he'd kept on ticking this long. That cupful of brandy alone might have been enough to finish him off."

"That's the sensible view," I agreed, wishing that I didn't sound so stilted but not able to help myself. Had Ben swept me into his arms I would have felt he brought Val in tow. Perhaps sensing this, he put his hands in his trouser pockets and began talking about Betty.

"You can't go by what she says, Ellie, she's dealing with a lot of issues: the lottery win, her problems with Ariel, and . . . whatever else she's got on her mind."

"Such as?"

"Tom. You could see how he reacted to her behavior at that ridiculous séance." This was the moment to tell him about the false Madam LaGrange, but I didn't. Childishly, I decided that if he could have secrets so could I. Receiving no response, he continued. "There's always stuff going on in any marriage that outsiders aren't tuned in to."

"Are you speaking about them or about us?" It was out. I told myself I felt better. Nothing was worse than the distance growing between us. I saw the hesitation in his eyes, waited for him to say something—anything—but when he did I wished I'd left things alone.

"Ellie, I'm caught up in a situation that I would have given anything to avoid. But it was flung at me, and there it is. I want to talk to you about it, but that might complicate things even more. Also I gave my word to—"

"Val? Or, as you call her, Valeria?" I almost choked on the words.

A muscle tensed in his cheek, but he kept his hands in his pockets. "She feels so guilty. Ellie, you've probably come to your own conclusion and think I'm behaving like a cad."

"Heaven forbid! You're my knight in shining armor!"

The drawing room door opened, making an end to our tête-à-tête. All at once there was activity. By the time the body was removed and its entourage, including Mr. Hardcastle, had departed, I was not the only person looking less than cheery when we gathered in the drawing room. Ben and Tom stood in silence; Mrs. Malloy said her feet were killing her and sank into a chair. Only Betty displayed an interest in chatting about the death, and even she gave up on this idea when Ariel flung herself down on a sofa and began sobbing uncontrollably. Galvanized into unexpected speed, Tom knelt at her side, patting her heaving shoulders and looking around in accusatory alarm at his wife.

"Betty, what's set her off?"

"How should I know?"

"You're always getting at her."

"That's not true." The green eyes flashed. "Most often it's the other way round. Oh, move over, do!" Betty knelt down beside him. For that moment they looked like a set of concerned parents, thinking only of their child.

"What's the matter, Ariel love?" Mrs. Malloy asked from her chair, while Ben and I hovered in the background.

"It was so sad! His eyes were open and he was looking at me, like he was asking me to tell him he wasn't really dead. He was such a tiny little old man, not big enough to look after himself properly." Ariel raised a tear-drenched face. "It's different talking about death when you've never seen it. I wish I'd never made cracks about wanting people out of the way." She turned away from Betty and her father. "And I never again want to hear about murders. It's like tempting fate to come up with another dead person."

"You see, Betty!" Tom got to his feet. "What have I been saying for weeks about this nonsense of yours regarding Lady Fiona? It was bound to lead to trouble, and now it has! You've filled my daughter's head with fear. If she doesn't have a nervous breakdown, it won't be your fault!"

It was time for Ben, Mrs. Malloy, and myself to clear out. Seeing that Mrs. M wanted to talk and not feeling up to a heart-to-heart, I said I had a headache that would only cure itself if I went for a lie-down in a darkened bedroom. Ben started to say something, but I waved a hand and headed upstairs.

I rarely get headaches, but I was not fibbing about this one. A couple of aspirins later, I crawled under the bedclothes and willed myself to sleep. It took some doing, but finally Val's triumphant voice stopped telling me she was an Irish rose and I was a dandelion growing where it wasn't wanted. Ben reduced his pleas for my forgiveness to an incoherent muddle. Blessed oblivion.

When I opened my eyes and looked groggily at the bedside clock, it was several hours later. I would still have benefited from taking off my head and putting it on a hat stand, but that was

mostly because doing so would have made thinking more difficult. The physical pain had eased considerably. For several minutes I contemplated the advisability of getting up. I was thinking
that perhaps I had better do so when Ariel stuck her head
around the door and asked if I would like something brought up
on a tray, everyone else already having had dinner. Her eyelids
were still puffy and she looked in need of a good night's rest.

"Or perhaps you'd rather just go back to sleep, Ellie."

"I think I'll do that. Good night, Ariel." Suddenly the best
possible move seemed to be total inaction. No thanking anyone, especially Ben, for bringing me a heartening bowl of
broth; no being drawn back into the Hopkinses' emotional
turmoil. Tomorrow would be better or worse. Either way it
would be there. For now I would burrow back down and hope
to be asleep when my husband came to bed . . . or didn't.

When I awoke the next morning, the other side of the bed was
still warm. Ben had come and gone, like a visitor showing up
when no one was home. I was filled with a wild longing to run
and find him, to tell him the business with Val was madness
and when we got back to Merlin's Court he would realize it
had been no more than a midsummer night's dream. But I realized, as I set one foot on the floor, that I couldn't bring myself to grovel. Pride balked at the idea, and fear raised the ugly
possibility that he had no wish to be saved from his folly.

After taking a hot shower that did nothing to warm me, I
went downstairs in the wake of Mrs. Malloy, who had just
come out of her bedroom.

"How's the head, Mrs. H?"

"I'm still wearing it."

"Now, don't go getting snappy with me." She eyed me severely.

179

"Sorry." I folded my arms.

"You should see yourself, standing there all defensive. Come on, what's the bother?" She can always get to me when that kindly light beams from her eyes, like the last hope for a drowning sailor. "Trouble with Mr. H over that Val woman?"

"However did you guess, Mrs. Private Detective?"

"From the soppy way she was looking at him at tea. If you ask me, he looked downright embarrassed."

"An awkward situation for both of them."

"Yes. Well, don't go thinking yourself into trouble, like Tom accused Betty of doing. Just you cling to the thought that it's always darkest before dawn."

"It *is* dawn." I looked at the long case clock. "In fact, it's nearly ten."

"You're right." She followed my gaze. "Unless it's telling wicked falsehoods, as wouldn't surprise me in this house, where—present company excluded—taking what anyone says for fact could be a big mistake."

"Does that include Mrs. Cake?"

"Why?"

"Breakfast doesn't have its usual appeal. Ben and I aside, Tom and Betty could benefit from some time with Ariel without our looming presence. Why don't you grab a slice of toast and come with me to talk to Mrs. Cake?"

"I've already had several chats with her. That's what I wanted to bring you up to speed on, Mrs. H, when you went and got your headache. Have a word with her on your own, and afterward you and me can decide if anything she has to say about Mr. Gallagher's disappearance is important. As for now, I'm off to ring Milk Jugg and ask him to find out whether her ladyship forgot to untie the first knot, so to speak."

"You brave soul! I'll keep my fingers crossed that he doesn't bang down the phone."

"Look for Mrs. Cake in the room next to the butler's pantry. That's where she sits most of the time, resting her foot and doing a bit of mending."

"Should she be hobbling downstairs each morning?"

"I suppose she feels she'd better. The things some women do for fear of losing their jobs!" Mrs. Malloy sighed heavily. I assured her that under similar circumstances I would hire an around-the-clock nurse for her who looked like Cary Grant and sang like Elvis, and we went our separate ways: she to the library, where she could telephone in privacy, and I down the passageway to the left of the kitchen. No sign of anyone else about. No footsteps hurrying to catch up with me. No anguished male voice begging me to turn around and fall into his arms. It was a relief, I told myself staunchly. Ben could at least have left a note on the pillow. No, scrap that thought! Pillows, like mantelpieces, are rarely the deposits for good news. They are for missives that begin: *Forgive me for leaving you destitute, pregnant, and with the pox. . . .*

It was pleasant to remind myself that I was none of those things as I entered a cozy parlor. Maybe it was the quarry-tiled floor and deep windowsill that made me feel more at home than I had yet done since coming to Cragstone. There was a feeling here that reminded me of my kitchen. Instead of copper pots and pans hanging from a rack above the cooker, there were equally well-polished kettles and platters on shelves around the walls. I stood in the doorway drinking in the atmosphere as if it were a life-restoring elixir. The most comforting sight of all was the woman seated in a worn easy chair with her feet on a hassock, the left one was bandaged to the ankle. She was stout and cheerful-looking, with a rough red face and gray hair permed to last.

"Good morning," she said. "I expect you're that nice young gentleman's wife. Such a relief, him taking over the cooking,

181

especially with the caterers letting Mr. and Mrs. Hopkins down for Thursday."

"Yes, I'm Ellie Haskell. I do hope your ankle is better."

"On the mend. You sound a bit choked up. Coming down with a cold?"

"I don't think so." But was it something to consider? It could be my excuse for holing up in my bedroom. I could claim that the headache had been the precursor. Thank goodness I had gone straight to bed! How wretched I would feel if anyone, especially Ben—with the Hopkinses so dependent upon his help—were to catch what might even turn out to be the flu! And—I didn't grind my teeth because it might have frightened Mrs. Cake—what anguish for my once-devoted husband if I should pass from this world without ever telling him I forgave him and that venomous woman. . . . I returned to what senses I had left. Death was out. Ariel had said she couldn't take any more of it. And, most important of all, there were my own children to consider.

"I've been wanting to meet you, Mrs. Cake."

"Sit yourself down in that chair opposite mine. It's right pleased I am to make your acquaintance, Mrs. Haskell."

"Thank you." I did as directed. "Ariel speaks of you fondly."

"The little lost lass is what I call her." The voice was kindness itself. "She doesn't know what she wants and takes it out on Mrs. Hopkins; then around they go with the dad in the middle. And now they've had that poor old vicar drop dead in the conservatory, adding fuel to the fire." She picked up a pillow slip from the table next to her chair and began stitching up a seam.

I didn't pretend not to know what she was getting at. "You're talking about Mrs. Hopkins's idea that Lady Fiona murdered her husband."

"I wouldn't have brought it up if your friend Mrs. Malloy hadn't broached the matter in our talks. It's upsetting, and not just for Ariel and her dad. Mavis has got wind of Mrs. Hopkins's suspicions. She's not usually a gabber, but she hasn't taken to Mrs. Hopkins, and if there was to be a real blowup she might do some repeating of what she's heard in this house. I'd hate for Lady Fiona to be upset."

"You like her?"

"Yes, I do. She's odd, there's no getting round that. She and Mr. Gallagher made quite a pair that way. Eccentric wouldn't be putting it too strongly. I suppose that's why they got along."

"They were happy?"

"Very, I would say. And I've worked for them these twenty years or more." Mrs. Cake rethreaded her needle and started on another seam. "They weren't the sort to show their feelings, not in a public way. But it was clear they meant the world to each other. Surprising, you might say, because from what I've heard theirs didn't start off as a great romance. But they each knew how the other thought, and in my book that's a good foundation for the sort of love that grows and lasts."

"Mrs. Malloy and I have been told this wasn't the first time that Mr. Gallagher left home on the spur of the moment."

"She said you got that from her sister, Miss Tabby. There's a woman you can tell has had her heart broken." Mrs. Cake shook her head sadly. "Same old story—married man—but new every time it hits home. A pity if she lets the past stop her from making things permanent with the good man she's now found."

I didn't advance the information that the previous love interest had been Mr. Rochester from *Jane Eyre*. That would have been gossiping. Besides which, I was too surprised. "Melody Tabby has a gentleman friend?"

"There!" Mrs. Cake slapped herself on the wrist. "What a one I am for spilling the beans! But at least I haven't said his name. I'm a talker right enough, but that doesn't mean I can't keep the occasional secret. As I've said to Ariel, my lips are always sealed when I'm told straight out to keep mum."

I wanted to say she had that in common with my husband; instead, I brought her back to Mr. Gallagher by asking how frequent had been his disappearances.

"I'd say he's taken off half a dozen times since I've been here," responded Mrs. Cake. "Some bee would land on his bonnet and away he'd flit to a place in the back of beyond with a name only the native inhabitants can pronounce. Even Lady Fiona wouldn't know where he'd gone until a letter or postcard would arrive."

"Didn't she get upset?"

"You've met her, Mrs. Haskell. She floats through life; most things slide right off her shoulders."

"She never got angry with him for not bothering to let her know he was going away?"

"It does seem odd to the likes of you and me." Mrs. Cake smiled comfortably. "But we're talking about two people living on a totally different plane from the rest of us. All her ladyship ever said to me was that Mr. Gallagher couldn't bear goodbyes. And my guess is that came from being brought up by Nanny Pierce. I wouldn't be surprised if every time he said he was going out, either by himself or with friends, she got upset and he ended up staying home. Far too possessive, that woman! I'm not surprised her great nephew has stayed clear of her over the years. She explains that by saying he married a woman that's not up to snuff, but who knows? Anything less than him being Lord Mayor of London wouldn't count for much. Having her great-niece come to live with her should make her happy. But Nanny blows hot and cold with her too."

"Really?" Was there any hope of Val being booted out in the next ten minutes?

"One minute it's all working out wonderfully, and the next

you hear a long list of complaints from Nanny. Something has been misplaced, she's left on her own too much: that sort of thing. I really don't know how her ladyship managed with having her underfoot for so long. Finally, it was Mr. Gallagher who put his foot down and said it would be best if Nanny was moved to the Dower House. There was a scene I couldn't help hearing. She was shouting and carrying on like you wouldn't believe."

"When was that?"

"Just a couple of days before he left." Mrs. Cake, having finished with the pillow slip, picked up a linen table runner to work on.

"So she had a reprieve on going to the Dower House?"

"That's right. She didn't move in there until this house was sold."

"How did Miss Pierce react to Mr. Gallagher's most recent departure?"

"As always, she blamed Lady Fiona for his need to get away, this time because of the upset—that had to be all her doing. But—and I could be wrong—I sensed some relief on Nanny's part. And looking at it from her side, the timing couldn't have been better. It gave her the opportunity to put that row behind her, perhaps forget it even happened. There's no doubt her memory is failing some; she's old. I should be kinder in my thoughts." Mrs. Cake stopped stitching and sat staring at her needle.

Noticing an electric kettle on a cupboard shelf, I asked if she would like me to make her some tea and, upon her ready acceptance, made a strong brew, which was how she said she liked it. Having found milk and sugar and a tin of biscuits, I set a loaded tray down on the table, from which she had now cleared her mending, before sitting back down with my own cup and saucer.

"Thanks, love. I was gasping for a cuppa."

"You're very welcome." I took an invigorating sip. "Why do

you think Lady Fiona reacted with more than usual concern to Mr. Gallagher's most recent departure?"

"It was like this." Mrs. Cake dipped a ginger biscuit into her tea. "There'd been a recent rash of burglaries in the area. I used to say to both of them they were asking for trouble with that outside door to the west wing always left unlocked. How much bother would it have been to get a new lock fitted? But they never got round to it. Neither have the Hopkinses, for that matter. Anyway, that night—the last night Mr. Gallagher was home—her ladyship went up to bed earlier than usual, with a headache. She gets them bad sometimes."

"I can sympathize, having just had one."

"There'd been some tension between them that day. The police asked me if there'd been anything wrong and I told them, there being no reason to hide it. Mr. Gallagher had tried several times that day to reach Mr. Scrimshank on the telephone. Each time he couldn't get hold of him, he'd come into the kitchen and I'd hear his nerves jangling. Mr. Gallagher had been holed up in his study for the previous couple of days, so I guessed it had to do with business. I don't know anything about stocks and bonds, except that sometimes they need to be bought or sold in a hurry, so that may have been it."

"What about Lady Fiona? Do you think she knew why her husband was trying to contact Mr. Scrimshank?"

"I'm sure she didn't, because the one time she came into the kitchen when he was there telling me he still wasn't having any luck with phoning, he changed the subject right quick. Wants to surprise her with the good news that there's a windfall in the offing, was what I hoped. As the day went on, it could be he saw a golden opportunity slipping away, because it was clear he was getting tense and finally irritable, which wasn't like him at all—there never being an easier-going man. Floated aloft he did, as a rule, just like her ladyship. It ended with them having words, which I don't remember them doing before. I'm sure that's what gave her ladyship the headache that sent her to bed about eight o'clock."

"Did you tell that to the police about the argument?"

"I'm not one for causing trouble, but there wasn't any reason not to." Mrs. Cake set down her teacup and picked up another piece of mending. "Lady Fiona would have told them herself. There was nothing to it. Just Mr. Gallagher carrying on about his clean socks. He always laid them out each evening, well before he went to bed—something Nanny Pierce had insisted upon when he was a child, I expect. I heard him grumbling about how he couldn't find the pair he wanted, a sure sign he wasn't himself, considering Mavis always put them away as tidy as you please, all in the same drawer that could be pulled out from here to next week for a good look. It was the blue-and-black Argyle pair he couldn't find. And Lady Fiona lost her temper, if you could even call it that, she's so mild. I remember thinking the upset with Nanny was what had them both on edge, but that they'd both forget about it if she'd ever let them, instead of bearing a grudge, which is her way. Always best to keep on Nanny's good side has been my motto; that's what I've told Mavis." Mrs. Cake rethreaded her needle. "And that's why I had your husband go down and ask Nanny for her scone recipe."

"What about the burglaries?" I got up to pour her more tea.

"Thanks, love." She picked up her cup. "It was like this, you see. There was a lot of nervousness about the houses that had been broken into over the previous few weeks. We'd never had much of that before. Anyway, there was a Mrs. Johnson living about half a mile from here at the time who always walked her dog this way around ten-thirty of an evening. A nice animal, a sheepdog."

"I've seen a man walking a black-and-white one."

"Probably the same. Mrs. Johnson recently moved in with

her sister that owns the bed and breakfast on the corner by the traffic light where you turn onto the high street. Some of the guests enjoy taking Keeper for a walk. He's named for Emily Brontë's dog, Mrs. Johnson told me. Lovely animal. Anyway, on the night we're talking about they stopped at the gate out front because the dog had to go, and Mrs. Johnson saw a man come running out of the house. Like his life depended on it, she said. She always carried a torch with her because the road isn't well lit, but she only got a brief glimpse of him because he dodged around the shrubbery. She went straight home and rang the police, and they came round quick as a wink, waking me and Lady Fiona up with their wailing sirens and flashing lights."

"Was Mrs. Johnson able to describe the man?" I set down my cup and saucer.

"She said she thought he had gray hair, but it could have been fair, and perhaps she had leaped to the other conclusion because she'd assumed the man was Mr. Gallagher, fleeing because of a problem inside. She imagined a fire or a gas leak. When the house was checked and him not in it, the thought was that there'd been another break-in and he'd surprised the burglar and gone chasing after him. Under those circumstances, her ladyship did get quite worked up— for her, that is. Even when Mr. Scrimshank got the phone call and the police accepted that Mr. Gallagher had gone off on another of his holidays, I could tell she wasn't easy in her mind."

"If that's all there was to it, why would he have raced out of the house in the manner Mrs. Johnson described?"

"Police Sergeant Walters said that could've been the burglar." Mrs. Cake looked up at me from her sewing. "Such a lovely man—and a wonderful knitter—is the Sergeant, a shame he's still not married. If I could have a word with his lady friend, I'd tell her not to keep him waiting."

"Rather a coincidence, a break-in on the night Mr. Gallagher disappeared."

"They do happen. Or it could be Mrs. Johnson saw things her own way."

"Presumably a check was made to see if Mr. Gallagher had taken a suitcase and some of his clothes."

"Her ladyship wasn't sure. She said he always kept one packed, ready to go, but she couldn't remember where, and with a house this size it's hard to track things down. She did look, so did Mavis and myself. It was Mr. Gallagher not taking his walking stick with the lion's head that bothered Lady Fiona. But like I told her if he was in a hurry to be off, it would be easy to forget."

"What was the weather like that night?"

"Cold and damp, it being January."

"So he'd have taken a coat?"

"His waterproof jacket was gone from the hall closet."

"Mrs. Cake," I said, "is Mr. Gallagher of a similar height and weight to Mr. Scrimshank?"

"Not far off." She stopped sewing, her kindly face puzzled.

"I'm wondering if it was Mr. Scrimshank Mrs. Johnson saw leaving the house and, because of the resemblance, assumed he was Mr. Gallagher."

"Could've been, I suppose. There'd been all those attempts by Mr. Gallagher to get hold of him that day. That's why it made sense that it was him he phoned a few days later. But if Mr. Scrimshank had been here at the house that night, he'd have told the police, wouldn't he?"

"Perhaps not, if there'd been an argument."

"About what, for instance?" Mrs. Cake moved her bandaged foot gingerly, as if it had begun to hurt.

"Problems with the Gallaghers' finances?"

"Now you've said it, Mrs. Haskell. I have wondered why they were in a bad state and, nasty as it is for me to say, I never took to Mr. Scrimshank. I've always been sorry for Miss Tabby having to work for him. There's something about his eyes, sort of a dead look, that gives me the creeps. Even so, it's a big leap from not liking someone to thinking he could be wickedly dishonest. It never crossed my mind; but I do see where you're going. Oh, dear, this does frighten me! What if Mrs. Hopkins has it right about Mr. Gallagher being murdered, even though she's off the mark in thinking it was her ladyship that did it?"

"Would you like another cup of tea?" I asked her, noting that Mrs. Cake's red face had paled.

"I could do with one, love. Don't bother to make fresh, just heat up what's in the pot and give it a good stir. . . . Thanks," she said, when I handed back her cup. "One thing that's struck me as strange is that Mr. Gallagher would have gone away right after that row with Nanny Pierce, leaving her ladyship to deal with the old girl. She has her ways of getting even. I think that's the reason her ladyship, leaving aside the shock of the police being brought in, has never felt quite settled in her mind that this was just another of Mr. Gallagher's adventure trips."

"That's a lovely portrait of her in the gallery." I sat warming my hands on my teacup, the brew being too stewed for my taste. Mrs. Cake didn't seem to mind.

"That was painted long before my time here."

"Ariel says that, prior to her marriage, Lady Fiona was very much in love with someone else."

"It'll be me that told her that. Like I said, my mouth can get going nonstop, but it wasn't a secret. Mrs. Johnson's sister told me about it, and so did several other people. From the sound of things he was very good-looking, quite like a film star, but her father thought him a bounder. Probably that was a good part of the attraction for a gently brought up young lady. Anyway, her parents put an end to it, threatened to cut her off with a shilling if she married the fellow."

"Do you know what became of him?"

"No." Mrs. Cake was still looking anxious. "But I'm sure her ladyship and Mr. Gallagher have some idea."

"Both of them?" I said in surprise.

"He was Mr. Gallagher's cousin. That's how her ladyship met him, at a house party that was intended to bring her and Mr. Gallagher together, or so the story goes."

I assimilated this piece of information. "Mrs. Cake, have you heard any rumors that Lady Fiona and this young man may have been secretly married?"

"Not a tweet." She looked bewildered, then anxious again. "Oh, Mrs. Haskell, now I can't get the idea out of my head that Mr. Scrimshank was here that night and"—a sob caught in her throat—"did something awful to Mr. Gallagher. But I can't see the police doing anything just because I've got a bad feeling, not if there isn't more to go on."

"That's the problem." I turned over an idea. "Mrs. Cake, is Mavis as fond of her ladyship as you are?"

"Every bit. Between you and me, we've both said we can't wait for her to have a place of her own so we can go back to taking care of her. Why do you ask?"

"Because I have the glimmering of an idea, but I'd like to talk with Mrs. Malloy before saying anything more."

As it happened, that was the end of my chat with Mrs. Cake. Betty poked her head around the door to ask if I'd seen Ariel. I told her I hadn't but, seeing she was worried, offered to help look for the child. Once out in the hall, Betty stood twisting her hands.

"Silly of me to get nervous," she said, "but you saw her reaction to Mr. Tribble's death, and she still didn't seem right at breakfast. Tom asked if she'd like to go for a walk, but she wouldn't so he left on his own. Here am I as usual with all the responsibility and none of the perks. What if she's run away again?"

"How long have you been looking for her?"

"At least an hour. I'd thought to take her out to buy something for her to wear at the garden party on Thursday. A little shopping trip and lunch, to help cheer her up."

"You'll have looked in all the obvious places?"

"I've gone through the house and searched the grounds. If only Tom would get back. I don't want to phone the police without talking to him." Betty raked her hands through her red hair, which as usual had a humanizing effect, although in this case it didn't seem necessary. She looked more real than I had yet seen her. Her eyes did not look like glass when misted with tears.

"Have you gone through to the west wing?" I asked her.

"What?"

"She took me up there yesterday. It's worth a try."

"Come with me," she said. "I always find it creepy at the best of times."

I thought of Lady Fiona's account of the priest who had been walled up behind the wainscoting. Had emanations from that ancient tragedy affected my mood during my former visit? Or did Nanny Pierce's presence still loom beyond the bedroom where she had kept her shrine to Mr. Gallagher's boyhood? Had she left his toys in place as a reminder to him and to her ladyship that she might have been ousted to the Dower House but there was no removing her influence, either past or future?

We passed through what I thought of as the ballroom and entered Nanny's personal domain. All was as I remembered, neat and organized, apart from a slightly rumpled bed and a small blue and gold object placed in the middle.

Betty picked it up and held it out to me. "What can this be doing up here?"

Not Frances Edmonds, I thought. Surely she would have taken the snuffbox from the Chinese chest home with her if she had bothered to steal it. I shook my head, hesitant to suggest the most likely scenario, which seemed confirmed when Betty opened the lid and drew out a twist of toffee papers.

"I suppose it must have been Ariel; there's no one else, but I still have trouble believing it. Whatever that girl's faults, she's not sneaky: too much the other way round, with her in-your-face rudeness. And she's not one to want someone else blamed for what she gets up to. She had to know that if I'd realized the snuffbox was missing, I'd have thought Frances had taken it to get back at me for not helping her and Stan out after we came into the money. No, I just can't—"

"It wasn't me, Betty." Ariel came around the door. "I saw it when I came up here and have been trying to figure it out myself. I was going to bring it back down with me, but I wasn't ready. I wanted more time to think. This is always where I come when I want to be alone."

"Now that I know," Betty said tartly, "I won't panic the next time I can't find you. Do you have any idea what you've put me through this past hour, searching every nook and cranny, afraid something was terribly wrong and your dad and I would never find you?"

"Nice to know you care." It was a familiar pert reply, but Ariel brushed at her eyes and her voice trembled.

It was time for me to slip away. I went down the back stairs, as Ariel and I had done on the previous occasion, and entered the passageway connecting the two parts of the house. I was about to go out into the garden when I heard Ben's voice.

"I can't go on like this," he said. "I've never kept Ellie in the dark about anything, so with or without your agreement, Valeria, I'm going to tell her what's been going on here."

"And what would that be?" I said, coming out into the open.

11

꿎

Ben took a step toward me, but Val laid a hand on his arm. "Please," she begged, "let me tell her." Women shouldn't plead, I thought, from someplace off in the distance, not unless they are incredibly lovely and nothing they do can reduce them. And Val was at her most beautiful at that moment, with the blue of the sky in her eyes and her black hair as glossy as a raven's wing in the sunlight. I felt all color seep out of me, as Ben nodded and, after looking at me intently, turned on his heel and went into the house.

"So what do you have to tell me?" I asked the woman of the hour, as if this were an entirely casual conversation, with nothing dependent on it other than whether we should stand or sit while it took place. She would have looked good anywhere, in her rose-colored skirt and pale pink top. Would it be rude to nip upstairs and change into something better suited to the moment when my life fell apart?

"Why don't we get comfortable?" She pointed to a couple of garden chairs under the draped fringe of a willow tree, and we settled ourselves facing each other. It was lovely and warm, so there was no need to hug my arms or battle to repress a shiver. The sky seen through the green canopy showed no sign of raining, as conservatory ceilings sometimes do. There were no heavenly bodies clad only in laurel wreaths on display, no clouds to flake off and drop into our teacups. But I thought determinedly of Mr. Tribble and how cold he must be now. It would be appropriate to send flowers, but should the card be signed from Ben as well as myself? Suddenly I would have given anything for a plate of chocolate biscuits to float my way or to be wearing red. I look horrible in red, but it is a brave, defiant color. All I could do was put a wobbly smile on my face and say, "I'm all ears, Val."

"You're going to think me a deceiving wretch."

"Whatever makes you think that?" Sarcasm was wasted on her.

"Ben told me that one of things he most loves about you is your honesty."

"That was kind of him." I would have preferred a mention of my fabulous figure, winning charm, and ineffable grace, but at such times one settles for crumbs.

"He said"—she looked at me with wonderfully sad eyes—"you hate deceit, and if you knew what was going on it would be bound to show in your face, and every time you looked at either Tom or Betty you'd be miserably uncomfortable."

"Why them in particular?" I asked, and again the sarcasm sailed overhead like a bluebird.

"Because Betty doesn't know that, long before she met Tom, he and I planned on getting married."

"*What?*"

"His parents broke it up because I wasn't a Roman Catholic, and that was a must for their daughter-in-law."

I sat utterly still for fear that if I didn't I would fall through my chair.

"Shortly afterward, Tom married his first wife. I heard they'd had a daughter, but I never saw him again until I came here to see my great-aunt and discovered that he and Betty had bought this house. My immediate reaction was to turn tail and run, but once I saw Aunt Valeria was declining rapidly and was no longer fit to be left alone, I knew I had to stay. So I talked to Tom, and we both agreed there was no good reason to tell Betty about us. It was well in the past. . . ."

"Yes?" I prompted, as life and feeling flowed back into me.

"I'm sure you've noticed she's the insecure, volatile type. Why upset her unnecessarily, particularly when Ariel would probably get the backlash?"

"And Ben was worried that if I knew I'd give the game away?"

"I was the one who was afraid you might unintentionally let something slip." Val leaned toward me, full of apology. "Ben's concern was that being in the secret would make you intensely uncomfortable and you'd think it wrong of him not to have things out with Tom, which I didn't want him to do. Finally, he gave me his promise that he wouldn't tell you. But just now he said he couldn't continue to keep you in the dark. That the two of you don't have that sort of marriage; it was causing a strain between you and he wasn't prepared to sacrifice your peace of mind for mine."

I became aware that the air was sprinkled with birdsong and the sun had laid a golden scarf around my shoulders. Every breath was perfumed; every flower bloomed more brightly than it had done moments before. This was not the moment to dwell on my folly in doubting Ben's love for me. He had told me about Tom's broken love affair with a girl he had called his wild Irish Rose. No wonder that term had kept popping into my mind. But I had been prey to my insecurities. Who better than I to understand how Betty might have reacted to the reality?

"Has Tom said anything to Ben about his recognizing you?"

"Not a word. I knew he wouldn't if not confronted. Tom was always an ostrich, ready to put his head in the sand and let the world sort itself out. It's what made it easy for his parents to decide what was best for him. By the time he looked back up it was all settled."

"You know him very well."

"Do you think me wretchedly deceitful?" Her smile was rueful, her eyes shadowed with unhappiness.

"You found yourself in a situation that you tried to make less difficult."

"Thank you."

Impossible not to warm to her. Her beauty had such a wholesome quality. She was this lovely garden, she was a leafy lane in the dew of morning. . . . Happiness was turning me into a poet almost of Mrs. Malloy's equal. The thought of this personage brought her sharply to mind. I even imagined for a couple of seconds that I caught a glimpse of a black-and-white head topping a row of shrubbery. How, I wondered, had I previously seen Val as the scheming femme fatale? Envy gave way to sympathy for her . . . and Betty. Which of them, if either, did Tom truly love?

"It must have been a shock Saturday when you walked through the door and saw Ben in the hall," I said.

"Yes." The rose-petal lips trembled. "I'd only met him a few times. He was Tom's cousin; they both worked in his uncle Sol's restaurant. He didn't know me well enough to call me

Val. Only my closest friends used the shortened version of my name at that time. In those days I thought Valeria sounded more sophisticated, but it's always been a bit of a mouthful for everyday conversation."

"Was Tom worried when Ben recognized you?"

She looked away from me and glanced over her shoulder as if looking to see if anyone was about. But when she turned back I wondered if she'd needed a moment to collect her thoughts. Her voice came out tight and higher than usual, and there was a suspicion of tears in her eyes.

"I think what really upset Tom was that he realized something when he saw me looking at Ben that I had never wanted anyone to know, let alone him . . . and now you."

"What's that?"

"Even though I had only met him a few times, it was Ben I fell in love with. One of those at-first-sight things. You more than anyone else would know why." Her eyes implored me to understand. "He had no idea. I made no impression on him at all; I might have been the wallpaper. Believe me"—she laughed shakily—"if I'd thought I had the whisper of a chance I'd have tried for him, but I knew it was hopeless. He's not a man who can be manipulated into falling in love. I really should be unbearably jealous of you, Ellie, but I can't be. There isn't room for any other strong emotion. Good to hear?"

"I hope one day you meet the ideal person." I meant it. "Do you think Tom recognized the true state of your feelings when he saw you standing with Ben?"

"I'm sure he did. I know it was there—in my eyes, my whole body language. You must have realized too."

I nodded.

"That's why I thought I should get everything out in the open with you. Ben hasn't a clue as to how I felt about him. It's up to you if you want to tell him." She sounded tired.

"There *are* some secrets I can keep." I sounded like Mrs. Cake. "It's a matter of deciding which ones they should be."

"It would only hurt Tom if I told him at this juncture that the only reason I agreed to marry him all those years ago was that it might as well have been him as anyone else. He's a dear man, I really cared about him and still do, but when it came down to it I was relieved that his parents broke up the match." I kept listening, as I would have with a friend.

"Aunt Valeria has a feeling she won't live much longer, and I sense she may be right. The moment I'm no longer needed here, I'll get out of Tom and Betty's lives. It's been so awkward. I've felt so guilty toward her that I've probably gone overboard trying to be helpful. The decorating started with her asking my advice about wallpaper and mushroomed into her asking me to do all the decorating and help her pick new clothes. You've no idea how I've felt at times, with her being so trusting. I've tried so hard to encourage her to make her own choices, particularly about what to wear. She would look so much better if she got the right fit."

"I know," I said, thinking of the too-large suits. "It'll take time for Betty to adjust to her new lifestyle, but what will make the real difference is if she and Ariel can reach a better understanding and Tom helps to pull them all together as a family."

"Thank you, Ellie, for hearing me out." Val got to her feet. "I'd better get back to the Dower House. Aunt Valeria was in a real tizzy this morning."

"I'm sorry." I also stood up. "Old age can be sad."

"I'm fond of her. She gave my brother, Simon, and me a wonderful holiday here when were children. Of course I always knew she could be difficult with others, but she never was with me, until now, and that's only occasionally when her mind really seems to slip."

"It must be a strain," I said.

"She kept talking this morning about there being people she hasn't seen in years who've snubbed her by passing down the road in full view of the Dower House without coming in to see her. And then she got really worked up because there were letters or photos she wanted to look at in the top of her bureau and she couldn't find the key. She's always misplacing it. But she accused me of hiding it, to prevent her from finding evidence that old Reverend Mr. Tribble was not talking through his hat when he said he was sure he'd officiated at Lady Fiona's marriage to someone other than Nigel Gallagher. I only hope Aunt Valeria forgets all about it before her ladyship takes her out on Wednesday, or things could turn nasty. She told me she's primed to speak her piece. Even if I hadn't known Ben wanted to talk to me, I would have needed to get away to clear my head."

Val looked at her watch.

"I've been gone long enough, I have to get back before she comes out looking for me, the way she did Saturday night."

I said I remembered, and we parted a little awkwardly. We were two strangers who had shared an unusual conversation. Under the circumstances, I couldn't resent her telling me that she was in love with my husband. She had been right to do so. Perhaps she realized that I had made unfounded assumptions about Ben's feelings for her. I found myself somewhat embarrassed at the thought of facing him but was delayed in going back into the house when Mrs. Malloy popped around the shrubbery.

"Well, that was interesting." She enthroned herself in the chair Val had vacated. And to think I hadn't even requested an audience. "Of course I'd not the least intention of listening, Mrs. H. I came looking for you to see how your talk with Mrs. Cake went."

"How much did you hear without your ear trumpet?"

"No need to be snippy; I didn't want to move in case she heard me and got extra embarrassed. Too sensitive to other people's feelings, I am, but isn't it a relief all's cleared up for you and Mr. H? I can tell you now I was worried meself, for all I made light of things to you. It kept coming back to me what the real Madam LaGrange said about an old girlfriend showing up and causing problems for a woman with the name beginning with *E*."

I sat back down. "When you saw my reaction, you said it might have been a *B*. Did Madam LaGrange add that, or did you throw it in to make me feel better?"

"If I told you she said it, then she did," Mrs. Malloy replied huffily; then her painted eyebrows shot up. "I see what you're getting at! It was *Betty* that Madam was talking about. She has the gift for sure! Now I'm back to being worried about what else she said."

"That's understandable." My mind had drifted to Ben and what I would say to him. *Wives are such fools* might be a good beginning. When I said this to Mrs. Malloy, she poked me with her finger.

"You'll continue being one if you believe everything you hear. I'll tell you, now you're so keen on Val, that there's something about her gets right up my snout."

I changed the subject. "Any more tries to get hold of Madam LaGrange?"

"Still getting her voice mail. Mrs. Cake say anything interesting?"

"I expect it was much the same as what she told you. Did she mention that your sister, Melody, does have a gentleman friend?"

"She did, but I couldn't get a name out of her. Said it wasn't for her to say. My guess is he's the friend Mel was seeing Saturday night but canceled to spend time with me. She made it sound like it was a woman."

"That's probably because she talked about a shared love of knitting."

"I suppose." Mrs. Malloy pursed her lips. "If she wants to keep him interested, she needs to do something about her appearance. Wear bright colors and stay away from black."

"No, I don't suppose it suits her as well as it does you."

"Never did. Even when Mel was a baby she didn't look good in black."

"And maybe if she were to do something about that bad perm." It was something to say, rather than a desire to be catty. I was wondering if I had been too eager to believe Val when she'd assured me Ben had no feelings for her.

"Melody doesn't need a perm. That's her natural curl."

"Conditioner," I murmured.

While my mind continued to float, Mrs. Malloy recounted her conversation with Mrs. Cake. When she finished, I said that when it came to the main points the story was the same. Forcing myself to concentrate, I asked if she had managed to connect with Milk Jugg on the phone.

"He wasn't what you'd call thrilled to hear from me, but I soon put him in his place, Mrs. H, the upshot being that he's going to check into whether Lady Fiona was married to this other man, who from what Mrs. Cake said would be Mr. Gallagher's cousin. I told Milk as how you and me needed all the particulars he could come up with, and we didn't want to be left tapping our feet too long. 'Course, he went on about how strapped he is for time right now."

"That may well be true." I was once more convinced Val had told me the unabridged truth.

"Whatever, Mrs. H! The best I could get out of him was that he'd get back to me in a few days."

"There's an idea that came to me while I was talking with Mrs. Cake. It has to do with Melody and her desire to get into Mr. Scrimshank's safe and have a look at his records of the Gallaghers' finances. Mavis told me yesterday when I stopped to chat with her in the hall that her husband is a locksmith. According to her, he's so good he can break into anything. I've also learned, via Mrs. Cake, that Mavis is extremely fond of her ladyship. Perhaps if Mavis were to speak to her husband and got his okay, Melody could phone and ask the husband to come to the office and try and open the safe at a time when Mr. Scrimshank won't be around. What do you think?"

"Maybe it'd be best to say as little as possible to the man, in case he refuses for fear of getting into trouble with the law. I'm going to see Melody later; she told me this evening would suit her. I'll tell her what we've been thinking, and if she's for it you and me can have a word on the subject with Mrs. Cake tomorrow."

We agreed it was a plan, and I went into the house to face my husband. He was in the kitchen and fortunately alone. Not for the first time, I wondered how many men looked as wonderful as he did in a pair of faded jeans and an equally old sweatshirt, especially when holding a saucepan in one hand and a couple of tomatoes with the other. On seeing me, he laid these items down and came toward me.

"You and Valeria talked?" He placed his hands on my shoulders.

"She said you insisted she do so."

"I should never have made that promise not to tell you about her and Tom. I have this thing about keeping my word, even if it's nonsense."

"I know."

"At first it seemed to make sense. I didn't want you to feel uncomfortable every time you looked at Tom and Betty when

Valeria was there or her name was mentioned. What I overlooked was the fact that you were bound to figure out the state of affairs for yourself and wonder why I was in collusion with a woman I barely knew."

"I thought you did know her . . . very well. I convinced myself that you were in love with each other."

"*What?*"

I pressed my fingers to his lips. "That's the way it looked to me, the way you froze before walking blindly toward her. How your face shut down when your eyes met mine."

He gently removed my hand. "Ellie, I was trying to contain my shock. Here was the girl—the woman Tom had been madly in love with. She was right there in his house, and Betty obviously didn't have a clue. I felt as though I were in the middle of a minefield. If I were to so much as change expression, there'd be an explosion."

"It's all clear as glass now, but . . . I was a fool."

"Don't say that." He spun a chair away from the table and sat down, drawing me onto his lap. "I can see now how it may have looked."

"You called her Valeria when no one else did."

"It has to be one of the worst names ever. Rhymes with *malaria*."

"That's what Ariel said." I laid my cheek against his and stroked his dark hair.

"And why it stuck in my mind." He kissed me slowly, and I melted into his warmth, loving his tenderness, his strength, our knowledge of each other that was the reward of having been together for so long, coupled with the feeling of beginning all over again.

I continued to nestle in his arms when speaking about Tom and Betty. "Do you think he had forgotten that you'd met her and was appalled when he saw you recognize each other?"

"Tom has always had the ability to block out what he didn't want to remember, but in this case it isn't that surprising that he'd forget. I only saw him with Val, as she's now called, on a few brief occasions. But I happen to be good with faces."

"Hers is particularly beautiful." I was able to say this without rancor.

"Yes, she's lovely."

"She's also a great decorator."

"There's no better judge of that than you." He kissed me again.

"Mmm!" I savored the taste and texture of his lips. "Ben, I don't think I would have been quite so ready to leap to the wrong conclusion about Val if we hadn't had the evening we did, before leaving home. I said all the wrong things about that review in *Cuisine Anglaise* and then got in a snit, as Mrs. Malloy would say, when you went off to the Dark Horse with Freddy."

"I was the one in a foul mood."

"I shouldn't have agreed to Mrs. M's spending the night, when it was our first chance to be alone with the children gone."

"It all worked out for the best. We've discovered from being here with Tom and Betty how very blessed we are." He gathered me closer and the kitchen was really heating up when the door creaked open. We got to our feet as Betty came in. He had been right; I did feel uncomfortable with her, knowing what I did. I would probably have blushed regardless of my tousled appearance. Fortunately, she appeared oblivious. Was that her Achilles' heel? Did she generally fail to see what was right in front of her, I wondered, or was she exceptionally good at hiding her true emotions?

She asked me if I would like to join her and Ariel on a shopping trip.

"Please come, Ellie. We'll stop somewhere fun for lunch,

and then we'll scour every boutique we can find for an outfit for Ariel to wear on Thursday. I think she'd like it better if you're with us."

"Don't you think the two of you should have the time alone?" I was hesitant to intrude, but at the same time it would be a good idea to get over the hump of being around any of the Hopkinses, especially Betty.

"Getting Ariel to agree to the outing is triumph enough for me. I don't intend to rush things by foisting myself on her without any distractions."

"Ellie is the best of distractions," Ben assured her. "You need to take her with you if I'm going to get started planning the food for the garden party."

"Well, if it's like that!" I pretended to glower at him in lieu of kissing him good-bye. Somehow that wouldn't have seemed kind in front of Betty.

Ten minutes later, she and I met up with Ariel on the drive in front of the coverted carriage house, now used as a garage. Betty proved to be a relaxed and skillful driver. I had been quick to get in the back so Ariel could sit beside her. The expedition began well. They chatted, almost like any other mother and daughter, bringing me into the conversation and occasionally pointing out passing places of interest. Lunch was everything to be hoped: delicious food in a charming Georgian house converted into restaurant and gift shop.

It was while we were eating our treacle pudding and custard that Betty brought up her husband's name for the first time.

"The thought has crossed my mind a few times, Ellie, since you and Ben came to Cragstone, that maybe Tom and I should consider converting the west wing into a place similar to this one. He's so handy he could do much of the remodeling himself. Also, he did have that experience working in Ben's uncle's restaurant in London. I know he was at the cash register, not in management or involved with the meals. I think he may regret having gone in a different direction. He had a lot going on at the time."

"Oh?" I spooned up custard while blocking out Val's image.

"That's when he was about to get married."

"Really?"

"To Angela." Betty looked at Ariel.

"My mother." The girl continued a composed demolition of her pudding.

"That would have preoccupied him," I said, wondering if it would appear odd if I jumped up and suggested we explore the gift shop.

"As I've said, Tom knows the restaurant environment and I've seen him watching Ben while he's cooking. Maybe he's thinking he might like to have a go at learning to be a chef."

Was that the only reason for those looks? Or was her mild-eyed husband inwardly seething with jealousy and resentment over Val? If so, was this why Tom had said he didn't feel well in church and had gone outside for some air? I felt sorry for him, even while thinking he had brought most of his problems on himself by buckling under to his parents instead of waiting for the right woman to turn up. Angela would probably still be alive, married to someone else, and Betty might be with a man who worshiped her, from the top of her red head to her Barbie-doll shoes. But of course there wouldn't have been Ariel.

Half an hour later, she said she wished she were home; she was bored, she was tired, and she was sick of looking in stupid shops at stupid clothes. It didn't matter, anyway, what she wore to the garden party; nobody would be looking at her even if she did go outside for it. And Betty needn't expect her to play any childish games, or run any three-legged races, because she wouldn't. She'd just sit at a table under an umbrella and pretend she was having a wonderful time in school doing algebra.

My patience was soon exhausted and Betty, having showed magnificent restraint, flared at her. "Keep this up," she said, "and it will be boarding school for you."

"You don't think I'd like that?"

"At this point I really don't care, Ariel."

"Well, isn't that nice, after you pretended to be so sympathetic when I was upset about Mr. Tribble dying!"

Betty pressed a hand to her brow, and we returned to the car. This time it was Ariel who nipped into the back and we made the return journey to Cragstone House in silence. Anything I could have said would have been jarring. I truly felt sorry for both of them. Ariel had been a little snot, but there was something about her current quiet that tugged at my heart. It seemed fitting that it should start to rain as we drove between the gateposts.

"Probably only a shower," said Betty, as we pulled into the garage.

But she was wrong about that. Mother Nature having been dry-eyed and eager to show her best colors, by being sunshine and light over the past few days, decided on making up for it by being utterly miserable. It drizzled continuously for the rest of that day and evening.

There was a brief letup the next morning, which was particularly welcome because a team of gardeners arrived and got to work, as apparently they did every other Tuesday. The lawns were too damp for mowing, but there was plenty of weeding and clipping to keep them occupied until the skies, which had darkened rapidly, unleashed a deluge that sent them scurrying into their vans. I watched this from the conservatory windows while halfway occupying myself arranging cut flowers in vases. Tom ambled in and said the gardeners had promised to return early Thursday morning, weather permitting, to do the mowing and set up the marquees and umbrella tables that would have been delivered by then. I had the feeling that he would have liked to follow this up with something more but didn't know how to begin. After shifting from one foot to the other, he wandered out. Mrs. Malloy, who came in to tell me about her evening with Melody, replaced him.

"She's got a nice little flat. The furnishings wouldn't be my choice, but they suit her. I don't care for knitted curtains."

"Although interesting," I commented.

"Or wall arrangements of tea cozies. 'Course I didn't let on. I said she'd fixed the place up a treat and asked if her gentleman friend had contributed his handiwork. She shied away from that one, and I knew there was no use trying get more out of her about him. Mel always did clam up when she'd the mind. But that had its good side last night."

"How?"

"It gave me the chance to bring up Mavis's husband. I told Mel she was like a safe that only a locksmith could open without knowing the combination. And I'm pleased to tell you, Mrs. H, that she was all for the idea of phoning him up. She's going to choose her time, when Mr. Scrimshank is out of the office."

"Yes?"

"She'll tell Mavis's hubby as how there's some important papers she needs on the double but can't get into the safe because she's forgotten the numbers."

"Have you run this by Mrs. Cake?" I asked, feeling more and more doubtful, being the one who had come up with the idea.

"Just now. She don't think it would be right to drag Mavis and her husband further in than necessary by telling them what's really going on. She thinks Mel should just say the papers have to do with Lady Fiona's future financial welfare. Seeing as Mavis is so fond of her ladyship and eager to see her back on her feet, Mrs. Cake is sure that'll do the trick with the husband. Otherwise, he might say he'd only come out if he had Mr. Scrimshank's okay."

"It may still take some persuasion on Melody's part. Do you have a phone number to give her?"

"Mrs. Cake said it's in the directory under Ed the Locksmith."

"Oh, do let's hope that nothing goes wrong if he agrees." I shivered, not only because it was chill and damp in the conservatory, even without water dripping from the ceiling, but I also kept seeing little Mr. Tribble's ghost sitting perilously close to the edge of his chair. If only he had been wearing a seat belt and not been drinking while perched. O vain regrets!

"Death casts a long shadow," quoth Mrs. Malloy.

"Shadows I can take," I replied. "I just don't want any more of the real thing."

"I'm not going to phone Mel at the office, just in case Big Ears should be listening; I'll go round and see her again this evening. For right now, if you should want me I'll be in me bedroom, writing a eulogy to Mr. Tribble. It's amazing how I'm getting the hang of this poetry business."

The rest of that day blurred into the rain that sheeted down the windows with very few letups. Ben was fully occupied in shopping for and preparing what could be made ahead for the garden party. We had the occasional idyll, when meeting on the stairs or in the hall. But I stayed out of the kitchen and mealtimes naturally included other people, making it impossible for any real conversation between the two of us. But given what had so recently transpired, I would have basked in our restored happiness, had the feeling not lingered that something of a distressing nature was about to happen.

Wednesday arrived in an uncertain mood. The sky was a watery blue, and the sun peeked out from behind the clouds every now and then. The rain had turned to fitful drizzle, but every so often there was a rumble of thunder. When I met Mavis on the stairs, as I was going down and she was coming up, she said, somewhat morosely, that this looked to be a better day than yesterday. I hoped she would be proved right, as I was eager to get out of the house, if only for ten minutes. This became increasingly appealing when an army of cleaners came marching through with enough equipment to scour Buckingham Palace from top to bottom in no time flat.

This convergence put Ariel, who had come fairly speedily out of her Monday shopping sulk, back in a snit. This time it was her father who annoyed her by getting on her again about her hair.

"He's mad because I wouldn't go with Betty when she left to have hers done," she told me. "But I didn't feel like sticking my head in one of those cooker things."

"You could have told the hairdresser you like to let your hair dry naturally."

"I don't. I hate having it damp around my face."

I was tempted to tell her to suit herself, as Betty might have done, but a peek out the front door showed clearing skies and I decided not to delay my walk in the grounds any longer. It was not yet noon, which would give me sufficient time before lunch. I felt a little guilty slinking off when the house was swarming with workers, which included Ben in the kitchen and Mavis, whom I'd not seen since she had gone upstairs.

Begrudgingly, Ariel offered to accompany me. So we each donned a waterproof jacket and set off down the drive before crossing onto the lawn that separated Cragstone from the Dower House.

"What does Mavis do when the cleaning crew comes in?" I asked, as we trudged soggily past ornamental trellises and beds filled with flowers now even more lush and fragrant for their good soaking.

"I think she sorts out cupboards, that sort of thing." Ariel dragged her hood over her head. "Betty says it isn't fair to make her take every other Wednesday off. It would mess her about where her pay is concerned."

"That's thoughtful of Betty."

"I've said she doesn't have a lot of good qualities. I didn't mean she has none."

"She tried hard to find you something nice to wear on Thursday." Suddenly I realized that was tomorrow.

"I know." Ariel plodded on, head down. "Next you'll be telling me a psychologist would say I'm afraid of getting close to her in case one day she isn't there—just like with my mother."

"There are always huge risks in loving anyone," I said.

"Speaking from experience?" She stopped and pushed back the hood.

"Absolutely. I've been the worst coward when it came to relationships, and I still have relapses."

I felt her hand slip into mine as we continued walking. A small glimpse of sunlight warmed my heart. Let her be happy, I thought; she has the possibility of growing into a special woman if her family of three can find their way to one another.

"See who's coming our way." She pointed toward the Dower House. "She looks like she's in a hurry from the way she's galloping along."

"She certainly does." As we drew closer, I could see that Val's black hair was windblown and heightened color had been whipped into her face. She was wearing a raincoat that was misbuttoned, the belt left dangling.

"Oh, dear!" She shoved back her sleeve to look at her watch. "I'll have missed it. The bus, I mean. I didn't hear Aunt Valeria leave and was hoping she was only a few moments ahead and I could catch her on foot. But she must have set off at least ten minutes ago to walk to the bus stop. She's meeting Lady Fiona in the high street for lunch and she's forgotten her senior citizen pass, which will ruin her whole afternoon."

"What a shame," I said.

Val smiled distractedly. "I don't understand why she always refuses to let me drive her. . . . Yes, I do." She paused to exhale. "She wants to keep doing things the way she always has. And everything about her Wednesday afternoon has its routine: the ten-past-twelve bus going and the four-thirty coming back."

"Ritual has its security," I said lamely, and heard Ariel giggle.

"It's not fair for me to try and change her at this stage of her life." Val plucked at her black curls, and they responded charmingly. "I'll get my car and go after her. There are several places where she and Lady Fiona could have lunch, but I'll find them. And if Aunt Valeria has her pass for coming back it should cheer her up a bit."

"Wouldn't the driver, seeing her age, overlook her not having it with her?"

"You'd think so, wouldn't you? But there are always those officious types who insist on going by the book." Val waved as she walked back to the Dower House, where I could see the outline of a car parked outside. In the short time we had spent talking, the mist had thickened.

"Let's go back inside." Ariel gave an elaborate shiver.

"Okay." I turned with her toward Cragstone's soaring

roofline and imposing gloom. "Now tell me, why did you giggle just now when I was talking to Val?"

"You sounded so preachy!"

"Grown-ups do that. It's to mask our horrible sense of inferiority in the presence of children. We know we are doomed to disappointment where most of them are concerned, and it inevitably takes its toll."

"You are ridiculous!" She skipped along beside me.

"You need to talk to my brood of three sometime; they'll be in complete agreement. They don't find Ben quite so trying. It's a scientifically proven fact of nature that fathers in seventy-two point three percent of cases get off easier than mothers."

"Men being the weaker sex? Poor things!" Ariel raised her face to the now sharply blowing wind.

"I hope Val catches up with her aunt," I said, as we walked up the drive.

"She doesn't approve of us."

"Val?"

"No, silly, Nanny Pierce. For one thing, she's made it clear that she's not keen on Roman Catholics. That's why she's upset that Val's brother went to live in Ireland, where the place is full of them."

"But aren't they Irish?"

"Only way way back, Miss Pierce told me, and she added, 'Thank God.' I'm sorry she's old, but she's not a nice person. She disapproves of everyone except her dear Mr. Nigel. Would you believe that the other reason she disapproves of us is that she thinks Dad and Betty have a wild lifestyle?"

"Whatever gave her that idea?" We were approaching the steps leading to the front door.

"She said she's seen car lights coming down the drive several times in the middle of the night. She said so the morning after Mrs. Cake fell down the stairs. She told me the glare through her bedroom window had woken her up at three A.M. I didn't want to repeat that to Betty and get her going on her murder mystery merry-go-round." Ariel turned to me and clutched my hand. "But it did worry me, just on the off chance that Nanny Pierce wasn't hallucinating." She looked away from me, and I wondered sharply if her reason for wanting Mrs. Malloy and me to come to Cragstone had less to do with proving Betty wrong than with setting her own fears at rest.

I put an arm around her as we entered the hall. The lights were on, but I found myself overwhelmed by the same feeling of oppression that had filled me on my arrival at Cragstone. It was a feeling that lingered all afternoon and culminated in the news that Nanny Pierce had stumbled off the high street pavement into the path of the four-thirty bus.

12

❦

"If it had to happen," Tom repeated, for at least the fourth time the next morning, "it's for the best that she died instantly."

"There is no looking on the bright side," said Betty. "The woman was murdered, and we know who did it."

"Are you saying Val was responsible?" His face whitened. The three of us were in the drawing room, which was incongruously flooded with sunlight, the rain having finally stopped yesterday shortly after Val had blundered weeping into the house to break the news.

"Don't make this harder than necessary, Tom." Betty stood with arms akimbo, tapping a foot. "You know I'm talking about Lady Fiona. She planned it when she invited Nanny Pierce out for the afternoon. She must have been worried that the old girl had realized that she'd done away with Nigel. Perhaps she'd even found proof—at least of the motive—and decided a shove under a bus was the answer. She got lucky with the weather. Mist and rain made a good screen against the other people at the stop seeing what she did. She has to be stopped, but it won't be by the police. Val said they didn't question its being an accident."

"You didn't voice your suspicions to her?" Tom's protuberant blue eyes spoke volumes. They both seemed to have forgotten I was in the room.

"Yes, I did." Betty spoke with an assurance she had not possessed before the séance. Her belief that Nigel Gallagher needed her had done wonders for her morale. "If you're prepared to listen, Tom, I don't think Val was surprised. In fact, I think the idea of murder had already crossed her mind. She kept repeating that there was something odd about the way her aunt pitched forward as she did. She said she'd been looking for her and Lady Fiona up and down the high street a good part of the afternoon. Having no luck, she finally went and had a meal herself before going to the stop, knowing they would be there to catch the four-thirty bus. The accident"—Betty's voice was laden with sarcasm—"happened just as Val was about to tap her aunt on the shoulder and tell her she had her senior citizen pass."

"Do you think Val will be up to attending the garden party this afternoon?" Tom sank into a chair.

"Oh, for heaven's sake! Of course she won't! I feel bad about going on with it, but I have no choice. Ben has all the catering done and it would be wretched to disappoint the schoolchildren. Their parents and families I don't care about." Betty gripped her hands. "This was never about them. But they'll come in droves, no doubt to see if we've polluted the grounds of Cragstone."

This wasn't *Pride and Prejudice*, but I wished it had been. I would have given anything to crawl between the covers of a book.

"Where's Ariel?" Tom asked sharply.

"In the little parlor with Mrs. Cake," I told him.

"Thank heaven for some normalcy," said Betty.

"Ariel isn't feeling normal," Tom retorted, "she's all to pieces. She was sobbing and crying when I saw her after breakfast. She's got it in her head that Miss Pierce's death is her fault because she's been thinking nasty thoughts about the woman. I did my best to settle her down, but I don't think I was successful."

"Then why don't you . . . we . . . go to her and start acting like parents?" Betty said.

It was another of those times when I found myself sliding out the door. I would have given anything to go into the kitchen and seek the safe harbor of Ben's arms, but he didn't need me chewing up his time. The garden party was due to begin at one o'clock and would continue until four. I wandered out into the grounds to survey the umbrella tables and the two marquees that had sprung up earlier as if because of the heavy rainfall. The clouds were white and fluffy, the sky a guiless blue, the breeze a gentle caress. What a festive scene, what a place for merriment and childish laughter while their elders sipped tea or lemonade and sampled the delicacies that would be provided!

I was about to go back into the house when Mrs. Malloy came out to stand beside me. It was my hope that she wouldn't pick up where she had left off, about how the real Madam La-Grange's vision of a woman going under a bus had tragically come to pass. It had made me feel intensely creepy when she brought it up the first time . . . and the second. Fortunately, she brought up the subject of her sister, Melody, instead.

"She's disappointed like you'd expect that she can't be here this afternoon. I told you how good she always was at the egg-

and-spoon race, and it would have been nice to see her win another ribbon to add to her collection. But with Mr. Scrimshank planning to attend as always, she's decided this is her best opportunity, while the cat's away, so to speak, to have Mavis's husband come to the office and try to open that safe. If all goes well, she's going to copy what's in the Gallaghers' file, put the originals back, and take her set home with her to go through this evening, to see if she can discover how Mr. Scrimshank managed to diddle them."

"I wonder if he was at that bus stop when Nanny Pierce took her spill."

"It's a thought, isn't it?"

"Did you talk to Melody about Nanny's death?"

"Some. But she wasn't listening. Her mind was on whether Ed could open the safe."

"No word yet from Milk Jugg?" We reentered the house by the side door.

"Not a dicky."

"At least you can fill in the time, Mrs. Malloy, by writing another eulogy: this one for Nanny."

"The one I did for Mr. Tribble never got going. I couldn't get past the first few lines."

I awaited the recitation, and it was forthcoming:

> *"No one could call him tall,*
> *In fact he was quite small,*
> *With a religious bent,*
> *And gentle, kind intent,*
> *To stand him in good stead,*
> *Now that he's dead."*

"The laureateship awaits," I said.

"Oh, bugger that," replied Mrs. Malloy. "I'm all out of poetry. If I was to meet the Queen herself this afternoon I couldn't come up with a verse." Luckily, she teetered off on her high heels before I could come up with a reply.

To my surprise, the next couple of hours passed rapidly. I showered and changed into the best of the few dresses I had brought with me, a simple sheath in a buttery yellow. Despite a lack of enthusiasm, I took pains with my hair and limited makeup. Ariel had said that no one would be looking at her, and the same could be more truly said of me. There would be few people present that I had yet met or would be likely to get to know much better. Ben came into the hall as I came down the stairs and caught me in his arms.

"You look delectable, sweetheart." He kissed my mouth and my throat, his hands making their wondrous way down until I laughingly pulled away.

"Will I see you out and about?" I asked.

"As soon as Tom and I have supplied the necessary replenishments after the five thousand have worked their way through what we've already set out. He's been a great help this last couple of days. He can't seem to stay busy enough. Every time there's been a lull he comes up with something else for us to cook. You'd think he was providing against an oncoming famine."

"Betty's been toying with the idea of their turning the west wing into a restaurant and gift shop. Maybe you could give Tom some ideas on how to go about it, if you think he's on board."

"It would be a good career solution, given the size of this place. He could hire a chef to get them started and learn as he goes. Now that the shock of winning the lottery has passed off a little, it might be the right time for him and Betty to come up with a plan to save them from the void they're now in."

Ben returned to the kitchen and I went forth into the garden party. At first I thought I was in a maze of people. Every time I put out an elbow I was afraid I would never see it again. But after a few minutes I was able to separate the adults from the squealing squalls of children. Girls with flying hair raced past; boys in T-shirts, blue jeans, and sneakers bumped into me. Their faces continued to blur, but occasionally I found myself returning a broad smile, some minus front teeth and others a silvery flash of braces. I eased my way between two women holding cups of tea and talking their heads off. They were raving about the sausage rolls, mini-Cornish pasties, and wonderful little cakes with fondant icing.

"Have you tried the salmon patties with the lemon dill sauce?" one woman, in a dwarfing broad-brimmed red hat, asked another.

"Not yet," floated the reply. "I'm devouring my fourth chicken wing. The fresh ginger glaze is divine. And I'd have two seafood tartlets left on my plate, if some fiend hadn't snatched them in passing."

"The food's much superior to what was served in previous years. I wonder who did the catering."

I stopped in my tracks but had no time to do more than draw a breath before Lady Fiona drifted up to me. Today she was attired in misty gray chiffon and a marvelous hat in the same shade. She was sufficiently tall that the wide brim accentuated her height rather than diminished it, as had been the fate of the woman in the red straw hat.

"Good afternoon, your ladyship." I held out my hand and she took it in a surprisingly firm clasp.

"How pleasant to see you again, Mrs. Honeywood. I remember, you did ask me to call you Edith. If you would be so kind, please mention this sad business about Nanny Pierce to your aunt when you next communicate. I am sure she would wish to know."

"Certainly," I murmured, catching sight of Betty standing with Mrs. Malloy.

"Not that they got on particularly well. Nanny once made a rather tactless remark to her, saying that Gibraltar was a rock even a seagull wouldn't land on willingly. I regret to say, not too many people liked her very well—not your aunt; I am referring to Nanny. I'm afraid being fond of her fell almost entirely on my husband's shoulders. It really is amazing he didn't run away from home more often, and why I never thought I could remonstrate with him about it when he did."

"How very awkward."

"We all have our trials. Nanny Pierce was ours. I wonder if that great-niece of hers will object to my moving into the Dower House? It was always Nigel's and my dream to retire there. A change of scene for people our age . . . a new beginning, so invigorating."

"Absolutely."

"My dear, you are so like your aunt. I do hope her hair stopped falling out. Ah, I believe I see Mr. Scrimshank; I want to ask him if he's had any more phone calls from Nigel. If you will excuse me. . . ." She ebbed away and I cut a path through the throng toward Betty and Mrs. Malloy. In getting to them, I passed Frances and Stan Edmonds, whose smiles had the determined sheen of people who have had their feet trodden on once too often. My impression of Stan was the same as formerly. He did resemble a weasel. But that meant nothing; looks can be deceiving. Although I doubted that was the case with Mr. Scrimshank, whose dead brown eyes were on Lady Fiona as she talked to him.

Reaching my targets, I asked Betty if Ariel had changed her mind about joining the madding crowd.

"I just saw her flit by with a couple of children her age."

"Her hair looked nice." Mrs. Malloy swallowed lemonade as if wishing it contained something stronger.

"She let me do it for her. She even agreed to wear the dress I bought her at the beginning of the summer, which hadn't been off the hanger. I'd be celebrating if I weren't scared half out of my mind, wondering who's going to end up dead next. It's not about playing detective anymore. It's a matter of how Tom and I are going to sleep at night, worrying whether Ariel is safe in her bed."

I could have said she was worrying about that unnecessarily; there was no reason to fear the girl was in danger, she being no threat requiring removal, even if Lady Fiona had murdered both her husband *and* Miss Pierce. I could have added that Mrs. Malloy and I were convinced, had her ladyship done so, it had been with Mr. Scrimshank's collaboration. But I didn't open my mouth. I hesitated a moment too long. Mrs. Malloy was complaining about her bra.

"It's that blasted underwire poking at me again. I didn't mean to wear this one again. It was for the ragbag when I got home, but I picked it up by mistake."

No time for commiserations; we were interrupted. A man came up and held out a spoon containing an egg to Betty, who was nearest.

"Would you mind taking this?" he said. "Some child just palmed it off on me, saying she'd be back in a minute, but I've seen someone I need to speak to, so if you wouldn't mind. . . ." He was there, and then he was gone. I had that nudging feeling you get when trying to place someone. His dark hair was threaded with silver, and I associated him somehow with the wild outdoors. He was Heathcliff in conventional clothing. Except for one thing. There was something sadly amiss with his ears. The left one was twice the size of the right one. Some afflictions, as in Lord Darkwood's interesting limp and noble scars, add to a man's heroic appeal. But, unfairly, mismatched ears didn't cut it.

"There's a piece of paper under that egg," said Mrs. Malloy.

"There is?" Betty stared down.

I removed the egg and set it in a saucer on a nearby table and, when Betty picked up the small folded square, did the same with the tablespoon.

"Go on, open it up. See what it's got written on it."

"There may not be anything." Betty's hand was shaking. "Maybe the child wanted something to hold the egg better in place."

"Don't be daft," said Mrs. Malloy. "That'd be more hindrance than help. If there's one thing I know about, it's egg-and-spoon races. Like I've told Mrs. H, if they was ever to put them in the Olympic games, me sister, Melody, would get a gold medal."

Betty unfolded the paper. After standing stock-still for the count of ten, she said she couldn't show it to us. "It's the message Nigel spoke about at the séance. He told me not to tell anyone."

"That doesn't mean us, we're Johnnies on the spot," retorted Mrs. Malloy. "Anyway, if that voice was from the spirit world, the man had his head in the clouds and can't be counted on to talk sense."

Betty held the paper as if afraid it would explode; then in a trembling voice read the words aloud: *"You'll find what you're looking for in the priest hole, main room upper west wing, fifth panel on left, third rose on right, top carving. Turn clockwise.*

"My goodness!" Mrs. Malloy's taffeta bosom heaved. "Should we take that to mean that's where we'll find—"

"No," I said, "because we won't go looking. Mr. Gallagher's grizzly remains can wait for the police."

"I won't!" Betty flared. "I gave Nigel my word and I intend to keep it."

"Let's at least find Tom," I urged.

"And waste time while he tries to talk us out of it? He's a wonderful man in many ways, but action has never been his forte. Besides, Nigel's instructions were specific. I'm to go alone."

"No, you're not," I said. "Like it or not, Mrs. Malloy and I are coming with you."

"If you insist." I glimpsed relief on Betty's face before she turned on her heel, weaving between and around the clusters of people still capable of enjoying the afternoon.

"I hope this isn't Ariel's idea of a practical joke," I said to Mrs. Malloy, as we followed closely behind. "Somehow I can't believe she'd pull something this unkind. She seems to have been making strides in her relationship with Betty, but that girl is so unpredictable."

"Only one way to find out, Mrs. H."

"If not Ariel, why the roundabout way of passing the note to Betty?"

"Maybe Nanny had a premonition that something would happen to her and left instructions with someone to get the information to Betty without Lady Fiona's knowledge, and whoever it was didn't want to be involved any more than possible." Mrs. Malloy marched ahead of me.

We caught up with Betty in the passageway between the two parts of the house and went up the back stairway and into the west wing through the heavy door. The unease I had experienced on my first visit returned in full force when we stepped into the wainscoted ballroom. Betty turned on all lights, but no amount of electricity could push back the crouching darkness. I glanced nervously at the wardrobe looming in the corner ahead of us. Was that where the menace hid? Were we being spied upon by some long-dead entity or something—someone—wickedly alive? The door appeared to be cracked open, and I braced myself to creep across the floorboards to take a look. Anything was better than this quivering uncertainty. But at that moment, Betty exclaimed that she had found it.

"This is the fifth panel, and here's the third rose on the right. I'm turning it clockwise as instructed. Oh, my God! Look!" At her touch, a rectangle of wainscoting swung open to reveal a shadowy void within.

"Why didn't we think to bring a torch?" I bemoaned.

"We'll have to feel our way around." Betty stepped heroically inside.

"Smells musty," said Mrs. Malloy, teetering after her, "but not unbearable, the way you'd think if there was a body."

"He could have mummified." I brought up the rear. "This is like being in a lift. Ben would have the most awful claustrophobia even with the door open." It was the wrong thing to have said. I had just finished squeezing my elbow into Mrs. M's middle when, as if in response to "Close sesame," we heard a creak, followed by a groan, and found ourselves swaddled in utter darkness.

"Nobody panic!" The words squeezed their way out of my throat. "It must have swung to, but it won't have shut completely. No door could possibly be that wicked."

Apparently this one was. No amount of pushing, shoving, frantic banging, or nasty name-calling would persuade it to relent.

13

❧

Mrs. Malloy, Betty, and I took turns exhausting ourselves, despite knowing it was absolutely the worst thing we could do, given that air was severely rationed. A national shortage, I supposed. I forgot about Mr. Gallagher. Indeed, it seemed to me that all the memories of my life till this moment were seeping from me. I struggled to think about Ben and our children, but they were fading. I sagged against Betty, but she wasn't there. She had crumpled to the floor. I could feel her grasping my calves, her hands clutching . . . then letting go. How sad for her, how anguishing for Tom that he was to lose another wife in an accident, how terrible for dear Ariel. Would she ever recover from this further devastation of her child-hood? Would it be any comfort for her to know that there were now three more faces looking down at her from heaven? I tried to come up with a prayer, but all I could manage were some starts and stops of Mrs. Malloy's poems. There was life left in her. I could feel her gyrations. A funny time to be doing her daily exercise routine, I thought with woolly affection. It was now, as the windows of my life were fogging up, that it came to me in a sort of vision why the man who handed Betty the egg and spoon had seemed familiar. He was the walker I had seen with the black-and-white sheepdog. I had a further revelation about his voice and his mismatched ears. A mosaic of scattered pieces of information floated together. I could be wrong, but I didn't think so. How to prove it, though; that was as ever the question. And the difficulties would increase monumentally when I was dead.

"You're not going to die." The clouds parted as Mrs. Malloy's voice boomed down on me from the sky. "None of us is. Now, move aside, there's a good girl. I had a bit of a tussle getting that underwire out of me bra. But it'll do the trick, see if it don't. Ed the locksmith's got nothing on me when the situation's desperate."

"That priest couldn't get out, the one Lady Fiona told me suffocated in here," I croaked, by way of encouragement.

"That's a man for you; they don't have our stamina. He'd probably never got locked out of the house after sneaking off at night as a teenager. Virtue isn't its own reward; it's a bloody handicap. Make yourself useful, Mrs. H." She was barely panting. "See what Betty's up to."

"I can't see, but I think she's passed out on the floor."

"I'm hurrying. There! I'm pushing the wire down a crack. It's hit something; it must be the catch. Careful, I mustn't lose me concentration."

"Please don't."

I waited, desperately hoping to hear a productive click, but I couldn't. Suddenly there was noise outside. Voices raised in panic, footsteps stumbling around. We were going to be rescued . . . if anyone out there knew how to open the panel. The fog returned, I felt my legs buckle, and then that same unearthly voice, the one that had spoken through the clouds, echoed through my head.

"That's it! The click! The bleeding pearly gates is opening."

Oh, dear! I thought, while falling forward. How many hours would Mrs. Malloy get in the heavenly slammer for swearing in front of St. Peter?

Obviously, there was a mistaken notion that I had led a blameless life. I was adrift in sunlight. There were no scolding voices, only one that was as gentle as a lullaby. I knew who was talking; it was Ben. How lovely of him to come after me, I reflected drowsily. But really he shouldn't have left the children! They needed him and I was quite safe here. I opened my eyes to find myself lying on a sofa in the drawing room at Cragstone.

"Are you back, sweetheart?" Ben asked, with a catch in his voice. He was seated in a chair beside me.

"Have I been laid out?"

"You fainted."

"How are—?"

"Tom fetched the doctor for Betty. She's going to be fine. At the moment she's as badly shocked as you are."

"No, I'm not." I sat up and kissed him absently. "What about Mrs. Malloy?"

"Right here." She came out of nowhere to stand over me. "A rare fright you've given us, Mrs. H! I thought you was gone and I'd never get to tell you I broke that pink vase you searched high and low after."

"That hideous thing?"

"The one my mother gave you?" Ben was laughing at me. I could feel the relieved exhilaration through his touch.

"The reason I kept quiet," said Mrs. M, "is that I did it on purpose."

"Thank you for that." I squeezed her hand. "As well as for saving my life and Betty's."

"Now don't go getting all soppy! If I hadn't managed, it wouldn't be the end of the world. The troops were already there."

"What troops?"

"Tom, Ariel, myself." Ben kissed my forehead. "Along with Mavis and Eddie."

"Her son?"

"I'll explain," said Mrs. Malloy, sitting down in a chair across from us. "That'll speed things, since it's me that had a proper talk with Mavis. Not that I'm blaming you for being out cold for over an hour. It's like this, Mrs. H; she's been bringing the boy to work on the q.t., seeing as how Betty had said she couldn't. It's been easy for her to slip him into the house unnoticed, because she comes in her car and parks close to the passageway outside the door that's left unlocked, there being no key. What she does is take Eddie up the back stairs to the west wing. She's drilled it into him to keep out of sight should anyone go up there. Today, when he heard us coming, he got in that big wardrobe."

"Go on," I urged.

"Seems he was peeking out and saw you, me, and Betty go into the priest hole."

"He must have been startled."

" 'Course he was, being only seven. Scared him, it did, when he heard us pounding on that door to try and get it open. But he kept his head on straight. Quite the little hero, our Eddie. He raced downstairs to tell his mum. Being Mavis, she didn't waste time asking a lot of questions. She found Tom, who was with Ariel and Mr. H, and they all came up on the double."

"That little boy deserves a medal," I said.

"Not quite the way Mavis sees it. She says he's a real scamp.

He'd get bored playing with Mr. Gallagher's old toys in Nanny Pierce's room and sneak downstairs. She caught him there a few times."

"It must have been him who took your toffees."

"And a snuffbox." Ben smiled. "Children love small containers. The poor little chap, he was bored out of his mind most of the time. But it wasn't Eddie who let the bathroom basin overflow. He and Mavis had left the house by that time." He shifted sideways, as I put my feet to the floor.

"Ariel told me Nanny Pierce thought Tom and Betty had a wild lifestyle because she'd seen car lights going down the drive in the middle of the night. Would that have been Mavis?"

"Mrs. Cake got her to fess up. Seems she had a set-to with her husband, Ed, one night." Mrs. Malloy displayed the air of importance that comes from being in the know. "They've been going through a difficult patch, what with him starting up his own business from home and not being quite as cooperative with Eddie as Mavis thinks he could be. One night, she told him she was walking out and taking the boy with her. Having said it, she had to follow through, and Cragstone was the only place she could think to come. Between us, I'd be surprised if it was just the one time. So easy to get in, with that door always unlocked."

"I suppose everything would have gone off without a hitch if Mrs. Cake hadn't heard them moving about on the night of her accident."

"It was one of Mr. Gallagher's old toys left on the stairs that caused her to fall when she come down to make her and Mavis a cup of tea. Put Mrs. Cake in a difficult position." Here Mrs. Malloy resorted to royal magnanimity. "She's fond of Mavis and didn't think Betty was treating her fair, not letting her bring Eddie to work when it was a case of needs must. So the next morning, when she was thinking clearer, she said she'd only imagined hearing someone. It was Betty's thinking it might have been Mr. Gallagher's ghost roaming about that made her press for details."

Ben put an arm around me, and I stood up to find the floor satisfactorily solid under my feet. "I expect Betty thinks it was her ladyship who crept after us into the house and closed the priest-hole door. It *is* possible, I suppose. She knew it was there and quite likely how to open it."

"Then she's barking up the wrong tree." Mrs. Malloy made a noble attempt at not preening. "Milk Jugg phoned while you was out of it, Mrs. H, to report he'd found evidence that her ladyship was married before she became Mrs. Gallagher, but there was an annulment. As for Mr. G not knowing about it at the time and only finding out right before he disappeared, that's a wash, seeing as the groom's cousin was one of the witnesses that signed the registry at the first wedding. So there goes Betty's theory that Lady Fiona murdered her husband because he found out she was a bigamist and then killed Mr. Tribble and Pierce because they might have exposed her secret."

"Something came to me before I passed out," I said.

"What was that?" Ben still had his arm around me.

"I think I know what's really been going on here. We have several villains and overlapping crimes. First up is Mr. Scrimshank who embezzled the Gallagher's money. Mr. Gallagher finally realized what was going on. We know from Melody and Mrs. Cake that on the day before his disappearance he repeatedly tried to reach Mr. Scrimshank on the phone."

"That's right," said Mrs. Malloy. "It's as clear as glass Mr. Scrimshank turned up at Cragstone that evening, after her ladyship had gone to bed. Probably the miserable bugger hoped to bluff his way out of the situation, but Mr. Gallagher didn't buy it. An argument followed and Mr. Scrimshank attacked him."

"Good so far." Ben handed me a glass of brandy.

"There's a quibble." I took a reviving sip. "A Mrs. Johnson saw a man race out of this house. Let us assume that man was Mr. Scrimshank. If so, where was Mr. Gallagher when the police arrived? Which they did fairly speedily, according to Mrs. Cake. No sign of him dying or dead on the floor, with a bloody blunt instrument lying beside him. But if he did recover sufficiently to get out of the house and try to reach help, why hasn't he been heard of since? He wouldn't have left Lady Fiona to Mr. Scrimshank's mercy."

"He may have crawled into a ditch and died." Ben gave Mrs. Malloy a glass of brandy.

"Go on! Keep talking this through, Mrs. H," she prodded. She'd had her moment of glory and was prepared to let me try for mine.

"This is the overlapping part. Someone unconnected with Mr. Gallagher's disappearance decided to use Betty's belief that he had been murdered to facilitate her death."

"Who'd want to kill her?" Ben asked sharply.

"I hate to say it," said Mrs. Malloy, "but the name that pops up in my mind is Ariel. And there was me getting so fond of her." Ducking her black-and-white head, she searched her dress pocket for a hanky.

"It was she who arranged the séance. And Ben"—I took a deeper sip of brandy—"there is something I haven't told you about that. The Madam LaGrange we saw was an imposter." I explained how Mrs. Malloy had failed to recognize the woman getting into the taxi.

"Ellie, I understand why you didn't tell me." He stood up, took a couple of paces, and sat back down. "We were at odds with each other. But why the switch?"

"To manipulate Betty into going into that priest hole when the time came. The garden party was the perfect opportunity.

People milling about in the grounds, general confusion: what were the chances of her being missed until it was too late?"

Mrs. Malloy produced the hanky again.

"Not Ariel," I reassured her. "We're not dealing with the Bad Seed here."

"Tom?" Ben's expression was grim.

"His first wife died in a car accident," said Mrs. Malloy, "and that can't be that hard to arrange, especially for someone as handy with tools as Tom. Ariel said he had recently been working in the west wing."

"Not him either." I shook my head. "None of the Hopkinses has a good way of showing it, but deep down I believe they're fond of one another. This could be just the wake-up call Tom has needed ever since Val showed up at Cragstone House. I'm wondering if he's had his suspicions."

"About her really being in love with Mr. H here all the time?" Mrs. Malloy was making matters worse for her face with the hanky.

"What?" Ben was shocked into shouting out the word.

"Don't worry, darling," I said, "I'm not going to let her get you. My supposition is that was a smoke screen. Val, as you're aware, turned up here shortly after the Hopkinses moved into Cragstone. She must have read about their winning the lottery in the newspapers. And whatever it took, she was going to get her hands on that lovely money. I think she was speaking the truth when she told me she wasn't devastated when Tom broke off their engagement. She probably has a knack for mixing fact with fiction. It makes what she says sound credible, although I could kick myself now for so gullibly accepting her misty-eyed performance. Her main problem in getting her hands on Tom and the lottery winnings is that he takes his Catholicism seriously. He'd never marry her while Betty lived."

"Agreed. Divorce for him isn't an option." Ben again got

up and paced around the furniture with his hands in his pockets, a clear sign that he was endeavoring forcibly to master his emotions.

"Val had to realize that when a wife is murdered the husband is the prime suspect, and Tom might not be keen to remarry if he was in prison. And there was the added complication of his first wife having died in an accident. This death had to appear to be Betty's own fault, a classic case of curiosity killed the cat. I think what gave Val the idea was hearing about the lights that went on and off by themselves and the front door being found open in the morning. Faulty wiring and carelessness? Or could it be blamed on an uneasy spirit, especially given Betty's belief that Lady Fiona had murdered her husband? You were another piece of luck, Ben. She saw your look of stunned surprise when she walked in. And right from the first, she played her scenes with you to great dramatic effect. Lady Fiona thought there was something between the two of you—and, yes, even I did for a while. And when she confessed her feelings for you to me so frankly in the garden, she raised her voice so the audience would be sure to hear."

"Me, that was," Mrs. Malloy explained to Ben. "The wicked vixen made sure I didn't miss a syllable."

"Insurance against its being said that there was something going on between her and Tom before Betty's death. While all the time her aim was to do everything in her power to undermine the Hopkinses' marriage. Causing Tom to realize what a mistake he had made in allowing his parents to part him from the woman he should have married in the first place.

"She already had set the action up for today," I went on. "Who else but Val would have made that phone call canceling the caterers? Betty would look totally inadequate when Val took over the job, as she would have done had Ben not saved the day. That's been her mode of operation ever since she arrived at the Dower House, eroding Betty's self-esteem, taking over the redecorating, and talking her into buying badly fitting clothes. The stunts she pulled—the dead birds, the wreath, and the deluge in the conservatory were all geared to one end. Val trusted in Betty's need to prove herself as a detective, if not an ideal wife or stepmother, to get her into the priest hole. But she was too clever to risk handing her that egg and spoon herself."

"So who helped out with that?"

"Very likely the one whose recorded image, as Mr. Gallagher, with the lion's head walking stick, appeared on Betty's bedroom wall. And whose shivery voice begged her to rescue him from the dark place. This she took to mean the grave Lady Fiona had dug for him; but, hopefully, would later connect with the priest hole."

"Any idea who this man would be?" Ben stood by the windows, which showed a darkening sky. In contrast the color and beauty of Val's décor struck a sickening false note.

"The one I've seen walking a sheepdog. Val's brother, Simon. When I was at the Dower House with Nanny Pierce she told me he was very good looking, although it was a pity about his ears. The man who came up to Betty today had a noticeably mismatched set. One being twice the size of the other. Maybe it explains why he's gone astray."

"Tough!" fired back Mrs. Malloy. "There's a woman at Bingo whose nose looks like it's on upside down and she don't go luring people into priest holes."

"I think Simon was one of the reasons Nanny had to die before today," I continued. "Left to roam around at the garden party, she'd have recognized him if she saw him close up."

"A less drastic approach would have been to drug her into a dead sleep so she wouldn't stir from the Dower House all afternoon," Ben responded contemptuously.

"I suspect Val wasn't in a mood to take any unnecessary risks at this late stage of the game. Nanny may have told her she had seen a man out walking who looked like Simon. Besides, she had that second reason for pushing Nanny under the bus. She needed to convince Betty that Lady Fiona had murdered yet again, so that no one would be surprised when she went looking for Mr. Gallagher's remains in the priest hole and accidentally got locked inside. Poor Betty! A sad case of a woman with a maniacal obsession! Winning the lottery had affected her mind! A tragedy, but why suspect foul play? And there would be Val on the spot to sweetly comfort Tom in his hour of need. She knew his persuadable nature. He wouldn't have had a chance against her. All that lovely money would have been hers when she led him by the nose to the altar."

"Apart from what she'd have to share with her brother, Simon," Mrs. Malloy pointed out.

"In addition to his role today, Val may also have needed instructions from him on opening up the priest hole. Lady Fiona said he wouldn't share the secret when they visited Cragstone as children. Maybe he kept it until Val promised to give him a share of the wealth when she married Tom."

"What a pair!" Ben removed my empty brandy glass and set it down on a table. "That poor old lady."

"Miss Pierce was lonely with Mr. Gallagher gone and she must have been glad of Val's company at first, but she wasn't a fool. She knew Val was up to something. She wanted to show me a photo of Simon and couldn't find it. Any guesses on who got rid of it?" I was getting angrier the more I talked. "What a gift of fate that her ladyship met Miss Pierce for lunch on Wednesday! But even if that hadn't happened, it's a sure bet that Betty would have put her at the scene. Another piece of luck for Val was meeting me in the grounds and telling me that Miss Pierce had forgotten her bus pass. It was a confirmation, should she be asked, of why she was at the bus stop when she never accompanied Miss Pierce on her weekly outings."

"But the thing is," Mrs. Malloy said bitterly, "convincing as all this sounds to us, we don't have a shred of evidence to take to the police. They'd laugh us out the door."

"You've made a believer of me, sweetheart"—Ben kissed my cheek—"but it looks to me as though she'll get away with it. Any thoughts on who she got to play Madam LaGrange?"

Before I could answer, the door opened and Melody Tabby came into the room. She was every bit as frumpy as I remembered from my one time of meeting her. Her hair didn't look as though it had been combed in a week, and she was wearing a pasty beige dress and clodhopping shoes. I saw Mrs. Malloy sneak a smug look at her own footwear, which happened to be the black pair of high-heeled sandals with the narrow crisscross straps she had worn on our visit to Mr. Scrimshank's office.

"So you're wearing those shoes again, Roxanne." Melody spoke in a great rush, with some concomitant huffing and puffing. "Remind me to say something about them in a minute." She paused for a half second to look at Ben and me. "Excuse me for barging in like this. A woman named Mavis let me into the house. She had a little boy with her who tried to put his toffee hands on me.

"Pesky kid!" Ben eyed her with enjoyment.

"Here's the news. Ed the locksmith arrived at the office at one twenty-seven. Three minutes early. But I didn't make an issue of it. He had black hair and eyes and a swarthy complexion. Memories of Edward Rochester came flooding back. The same Christian name—but I wasn't going down that road again. He got into the safe"—catching Mrs. Malloy's baleful eye—"let's say for speed, in a twiddle or two. I got out the Gallaghers' financial records and, like I said I would do, made copies. Seeing as Mr. Scrimshank had said he wouldn't be back at the office today, I took the copies home with me and started going through them page by page. It took me fifty-seven minutes and thirty-one seconds to find the relevant information. That evil man has swindled the Gallaghers out of—well, in the cause of haste I will say hundreds of thousands of pounds. I immediately phoned Police Sergeant Walters and got him on the case. He rang back to say he had spoken with some of the higher-ups at the station and would be round forthwith to collect the papers. And he was at my home in five and three-quarter minutes."

"That was very good of him," said Ben.

"I'd have blasted his ears off if he'd given me any flack!" Melody bristled assertively. "He's my gentleman friend. Has been for six and three-quarter years, two weeks, and four days. The least he can do is jump to it when I toss evidence of a crime in his lap. And that leads me back to what I wanted to say about your shoes, Roxanne. I didn't bring it up when we talked about Ed coming to open the safe because, as you know, I like to focus on one thing at a time."

"Spit it out, Melody."

"I was standing at the window in my office yesterday afternoon at precisely four-thirty. That's always the time when I get up from my chair and do my stretching exercises. If you remember the window, it is fairly wide but there's the blind cutting down the view. Meaning that when you stand in front of it you can't see all of a person, only their shoes and part of their legs. This is what I saw. A foot shod in one of those exact shoes, Roxanne, kicked forward, and the next minute there was the horrific sound of brakes being jammed on, followed by a lot of shouting and screaming. An old lady had gone under the bus. The death of Miss Valerie Pierce has been passed off as an accident, or so it said in this morning's newspaper, but I know that shoe kicked out on purpose, making it a case of murder. Though what good is that when I cannot provide a description of the person standing in them? Oh, I do hope it wasn't poor Frances Edmonds, roped in again by Mr. Scrimshank to do his evil bidding." Looking sad, Melody allowed Ben to help her into a chair.

"But we know who it was, don't we, Mrs. H? We talked about Val's having a pair exactly like these." Mrs. Malloy looked solemnly down at her feet. "Thank you, Mel, for giving us what it takes to battle on for justice." She was giving her sister a hug when Tom came in.

"How's Betty?" Ben asked him.

"Much better. In fact, she's gone for a drive with Val."

"What?"

"Val stopped by to see if she could borrow a cup of sugar, and when she found out about Betty and the others"—Tom glanced at Mrs. Malloy and me—"she suggested they both get away for an hour. It seemed a good idea, considering the two of them have been through a good deal in the past twenty-four hours."

"Unfortunately," I said, as gently as possible, "Val may be about to murder your wife."

"Good God!" Did some deep, unprobed awareness convince him? Tom would have swayed and fallen if Melody had not jumped up. Catching him under the arms, she continued to hold him up.

"The question is, where will they have gone?" Ben pounded a fist into his hand.

"To Lady Fiona's hotel," I said. "Val wouldn't act this quickly unless she thought she could turn Betty's escape from the priest hole to good account. Tom, do you or Betty own a gun?"

"Yes, I thought it might help her feel safer. It's in my bedside table drawer."

"Not anymore." I looked at him sadly, thinking how much more sensible it would have been to replace the missing outdoor key.

"It was Val who suggested..."

"Her story will be that Betty asked to be driven to the hotel so she could confront Lady Fiona. That she was beside herself with rage and distress and on arrival pulled the gun to force a confession. A scuffle followed in which her ladyship and Betty were both shot. A revised ending but not bad. Poor Betty! Already unbalanced and cracking completely after her horrible experience in the priest hole." I drew a ragged breath.

"How long ago did Val and Betty drive away?"

"I waved them off right before coming in here." Tom struggled free of Melody's sustaining hands.

"I've got to get to that hotel."

"You don't need to," said Melody, with a glow that made her look positively ravishing. "That's what my policeman gentleman is good for. It'll be Police Sergeant Walters to the rescue. He's at the jewelry shop around the corner from the Brontë Hotel, picking out my engagement ring."

14

On the Saturday morning two days later, Ben, Mrs. Malloy, and I made ready for our departure from Cragstone House. All was well. Betty's rescue had been accomplished before she and Val stepped into the hotel lift. Simon Pierce, in being questioned by the police, handed Val over on a silver plate in return for the deal he was offered. Val had attempted to put the blame on him but gave in when he started to talk. His wife had played the part of Madam LaGrange. She was the woman with orange hair I had seen outside Mrs. Johnson's bed and breakfast. When Mrs. Malloy finally got hold of the real Madam LaGrange, we learned she had been met on arriving at the train station by a man of Simon's description who said the Hopkinses' séance was called off. As he handed her twice what Ariel had promised, she was more than happy to take off for a few days' holiday.

Tom had barely let Betty out of his sight after her rescue. She was recovering rapidly from the shock of discovering she had been an intended murder victim. No more playing detective, she had vowed to me. From this point on, she would be entirely happy as a wife and mother. She even admitted to looking forward to the pleasure and responsibilities of great wealth. And she and Tom were making plans for what they would do for their friends the Edmondses.

Frances had been concerned that when Mr. Scrimshank was arrested she would be called in for interrogation by the police regarding the phone call she had made to him, which he said came from Mr. Gallagher. She had gone in voluntarily to talk to Sergeant Walters, with the result that she might be required to testify should Mr. Scrimshank plead not guilty to the criminal charges filed against him.

Ariel danced around Ben while he packed the Land Rover, issuing instructions with her customary bossiness.

"It's not an easy job, bringing up parents," I heard her telling him. "They can be a great trial at times, but I'm willing to accept my responsibilities if they'll promise to play nicely together."

Mrs. Malloy was delighted that Melody's love interest was a policeman with an intriguing middle-aged voice and most of his hair. Lady Fiona was in the process of moving into the Dower House, much to the joy of Mrs. Cake and Mavis, and I decided to go and say good-bye to her.

"How very kind of you to pay me a visit, Mrs. Honeywood." She ushered me into the pleasant sitting room, already made not quite the same as during Nanny Pierce's occupancy by the addition of several small pieces that created a comfortable disregard for whether things matched or didn't. "We've had rather a lot of flies in the house over the last couple of days, but otherwise moving has not been overwhelming. How is your brother, the artist model? No doubt you worry about his catching cold, but there are dangers in any career. One need think only of poor

Mr. Scrimshank. Such a stressful job, being an accountant. Let us hope he will get a good rest in his new environment."

"He may well have overworked, getting his sums to add up," I said.

"Indeed, yes. I myself never mastered long division, Enid—you did want me to call you that—shall I have Mrs. Cake make us a pot of tea? Her foot is so much better that she hobbled over here and is in the kitchen."

"Yes, I would love—"

"No, of course you don't. I'd forgotten that you don't take hot drinks, and I'm sorry to say I don't have any of that mango juice you enjoy so much." The French doors from the garden opened, and in walked a solidly built man of medium height and sparse gray hair.

"Sorry, m'dear," he said to Lady Fiona. "Didn't realize you had company. I'll go off again, shall I?"

"Of course not, Nigel, we can't have you starting up this wandering-off business again the moment you walk in the door. Do say hello to Enid Honeywood. Then sit down and tell us where you have been and whether or not it was a good trip."

After shaking my hand and saying the usual things, he sat down and strummed his fingers on his crossed knees. "Haven't had a bad time. Plenty of exercise! Been keeping fit yourself, my dear?" he inquired of her ladyship.

"I should be going," I said, but Mr. Gallagher waved me down. "No need to rush off. Good to see you again after all these years. Eyes just like your father. Would've known you anywhere, Elsie."

"Enid," corrected her ladyship. "Nigel, dear, I do have some sad news about Nanny."

It seemed to me that Mr. Gallagher's face brightened. "Hung up her butterfly net, has she?"

"I'm afraid so, but at least you're back in time to attend her funeral, and that of a clergyman who came to tea at Cragstone and seemed convinced that he and I had once been married. People can be exceedingly odd; the woman who bought Cragstone with her husband is definitely peculiar. She got it into her head that I had murdered you. And disposed of you in the strawberry patch, I suppose."

"Rubbish! Why would you do a thing like that, old girl? Knowing, as you do, that I've always been allergic to strawberries. Never mind that. Glad to see you're not miffed at my going off and leaving you to cope with Nanny when she was foaming at the mouth over being sent here to live."

"I'm always ready to hear your side of the story." Lady Fiona sounded ever so slightly impatient.

"The thing is, Fiona, I've had amnesia."

"Just as Mrs. Cake said would have happened. She was sure burglars had broken in and coshed—such a funny word—you on the head. Thereby causing you to wander off in a daze."

"Hit the nail on the head!" Mr. Gallagher smiled in the manner of a man who knows himself to be blessed with a wife in a million. "Won't go into details of everywhere I've been during the last year of a half, would take too long. But I have some lively anecdotes to share with you, my dear. Can be damned awkward not knowing who the devil one is! What brought me back to m'self was reading a mention in one of the daily rags about Cragstone being sold. Uh! Ha! I said to m'self. Something smells familiar! That place was my home! Better be heading back there. Was in the Scottish Highlands at the time, with nothing but holes in my pockets, making for something of a trek. Maybe we should take up hitchhiking together. The thing is, here I am, m'dear!"

"And very nice too."

"How about a cup of tea for the weary traveler?"

"You haven't told me the interesting part yet, Nigel. How did you happen to come down with amnesia?"

"Oh, that! Well, if you remember we had that little squiff

about my not being able to find my blue-and-black Argyle socks. Entirely my fault! I was out of sorts after trying all day to reach Scrimshank on the phone. You'd gone up to bed and there I was sitting in the drawing room, when he came ringing the doorbell. Damned inconsiderate! He could have woken Nanny, causing me to be up all night with her while she told me bedtime stories."

"She's in the past, Nigel. Please continue with what happened that evening after Archibald Scrimshank arrived."

"I'd done some figuring of my own, which brought me to the regrettable conclusion that the chap had been embezzling from us for years. Decided to do the gentlemanly thing and request an explanation. Honest, forthright, man-to-man. Wouldn't have wanted to take the fellow to court but saw no harm in asking him to begin making payments arranged to suit both parties."

"Exactly as I would have wished, Nigel. Unfortunately, the police have used very poor judgment by involving themselves in the situation. Archibald has been removed to one of those correctional facilities, as I believe they are called, where one isn't allowed to choose one's own pajamas. Fortunately, most men like stripes. I imagine your encounter with him deteriorated and ended in his attacking you."

"Most unpleasant business. Didn't recall it until the rest of my memory returned. I must have been knocked out cold for a while. Came round to an exploding head. Had no idea where I was, went for a walk hoping to shake things back into place, and couldn't find my way back to the house. All behind me now, old girl. Wouldn't be surprised if my trials and tribulations—and yours too, Fiona—will assist in our adjustment to a changing world." Mr. Gallagher stretched out his legs and, beaming blissfully, closed his eyes.

"Not color television, Nigel. I really don't think I could bear it."

"Good grief! Nothing that dreadful! I was talking about

living here at the Dower House instead of Cragstone. Regrets, m'dear?"

"None, Nigel. I think it may be rather fun."

"Good show! Wonder if Mrs. Cake and Mavis would object to working for us only part-time? I rather enjoy the thought of its just being the two of us occasionally."

"I think both of them have now warmed toward the new family and would probably enjoy working between both houses, with Mrs. Cake continuing to live at Cragstone."

I had sat absolutely still, so as not to disturb them. It had been like watching a play. But now the curtain must fall. It was time for me to leave. Ben would have the car sorted out and be eager to set off. I said my good-byes to the Gallaghers with a real twinge of regret. As the door was closing behind me, I heard her ladyship say to her husband, "She seems a lovely young woman, Nigel, but I do hope she doesn't take to popping in all the time. That was the problem with her aunt, the one they had to ship off to Gibraltar."

On reaching Cragstone's front steps, I found Ben and Mrs. Malloy ready to be off.

"Promise to come and stay with us again?" Ariel gave us each a kiss through the car window. We did not prolong our leave-taking, which would have made it harder. Having shared so much, it was my hope that we would remain close. The Hopkinses stood and waved until we turned through the gateposts.

"What now?" Ben asked. "Would you like to stop and see your sister before we take off, Mrs. Malloy?"

"I haven't known how to break it to you both, but I told Melody I'd stay with her for a few days and help her plan her trousseau. She's asked me to be her bridesmaid and I couldn't say no, although I'm scared silly she'll want me to wear brown. It's always been her favorite color. And I've got to say I think it suits her. . . . Could be she'll turn into a beauty yet."

"I wouldn't be at all surprised," I said.

"'Course she'll never be able to write poetry, but none of us gets to have it all."

Ben said he agreed heartily, and we drove in companionable silence to the house where Melody rented the top floor.

"Don't feel too lost without me!" Mrs. Malloy said, as she got out.

"Have a wonderful visit," I called after her.

"It will be good to get home," Ben told me as we drove away, "but if you're not in too much of a rush I'd like to make a stop first."

"Where?"

"Wait and see."

"You're being mysterious."

"That's the idea." Smiling, he laid his hand on mine. We left Milton Moor behind and entered a narrow road, not much more than a lane, bordered by gray stone walls brightened by bright yellow gorse. Ben slowed the Land Rover to a stop. Getting out, I saw an opening leading onto the moors. A moment later he was beside me, taking my hand. "Come, sweetheart," he said. "Let's walk."

And so we did: for miles, it seemed, across the unmown lawn that was the moor. A curlew or some sort of bird emitted a haunting cry as it flew past us. I unpinned my hair and let the wind take it. I lifted my face to the fine mist and knew I was happy.

"Is this far enough?" Ben finally asked.

"Far enough for what?"

"For this." He drew me to him.

"Oh, I do love you when you're masterful, Mr. Haskell," I whispered against his throat.

"Then I must take advantage of the situation, my very dear young lady." Ben's eyes were alight with love and laughter before he kissed me with tender passion. And that is almost . . . but not quite . . . the end of this story.